SIR ARTHUR'S LEGACY  BOOK 2

SARAH EDWARDS

Cover: Deranged Doctor Design

ISBN 978-1-990731-03-7
ISBN 978-1-990731-02-0

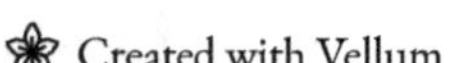 Created with Vellum

Chapter One

Faye must be an unnatural wife. She stood beside her father, Sir Arthur of Anglesea, and received the news of her husband's death. Behind her polite facade, she felt nothing. Perhaps the mask she'd spent so many years perfecting had seeped into her soul.

Not a wife anymore, but now a widow.

It was over. Calder was dead. The man who haunted the dark, hidden corners of her mind was no longer. She heard the words, understood their meaning, but still the numbness persisted.

"How did he die?" Her father spoke the question she could not bring herself to ask. If she asked, the squire might laugh and deny the news he carried. She had become accustomed to cruelty.

Young, fresh-faced and pretty, the squire colored to his hairline. "He...um..." His gaze flit to her and away again. "He choked. On a chicken bone."

Faye understood the boy's glance well. Her time as Calder's wife had been marked with looks just like that one. She almost took pity on him and told him to spare his blushes on her behalf. Calder had been with another woman at the time of his death. It wouldn't be the first time. Or the last—

1

Calder was dead. Perhaps if she repeated it enough times it would come to mean something.

Sir Arthur sat forward on his large, carved wooden chair before the great hearth of Anglesea. "He choked on a chicken bone?"

"Aye, my lord." The boy nodded. "It was a terrible accident."

Was it? Faye had been wrong to think she felt nothing. Nay, she felt relief. Calder was dead, she and her boys were safe. A year ago, she had run from him with her boys. Gregory had aided her and brought her here.

The thought of Gregory sent a shaft of agonizing pain through her middle, and she gasped. Tears sprung to her eyes and spilled over her cheeks.

"There now." Her father rose and tugged her into his embrace. "My lovely girl, I am so very sorry."

Faye pressed her face to her father's tunic and let him believe she wept for Calder. The truth would be so much harder to explain, and Father would blame himself for giving her to Calder.

"My lord?" The squire cleared his throat. "There is more to my message."

"God's bones, boy!" Sir Arthur thundered, his voice reverberating through her ear. "Can you not see the Lady Faye is overcome?"

Pushing herself from her father's comforting embrace, Faye drew a deep breath. Tears for Gregory were a waste of time. He was as lost to her as Calder. "It's all right, Father." She took the kerchief he offered and tidied her face. "He is only doing what he was told to do."

Sir Arthur growled and turned to the quaking squire. "Well, spit it out!"

"Sir Hugo...the earl's brother...um, he demands the return of the boy earl and his brother, with the Lady Faye to Calder Castle." The boy went paler than a duck feather. "Sir Hugo insists that as guardian to the young earl he has the right to demand the earl's return to his demesne."

"Never." Faye hadn't realized she had spoken aloud until her father and the squire's gazes locked on her. She didn't care. She would never go back there. Never put her boys or herself in that hideous place again. Seven years in that living hell before she'd finally worked up the courage to escape, and she would never return. Hugo was cut from the same cloth as Calder. "We stay here."

The squire gaped at her. "But—"

"You heard my daughter." Sir Arthur put his arm around her shoulder. "She and her boys remain here. If Sir Hugo wishes to take issue, explain to him that he takes issue with Sir Arthur of Anglesea."

* * *

Calder was dead. The axe bit into the wood and jarred Gregory's arm to his shoulder. He welcomed the impact. The bunch and release of his muscles soothed and kept him from the clattering noise between his ears. The news of Calder's death could mean nothing to him.

He swung and hit the wood clean. It shattered with a dull thwack and the halves dropped to either side of the chopping block. Would he had a blade to cleave Faye from his very being. Gregory picked up the largest piece and set it. He raised the axe.

Calder was dead and Faye was free.

"My son?" The Abbot's soft voice broke his solitude.

The Abbot and Brother Peter stood beside the neatly stacked wood. The height of the woodpile easily cleared their tonsures, the Abbot's pink and glistening from his daily nap in the orchard.

Brother Peter must have woken him. The smaller priest shifted his feet and folded his hands before him.

Insufferable, little toad. He resembled one with his protuberant eyes and rotund belly.

He needn't stand there wearing his pious face. Gregory saw right through him. Father Peter delighted in spreading tales throughout the abbey. Not a toad, more of a ferret. The name fit the man perfectly, busy, nosy and always where he shouldn't be. He had brought the news of Calder's death to Gregory with a smug gloat that Gregory itched to wipe from his face.

"You may leave us," the Abbot said to Father Peter.

Father Peter flushed, opened his mouth, and shut it under the abbot's unwavering stare. He scuttled away.

Probably lurking somewhere close enough to listen.

"What are you doing, Gregory?" The Abbot jammed his hands on his round hips.

"Chopping wood." It was fairly obvious, was it not?

"I can see that." Missing his nap made the Abbot peevish. "It was more a question of intent."

The sedentary existence of the Abbey near drove him out of his mind at times. It left his mind far too free to dwell on the fair phantom who walked his dreams. The same beautiful woman who had now been released from the bonds of her torturous marriage. *You could go to her*, his traitorous desire whispered. Instead, he brought the axe down again. "We need the wood."

"Then it is good we have enough kindling to stoke the fires of hell." The abbot raised his brow.

A snicker sounded from the other side of the mountain of wood.

"Thank you, Brother Peter," the Abbot called. "I will see you at prayers. You might reflect on Ecclesiastes seven, twenty-one whilst you pray."

Brother Peter scurried back across the kitchen garden.

"Now, my son." The Abbot turned back to him. "I take it you have heard the news?"

"Aye, Father Abbot." A raw burn rekindled in his gut and Gregory tightened his hold on the axe handle. He dropped his gaze to his feet. The Abbot would too quickly read the emotion in his eyes.

"You were Calder's vassal?"

"Aye, Father Abbot." That being the only thing that had prevented Gregory from killing the sod. That and Faye had begged him not to. She had not wanted him to forfeit his life for Calder's.

The Abbot moved to stand right before him. "You were knight protector to Calder's lady wife?" He did not wait for Gregory to answer his question. "And you aided her escape from Calder with her boys."

Gregory had never spoken of that night to anyone, or the reasons behind it. It was all in the past now, and he fought the suck and drag of his memories. He had a promise, far older than his history with Faye, to honor. A mother's dying wish he had vowed to fulfill. "Father Stephen denied my petition again this morning."

Denied permission to take his orders, again. For ten months he had been waiting. In that time countless other men were taken up as novice and still they refused him. It wasn't right. His father had insisted he take up the sword and he had, but he had been biding his time for when he could obey his true calling.

"Did Father Stephen explain our reasoning?"

"Aye, Father Abbot. He said I was not ready." Father Stephen had no idea of what he spoke. He'd been ready since before he attained adulthood. And yet, that miserable old priest stopped him this morning after prayers and smashed his hopes, again.

The Abbot studied his face keenly. "You disagree?"

"Aye, Father Abbot." He barely managed a civil tone. How did a man keep a civil tone when discussing cantankerous old Father Stephen? If he let free with his real thoughts, they would have yet another reason to deny him permission to take Holy Orders. "I want nothing more than to join the Abbey."

"Did you say as much to Father Stephen?"

"I did, Father Abbot."

"And?"

This part made him want to throw back his head and rage at

the Heavens. "Father Stephen questioned my motives for committing my life to the service of our Lord."

The Abbot nodded.

No immediate denial. Did this mean the Abbot considered overruling his spiritual advisor and admitting him to novice? Gregory sent a fervent prayer heavenwards.

He pointed to the axe in Gregory's hand. "My son, would you?"

Gregory laid the axe against the chopping block.

"Let us walk." The Abbot motioned with his plump, white hand. The nails of which always gleamed clear and meticulously clean.

Gregory stuffed his large, dirt encrusted meat-hooks into his belt as he shortened his stride to match the smaller man's.

A handful of monks toiled amongst the vegetables, their dark habits somber mounds in a sea of greenery as they bent to their labors.

They left the kitchen gardens through a small gate in the honeyed stone wall, which Gregory held open for the Abbot before ducking to clear the lintel. He must practice patience. The Abbot would speak when he was ready.

The breeze stiffened this side of the wall. Gregory drew the briny tang of the ocean deep into his lungs. Today, the sea spread in a calm, deep indigo that stretched to meet the arch of the sky. On the green swathes atop the cliffs, the abbey sheep dotted the hillside like tiny white clouds.

"Gregory, you present a problem." The Abbot tucked his hands into the sleeves of his habit. "And I cannot fault Brother Stephen's reasoning."

And there went his stupid hope. The wind cooled the sweat on his skin and he shivered. He should have picked up his tunic from the woodpile

"Here you are, a devout man and one with a pure and honest intention." The Abbot's habit flapped like a sail against his ankles.

"We see that in you. You are a powerful man, Gregory, and you would make a fine warrior for our Lord."

Please, Heavenly Father, anything but that. No more war or bloodshed or ceaseless violence. Let him live in peace and love, a man of God and not the sword. His final vow to his mother had been to fulfill her dream of him entering into mild and obedient service to his God. All his life, his size and strength cursed him and stood between him and his heart's desire.

"And yet, you would turn your back on your strength." The Abbot glanced at him.

"I would, Father Abbot."

"This life." The Abbot spread his arms wide and encompassed the Abbey roosting atop her cliff and nestled by her lands. "This life is not for everyone."

"It is the life for me." Gregory winced at the heat in his tone. He must master his anger or they would toss him out.

"Brother Stephen disagrees."

Brother Stephen. Bah! A miserable old woman who wouldn't know his sainted ass from his elbow. Best not to share his opinion and Gregory clenched his jaw shut.

The Abbot held up his hand. "And I agree with Father Stephen."

"But you cannot." The words burst out of him. Gregory drew in a long breath as he battled his temper into submission. "I feel the call to serve God."

"We are all on this earth to serve God." The Abbot stopped and gestured to the Abbey. "Yet, we are not all called to serve God in this manner."

The Abbot stopped walking and forced Gregory to stand still. He towered above the man by over a foot and he bent his knees slightly to lessen the height difference. "But I am."

He would be chopping until Judgment Day. Tension crept down from his shoulders until he bunched his fists by his sides. Yet another test for his patience faced him. Had he not practiced it all his life as a fighting man?

And his life at Calder, a testament to his patience. Seven years living side by side with Faye and not touching her. He had won his constant battle with the rage every time he saw the marks on her flesh her husband put there. God sanctified the bond between man and wife and he could not interfere, however sorely tested. All this he had done to earn his place amongst the holy brothers. And now to be denied when he was so close. It writhed inside him like a live beast.

"We believe your heart is not fully here, my son."

The words hit him like a slap in the face. All of it for naught?

"Brother Stephen and I believe there is a part of you that remains in the world of men."

Eyes bluer than the sky above him, a full, red mouth curved in a smile. *How solemn you are, Gregory. Do you never smile?*

Gregory's heart raced. They couldn't know the demons tormenting him. He prayed hours upon hours, purging his flesh of his lustful thoughts and cleansing his soul of the impotent fury. Here at the Abbey, he never spoke of it. Faye was a test, her husband a torment and he had mastered both.

The Abbot studied him. The breeze tugged his tonsure fringe into horns on either side of his head. "This life is a difficult one, my son. You cannot enter into it with any reservations in your heart."

He didn't have any reservations. None.

Liar.

His one huge reservation lived less than a day's ride away. His mind whirled sickeningly. The Abbot and Father Stephen must have seen into his soul and discovered the truth. "What should I do?"

"You must pray." The Abbot nodded. "You must pray for God to show you your true path."

"I have prayed." And prayed and prayed. And God had shown him his true path. This life, the life of a monk was the one chosen for him by God. He needed to lance the doubt from his soul. He must rid himself of the temptation. It was a trial.

Of course, it became so clear to him. If God had tested his Son in the desert, would He not test a man about to enter His service. "I believe you are right, Father Abbot."

The Abbot blinked at him and his mouth dropped open in surprise. "I am?"

"Aye." The certainty lit him within like a hearth blaze. "I believe I have held some part of myself back from the Lord. I shall pray for the strength to overcome this, so I may enter the service of the Lord with a free and willing heart."

"You are a stubborn man, Gregory." The Abbot shook his head. "While you are on your knees, you might ask God to deal with that for you, as well."

"But, Father Abbot, it has become clear to me whilst you spoke. God is testing me."

"I do not know about you." The Abbot sniffed. "But God is certainly testing my patience. Open your heart, Gregory." The Abbot tapped his chest. "Open your heart and receive the word of God."

He rapped his knuckles against Gregory's forehead, firmly. "Do not decide with this hard head of yours what you want to hear and twist the word of God to suit your desires."

The intense need to toss the Abbot on his plump ass staggered him. He knew what God wanted for him. God wanted him to be a monk.

Gregory dropped his gaze to his boots in case the man could read minds.

"Obedience, my son." The Abbot sighed. "First, begin with obedience."

He turned and trotted back toward the kitchen gardens.

Gregory followed behind. The Abbot was wrong. His hand itched for the heft of the axe. In former days, he would have grabbed up his sword and spent his anger in the practice yards. Here, he could only chop wood.

The Abbot left him at the woodpile.

The axe sat heavy and welcome in his hand. Gregory swung. It hit the wood with a jarring crunch.

He was obedient.

Thwack.

He was fated to serve God in mild and humble service.

Thwack.

He would pray harder.

Chapter Two

Two *months later*

Faye braced outside the hall where happy voices spilled into the corridor. Two days shy of St. John's Eve, almost a year to the day Gregory had brought her and her boys back to Anglesea. He'd left before the great bonfires lit that night were extinguished.

Gathered for the evening meal, Anglesea folk eagerly anticipated the festival marking the summer solstice. So many chattering, laughing people, many of them linked to her by blood and service, yet she still felt like an interloper in her childhood home. She couldn't stand out here all evening. Lady Faye, daughter of Sir Arthur of Anglesea, Dowager Countess of Calder, was expected to present herself for the evening meal and show a pleasant face.

She had so many secrets, so many pretty lies built behind her face. She could not afford to let her mask slip.

Calder. If only she could remove the memories now that he was dead and no longer a threat. But the fear clung tenaciously to her thoughts. Faye straightened her shoulders and drew a deep, soothing breath. Calder was the past, and it behooved her to face forward and embrace what the future brought. Faye smoothed her frown away with her fingers. She didn't want people to see her inner struggle on her face. Letting people see behind her mask would create more questions than she could answer.

A cooling breeze from the hall's open casements brushed her cheeks, stirring the great tapestries adorning the towering stone walls. Fresh rushes, scented with lavender at Mother's insistence, crunched beneath her feet as she wove her way through the trestle tables.

"Evening, my lady." A man-at-arms nodded his greeting as she passed.

More greetings followed her passage, and she returned them all with a smile. What a happy place this hall was, filled with love and laughter and a thousand different memories of a different girl. As a child she had imagined fey folk flitting and peering down at them through the mighty oak beams crisscrossed into arches along the ceiling.

A journeyman minstrel, his beard still a smattering of fuzz on his chin struggled to push his voice above the noise. He beamed a huge smile at her, strummed a chord, and paused for effect with his hand in the air.

A serving maid passed in front of him and ruined his brief flourish.

"Such beauty as was never seen,
In golden hair, sapphire eye and lily skin,
As Fairest of Fairest Faye's as has ever been,
And for her love my heart shall pine."

Heat climbed her cheeks as a handful of grinning people turned toward her. They saw what she wanted them to see. They saw *her*, Fairest Faye.

Fairest Faye, the mask that hid her truth. Dear God, she almost hated her.

The girl in the ballad wasn't her, not anymore. That girl's foolish heart had swelled with pride as she patted herself on her golden head. Stupid girl. Stupid, aye, but that girl's life had spread before her like a banquet of endless possibilities. Somewhere between her wedding night and her escape—

Nay, she would not be dragged into the past. No dwelling. Forward. The rise and fall of merriment wrapped around her and eased her turmoil. She smiled as Tom turned to greet her approach. He had grown larger since Faye last saw him. Nurse's son was not so often found in the hall since he had been gifted his allotment by her father. "Good evening, Tom."

"Good evening, Lady Faye." He flushed to his fair hairline.

Tom was a special friend of Beatrice's, but Faye was always glad to see him. "And how is your farm?"

His lanky frame had filled in with muscle very nicely, and he had a pair of shoulders on him that rivaled Roger's. Light blue eyes beneath heavy brows held her gaze for a moment before he dropped his chin to his broad chest. "Very well...um...my lady. Thank you for asking."

Ivy appeared at his elbow. Tiny and dark, Ivy possessed the sort of delicate beauty and cool distance that kept the men of Anglesea at her heels. Even William failed to thaw the lovely Ivy.

Tom's regular features split into a huge smile.

"Tom is preparing his north field for planting in the spring." Ivy put her small hand on Tom's arm. It lay against the rough sleeve of his tunic like a feather in a pile of wood shavings.

Tom's wide shoulders straightened. "Aye. I shall have the entire allotment planted by next harvest."

"Did you manage to finish the irrigation trenches?" Ivy's pale cheeks bore a delicate flush. Apparently Ivy was not as immune to all male charm as it would appear.

Over Ivy's head, Henry sent Faye a grave nod from the far end of the hall where he spoke earnestly to a man with a glazed expression. The poor man had her sympathy. Her youngest brother's fondness for delivering lectures to any recipient who would stand still long enough to receive one was well known throughout the keep.

Ivy and Tom's conversation moved on to animal husbandry and Faye excused herself.

"Faye." A boisterous kiss from Roger and the herb-honey waft of mead announced him well into his cups. Roger's blue eyes danced at her, a flush suffusing his broad, rough-hewn features. Many a lass sighed over her brother Roger. "Come and explain to William why he should be married."

"Dear sister." William's fine features broke into a smile. Faye couldn't imagine him relinquishing his position as keep heartbreaker in the near future. He bent his dark head and kissed her cheek.

"Should you be married?" Teasing William was always fun.

"Who would have me?" He quirked a dark brow and drained his cup of mead. If he tried to keep pace with the bigger Roger, he would be rolled out the hall before dinner ended.

"Look at that pretty face." Cupping William's carved jaw in his paw of a hand, Roger grinned at her. "There is not a girl for twenty leagues who would naysay our William."

"Leave him alone, Roger." Lord, they would be at each other's throats in a moment. They'd been doing it since they were lads. Roger toddled and William toddled faster, or at least near broke himself trying. It nearly always ended with fists flying.

She gave them a repressive stare as she slid past. It would accomplish nothing. Her brothers had too much time on their hands to get into mischief. Time they were married. Father hinted in that regard. William and Henry were rather sanguine about the idea. Roger had developed a case of deafness. As she was hardly in a position to advocate the benefits of matrimony, she stayed silent on the subject.

Her mother and father were settled at table and Faye took the seat to her father's left. As the first girl, born after Roger and William, she'd been accorded a special place in her father's affection.

His craggy face split into a grin. "Beautiful Faye." He kissed her cheek. "Tell me how you have been spending this day."

She dreaded the question. He asked it every night and every night she burrowed deep for some interesting morsel that wouldn't make her day seem as stale as old bread. "I am working on a new set of bed linens for Beatrice's baby. As we do not know the sex of the child, I thought green was a good choice."

"Marvelous." Her father rubbed his hands together.

She loved him for the attempt, but honestly, the mighty Sir Arthur of Anglesea had as much interest in bedding as, well, she did.

Twined up in each other like a pair of clinging vines, Garrett and Beatrice entered the hall. Beatrice waddled under the weight of the child she carried. Garrett strutted and preened like the first man to ever conceive a child, hovering about Beatrice constantly. So in love, it made her wish for things she couldn't have.

Nurse leaned forward from beside Lady Mary. "She carries a boy, you mark my words."

Faye itched to adjust her wimple. Nurse wore it so low and tight, it pressed her face inward and gave her the look of a spotted pudding.

"It is in the shape of the belly." Nurse made a circle with her hands. "If it is round like that, it's a boy. You were the same and your mother before you."

Both times Nurse had sworn up and down Faye carried a girl. Faye merely smiled and accepted a goblet from a serving woman. At least the wine at Anglesea was always good.

The chatter of confinements, reminded her that Simon and Arthur should be back by now.

"Nurse, have you seen the boys?" She leaned far forward to see past her father and mother. She had told Sir Arthur they should commission a curved table at Anglesea. It was one good thing she had taken from Calder Castle. She must not think of Calder Castle. Fairest Faye had gone to Calder Castle as a blushing new bride, and returned this husk of a woman who carried her dark shame and her darker secrets.

Nurse's bodice dropped in her trencher as she replied. A curved table would be a mercy to silk everywhere. "Nay." Nurse frowned. "I thought they were with young Oliver."

Oliver, the squire charged with watching the boys. There were so many squires around Anglesea, their names blurred into a crowd of eager young faces.

"Oliver missed weapons practice this evening." William took the seat beside her.

Why he did it baffled her because Roger would only insist he move one down.

Oliver should not have missed practice. Everyone knew Sir Arthur ran a disciplined keep, and squires did not miss practice. Not unless there was a problem. A tendril of alarm curled in her belly. She tried not to smother her boys, but worry was never missing for long.

"I saw them heading for the beech thicket." Roger rumbled from behind. He clapped William on the shoulder, his knuckles whitening as he increased his grip.

"The beech thicket? Did you not stop them? They told me they would go to the stream at the bottom of the hill. They were to remain in sight of the keep guards."

"I thought they had your permission." Roger won the battle with William and wedged huge shoulders in beside her.

Roger sipped his mead as if naught was amiss. She had told her boys right in front of Roger the thicket was not allowed, even accompanied. Roger should have stopped them. The beech thicket spread all the way to the village and the boys could be anywhere.

Breathe. The boys were safe now. She had brought them to Anglesea and they were finally safe.

Still, best she start looking. Simon forever led the way into mischief with little Arthur at his heels. She should never have let them go this morning.

Sir Arthur rose when she did. "Faye?"

"Forgive me." She managed a tight smile for the table. "If you will excuse me, I will go and find my sons."

Garrett stood. "I shall come with you."

"I am sure there is no reason for concern." She kept it light. Boys were boys and she did try not to coddle them, but for their bellies not to lead them to dinner was unusual.

"I will come." Garrett motioned for Beatrice to stay. "Where would you like to begin?"

Beatrice had a treasure in her husband. Faye gave him a grateful smile as she led the way out of the hall.

A bench scraped and William called out. "Hang about, Faye, we can split up and cover more ground."

Chapter Three

emain calm, Faye. The mask grew harder to wear as time wore on, the woman she was behind it screaming to escape.

The boys were not in their chamber, or the hall. The kitchen drudges hadn't seen them, and neither had the keep serving women. As a last resort, Faye even tried the chapel. Father Bernard shrugged and looked regretful, but the boys had not been there either. It had been a guess, at best. Two young boys could not disappear into air.

"They are not in the laundry." William dashed another hope.

The long summer evening gave way to full dark. The entire keep joined the search as it moved outside into the bailey. A tight knot of anxiety grew in Faye's chest as face after face turned down in regret. They must be somewhere. After all she had done to keep them safe, she had to find them.

Tom and Roger checked the stables. Nothing.

Lady Mary led the keep to Vespers. "We will pray you find them soon."

Simon could be anywhere. His sense of adventure needed to be curbed with some good sense. Earlier in the spring, he had led Arthur into the forests surrounding Calder while they played knights and dragons. They lost track of time in their game. Several anxious hours later, Faye found them, filthy and tired with Simon still engrossed in killing his "dragon" with a makeshift sword and Arthur fast asleep under a tree.

But they had never been gone this long before.

Torches flickered across the faces of the men gathered in the bailey.

Taking charge, Sir Arthur divided the men into groups to cover the area outside the walls.

"Never fear, sweeting." Her father hugged her. "They have lost track of time while about their mischief and got turned around in the dark. I am sure we will find them huddled together and telling grisly stories."

Stories like the ones Gregory told. Gregory. The name rocked through her. Gregory would know exactly where to look. Except, Gregory had left her. Left them.

Faye gave Sir Arthur a wan smile. She had naught more to give. Her boys were out there in the wicked dark. *Please God, let Simon not have gone anywhere near the sea.* Only last summer, the smith's youngest—

She needed to concentrate on finding her boys. A good mother would have noticed they were gone long before now. And what had she been doing while her sons were lost? Embroidering countless flowers and swirls on yet another piece of fabric. Heedless mother, thoughtless woman.

Beatrice slipped a warm hand into hers. "Let us search the stables."

"They have already searched the stables." Faye returned the pressure, grateful for her sister's presence.

"Aye, but men could not find their asses with both hands." Beatrice had picked up all sorts of unladylike expressions from her husband.

It drew a reluctant chuckle from her. Anything would be better than standing here waiting. Her father and brothers had forbade her joining the search outside the keep walls. Even Garrett turned mulish.

Beatrice tugged her toward the stable, their pace slow due to Beatrice's girth.

Hay and mud littered the floor of the stable, and Faye picked up her skirts as they tried the grain storage and hayloft first. They even peered into the great rain barrels kept beside the door.

Horses stirred and stamped at the intrusion as she and Beatrice checked each stall in turn. Hay, water troughs, and horses but empty of two, no doubt, dirty little faces. Faye's stomach ached from keeping it clenched. The boys were too little to be out there on their own. The smith's youngest child had wandered too close to the cliffs—

Claws fastened around her chest until each breath labored. They found the boy in the morning, his perfect, little body broken by the jagged rocks below. How did a mother bear such a thing? To live beyond your child, to never hold them in your arms again.

Beatrice stilled and raised her hand. She cocked her head as if listening to something outside.

"What is it?" Faye's heart drummed in her ears.

Shouts rang from the bailey. The men were back.

She left Beatrice in the stable, not able to bear her sister's slower pace.

William led a group of searchers through the gate.

And there, sweet merciful God, was a little form pressed against his shoulder.

They were found. Tears blurred her vision as she ran. She reached for her child, to hold his solid weight in her arms.

Arthur's face peered at her, streaked with dirt and tears, brown eyes huge and dark against the pallor of his skin.

Faye near wrenched him from William's arms. She wrapped his warm, little body beside her heart and buried her nose into his neck. She drew in deep, soothing breaths of his treacle, little-boy smell. Her tears wet both their faces. *Safe. Thank you, God.* He was here and he was safe.

William stood before the men, his face grave.

Nay, his face was all wrong. He should not cast his gaze to the ground like he bore grim tidings.

None of the men in the party would meet her eye. They shifted and murmured to themselves, their faces half-obscured by the dark.

"Simon." The name dragged up her throat like a rusty blade. "Where is Simon?"

William shook his head.

The edges of her vision darkened. Any moment now, William would grin, tug her braid and say he jested. She stared hard at William's face. He needed to smile, now, and tell her Simon was with him.

Arthur squirmed in her arms.

She squeezed until he whimpered, but her arms wouldn't release him. Spots danced in her vision. Nay. Simon was with them, must be with them.

William held out his arms to her, but she stepped back.

"Where is Simon?" Speech proved difficult past the pounding in her chest, robbing her of breath.

"They took him, Mam." Arthur's high, baby voice reached her down a growing tunnel of black. "The men came and took him. They hurt Oliver, and he fell down and I couldn't wake him."

Her knees hit the ground. She must have fallen or stumbled. She gripped the sides of Arthur's face. "Who? What men?"

Arthur's face crumpled and his breath hiccoughed.

"Faye?" William touched her arms. His hands pressed on her, weighty, ponderous, and she shook them off.

Arthur wriggled in her hold and tried to back away from her.

"Who, Arthur? Who took Simon?"

William crouched beside her. "You are frightening him, Faye."

Dear God, she was scaring her baby. She stared at her hands in horror. She had never lifted a hand against either child. Red marks on Arthur's sweet baby-soft cheeks shrieked condemnation at her.

Arthur's mouth twisted as he wailed, big eyes screaming her betrayal at her.

"I am sorry." She choked. The bailey dipped and swayed around her. She had to stop. *Think. Sweet Jesus, they had Simon.* "Mama is sorry, baby."

William gathered Arthur and handed him to Roger.

Her arms ached with the loss of her child. Another woman's child was also in peril. "Oliver?"

"Oliver will recover. He took a nasty blow to the head trying to defend the boys." William gripped her by the shoulders.

"Defend the boys? What happened? Merciful God, William, what happened?" She curled her fingers into his tunic, forcing him to look at her.

"Faye, Calder's family has Simon." Grim, his mouth harsh as a death mask.

Bile rose in her throat. It was not possible. She shook her head to clear the buzzing in her ears.

William was still speaking, and she had to hear what he said. "We will need Oliver to tell us what happened, but it appears they lured the boys into the thicket and took Simon. This was pinned to Arthur's tunic."

Parchment crackled in William's hand.

"Hugo cannot write." It couldn't be from Hugo. She grasped at the sliver of hope.

William shook his head. "He must have had a scribe write it. It bears his seal."

Faye snatched at the parchment. Tidy, sloping letters danced around the page, defying her attempt to make sense of it. She thrust the parchment at William. "What does it say?"

William stared at her. "It says, 'An Earl belongs upon his demesne.'"

Chapter Four

The ache in Gregory's knees brought him closer to God. Hunger gnawed at his belly and reminded him of his connection with the Lord. For three days, he had fasted and prayed, waited for God to show him the way to enter into service.

God remained silent.

He must pray harder and keep at it until he had his answer. God's way was not always the way of man and His divine timing did not always answer the impetuous call of sinners.

Something clattered through the bars of his cell.

Gregory started, but kept his eyes closed. He could afford no distractions in his wait for God to deign to speak with him. Sweat broke out on his brow. He bowed his head. "Dear Father in Heaven—"

Another skittering across the floor, and Gregory opened his eyes.

A pebble lay almost within reach at his knees, a pale trespasser against the dark stone floor of his bare cell. A thin pallet rested against one wall, stripped of linen except for a rough blanket. On the opposite wall a tiny barred window overlooked the fields where they worked each day. Above it, a stark wooden cross served as a reminder that all here was by Grace alone. Beneath the casement stood a plain wood table and a bench.

The Abbey bell tolled *Terce* over the undulating chant of the monks reciting the second of the Little Hours of the Divine Office. Father Abbott had understood his need for private meditation, but he would be expected at *Lauds*.

"Psst!"

Not God at all, unless the Almighty had grown a set of large hands and gripped the bars of his cells so tightly His knuckles turned white.

A dark head popped over the lip, followed by dark eyebrows and the sharply drawn planes of a face many a lass considered handsome.

"Garrett?" Gregory's knees creaked as he rose. Sharp pain lanced through his long-frozen muscles. Three days, most of which spent on your knees, would turn any man's limbs into a grandfather's. "Is that you?"

"Aye?" Garrett blinked away a sweat droplet that snaked down his brow and into his eye. His face turned redder. "Only could you come down, I am not sure how much longer I can hang on."

"Did you climb the side?"

Teeth clenched, Garret said, "Aye and I am about to go tumbling on my ass, so get down here."

Garrett's head disappeared from view as he scrabbled down the side of the two-story dormitory.

If Garrett was here, something was amiss at Anglesea. Sir Arthur might have sent him with news. *My Lady Faye.* His blood thrummed in his ears. Fresh sweat prickled over his skin as he wrenched open his door and dashed down the empty corridor. He took the stairs three at a time. Unease spurred him into a charge.

From the chapel the monk's voices called and responded in prayer as he entered the kitchen yard. Singing voices reminded him he had left his former life behind, but he needed to check all was well.

Garrett appeared out of the dark shadows around the dormitory.

The smell of incense hung heavy in the air.

"What is it?" Gregory closed the distance between them.

Garrett's expression was grim, his shoulders tense. "You must come."

"To Anglesea?"

"Aye." Garrett turned and motioned him to follow.

Gregory took a step and froze. He couldn't go with Garrett. Outside these walls was not his life anymore. His calling lay here at the Abbey, despite the Abbot's repeated refusals to admit him into orders. "I cannot."

Sharp strides driving divots into the soft, bare earth, Garrett strode back to him. "You must come. Sir Arthur sent me for you."

Sir Arthur would not have sent for him if it weren't urgent. Sir Arthur had sponsored him as a postulant to the Abbey and he owed the man for that. But he owed God his obedience and he had put his former life aside. "My place is here now."

"Your place is where you are needed, Knight." Movements sharp and jerky, Garrett gestured to outside the Abbey.

"I am no longer—"

"Did you take orders?" Garrett glowered at him.

Gregory hated the admission he was forced to make. "Nay, but I—"

"Then you are still a knight, and you are needed."

Gregory didn't want to ask the question; it did not concern him. Yet, his stubborn gut demanded an answer. "What has happened?"

Garrett clasped his arm. "It is Faye."

"What?" His muscles bunched in response. The words rasped from his throat. *Dear Father, please do not let her be...*

What? Hurt, or worse, married to another. He grabbed the other man's tunic, twisting his hand in the fabric.

Garrett shrugged him off. "I will explain as we ride."

He couldn't go. He couldn't not go. Again, the same tussle

within him. Faye or the Abbey, his lady versus his God. It never ended.

Garrett stepped closer until his face was inches away. "Beatrice is worrying herself sick. She carries our first child, and if I have to tie your saintly ass on a horse, you are coming with me. Faye needs you."

Faye needed him. The confusion cleared. It was all Garrett need say. Clean, crisp purpose flooded his being. "Do you have a horse for me?"

Garrett's grim face softened into a smile. "Come on, before one of your monks catches sight of me and tosses me in there."

* * *

The tide washed close and crashed over the large rocks beneath Faye's casement, back and forth it went, in an endless draw and suck. The walls of her chamber closed around her, robbing the air from her.

Women whispered all around her, driving her closer to the dark place. Like hens in a battery—Bea, her mother, and Nurse—heads clustered together and clucking over her near untouched dinner. They didn't understand. Hugo had her boy. Calder had been bad enough, but his brother, Hugo, did not even have the bond of fatherhood. Simon was merely to tool for Hugo's ambition. That monstrous brute had her child and she could not rest, could not eat. She sprang to her feet and paced to the hearth.

A roaring fire warmed her bedchamber, but left the ice within her untouched.

Her father wouldn't help her. Couldn't help her, he said. Hugo had been appointed Simon's guardian. Her teeth ground together. Sir Arthur of Anglesea was powerless to save his grandchild. He didn't know, didn't understand—because she had thought to spare him and not tell him—the darkness within the Calder blood. Hugo would stop at nothing. Only she really knew, and Gregory.

A golden, tousled angel amidst a feminine whirl of embroidered flowers and rich blue silk, Arthur slept on her bed. She wouldn't allow them to take him from her sight. She was all that stood between him and the devil who had his brother.

"Faye." Lady Mary caught her arm. "You must eat, sweeting."

"Aye." Faye disengaged her arm. She had not the strength to argue with them. They offered her food when she needed an army to rain vengeance down on Hugo's head. Her Arthur needed her strength for him. She must gather her inner resources and conserve them for the battle to win Simon. A hot shaft of anger wrenched up from her feet until it vibrated through her. She clenched her hands into her bliaut to hide their shaking. She had just started to feel safe after Calder's death. Hope had begun to peek through that she was finally free. Calder had won again, and this time from the grave.

"You will make yourself ill if you carry on in this manner." Lady Mary's eyes filled with tears.

"Do not cry." Tears were useless. No more tears. She turned her back on her mother and went to check on her son. Sleeping, his cheeks flushed.

Whispering came from the door. Talking about her she'd wager. Her eyes smarted, gritty from lack of sleep. She dared not sleep. If she closed her eyes for a moment, they would come and take Arthur as well. Never. She forced her legs to walk. She must stay awake like the tide, alert to danger.

A knock on the door.

She jerked to a stop. The knock must mean news of Simon. She stared at the door.

Beatrice went to answer, cracking the door open and peering through.

More infernal whispering. They worried she'd lost her mind. They kept her confined to this room like a madwoman. Her eyes burned from staring and she blinked.

Beatrice's face relaxed into a smile.

It must mean they had Simon, or news of him. Her throat felt raw from holding in the tears and her voice came out as a harsh rasp. "Is it Simon?"

"Nay." Beatrice's brow creased and her smile dropped.

Faye turned her back. Hope was almost worse than the constant fear. It was harsh in its flicker of life and left her only raging disappointment like a hook dragging through her lungs.

Arthur stirred in his sleep.

She went to him, touched the silk of his flaxen head with her hand. So warm and so alive, his soft breath raising and lowering his chest. They would not take him. Not while she still breathed. Whatever Calder had done to her, she had endured, to keep her boys safe from his rages. Until that day she had seen his anger turn on his son, and then she had found the fortitude to escape. She should have told her mother and father, should have revealed her shame to them. If she had, Simon might be safe.

Simon. She hunched her shoulders, hiding her face from the whisperers. The rawness inside her left her gasping for breath.

The door opened. Footfalls thumped the flags. The air stirred with a new presence.

"My lady?"

The hair on her nape rose. His voice, like a hot blade to an open wound. She had lost her mind; they were right. She could not turn and face the bitter anguish of the lie.

"My Lady Faye?"

Damn her legs! They turned her to face the door. Her head came up last, heavy on her stiff neck.

Strong, beautiful, outlined by the light in the corridor beyond. She had forgotten how tall and how broad. And his face. A crack opened in the hard ice within. Those eyes, darker than ebony in the harsh planes of his face. Her salvation. Her hope. The fissure widened and the anguish flooded in.

He walked toward her, his postulant robe fluttering about his powerful legs.

She would tear that robe to pieces. It had taken him from her, but the resentment was tiny, inconsequential, beside the rending asunder within her.

He was here to make Arthur safe, to bear her pain and her gnawing fear. Gregory would never let them take her boy. She could rest. Her legs buckled.

He caught her, his arms like steel around her as he drew her against his strength.

Faye rested there and drew in the scent of wool and horse and Gregory. A hundred images buffeted her, dark eyes so caring and sure, her anchor, her one safe point. Her fingers dug into the wool and touched the hewn strength beneath.

The first sob shook her.

His arms tightened.

She pressed her cheek to the rough homespun of his robe and absorbed the heat of him. The awful noise in her head stilled beneath the steady thump of his heart.

"My lady," he murmured against her hair. "My own lady."

"They took Simon," she said, the words muffled by his chest.

"I know and I am here."

His warmth curled into her and the ice splintered, driving hard into her wounded heart.

Her mask shattered, and Faye cried.

Drawing the covers up to Faye's chin, Gregory drank in the sight of her. Dark rings stood out in sharp contrast to the deathly pale of her skin. Still so damned beautiful and fragile she had near broken him as she sobbed in his arms. Every tear she had ever shed was carved on his soul.

He pressed his palm to his chest and tried to ease the ache inside. Since the moment he first saw her, he had not beheld anything as lovely. His failure tasted bitter in his mouth. She needed him, and he had been on his knees praying for his salvation.

"She sleeps?" Lady Mary nudged him aside. The torment of the last few days etched harsh lines around her mouth.

They told him Faye had not slept in three days, had barely eaten, just paced her chamber in a frightening, brittle calm. "It is better she rests."

"Thank you." Tears glittered as Lady Mary turned her head aside to hide them. "We did not know what else to do. She…"

Gregory waited for her to compose herself. Rage smoldered like a banked fire within him. That whoreson had Simon. The profanity shocked him a little, but it was apt. He knew the depth of Hugo's depravity. His lady knew, only too well, the beast to whom she had been wed. Hugo made Calder look like a saint. Seven years Gregory had lived with the cruelty and tyranny of Calder, an impotent witness with no power or right to intervene between a man and his wife. He had seen in Hugo's eyes the impotent lust for his brother's wife.

Faye's hair escaped confinement in wisps across her cheek, spun silk, the color of an early moon.

His fingers twitched to trace the creamy softness of her skin. He turned away. The desire, he could surrender to God; the tenderness always hit him like a stave to the knees.

"You will want to speak with Sir Arthur." Lady Mary straightened the covers about her daughter and little Arthur.

The boy had grown. He would be tall like his grandfather and those sturdy little limbs held all the promise of a fine, strong man. For the first two years of his life, all Arthur had managed to lisp of his name was "Gree." "Story, Gree!" or "Up, Gree!" His little face twisted in determination as he bellowed. "Nay, Gree!" Arthur had a will to match any man's.

Young Simon, in the hands of that satyr. It made him want to rip his robe off, grab his sword and ride like the devil himself to get his boy. Her boy, not his, only his for a short time. It became too easy to forget that.

He followed Lady Mary out of the chamber and into the

upper reaches of Anglesea. People nodded a greeting as he passed, subdued and wearing their sadness on their faces.

Lady Mary left him at the entrance to the hall.

Seated in one of two enormous carved chairs, Sir Arthur waited for him.

It was a fine hall, tall and majestic, proclaiming to all the might of its owner. On any other night, it would have been filled with castle folk, chatting away the hours before bedtime. Only Sir Arthur was here now, keeping silent vigil. Even the dogs lay silent by the hearth, their ears pricked, their gazes patient and watchful.

A pall hung over Anglesea and contrasted with his happy memories of the place. This hall should be a place filled with cheery, laughing faces, packed with love and good humor. The difference saddened him.

A large man with a barrel chest and the battle-hardened arms of a warrior, Sir Arthur's craggy face drew into grim lines. He rose to his impressive height. "Sir Gregory."

Not many men met him eye to eye. Sir Arthur stopped just shy. "Merely Gregory, now."

Sir Arthur flushed. "Indeed, Father, my apologies."

"Not Father either." The admission pinched at his gut. "I am still a postulant."

Sir Arthur's brows rose. "You have not become a novice?"

"Nay." Resentment sputtered and died. Hugo had Simon and his Lady Faye lay as a brittle shell in her chamber. Thank the Lord he could produce coherent speech with all warring inside him. "The Father Abbott has adjudged me not ready to take my vows."

"Indeed. It is perhaps fortunate for us this is so." Sir Arthur pressed his thumbs into his eyes. "You have seen my daughter?"

"I have." She still rendered him weak when they shared the same space. She always had.

"I have failed her." The older man's shoulders slumped. "My child has come to me in her hour of greatest need and I am impotent as a—" His gaze flickered over Gregory and he flushed.

The first glimmer of humor since Garrett dragged him from

the monastery tilted his mouth into a smile. "Not impotence, my lord, abstinence."

"Verily." Sir Arthur cleared his throat and motioned the chair beside him.

Gregory adjusted the skirts of his habit and sat. They seemed ridiculous beside the armor-clad Sir Arthur. Of course, they were not ridiculous. His robe served as a reminder of his inner conviction, the symbol of his chosen life. He shouldn't be here. Dear Father in Heaven, as if he would be anywhere else. "The abstinence is harder."

Sir Arthur gave a short bark of laughter. "I wager so."

A log popped in the hearth, and one of the coursing hounds raised his head. The hound trundled over to him as Gregory clicked his fingers. There were animals aplenty at the Abbey, but farming beasts, bullocks, chickens, and goats. He stroked the courser's brindle coat, and the animal settled again with a heavy sigh.

"I am given to understand your hands are tied." One of them had to broach the conversation and Sir Arthur seemed lost in his study of the fire.

"Simon is now the earl." Sir Arthur steepled his fingers in front of his mouth. "Hugo is his guardian. I have no legal right to keep Simon here."

Only fear of Sir Arthur and the men he commanded had stayed Calder's hand after Faye had left him. "You could demand him back."

"I could, but that would cause an uproar. I need move circumspectly." Sir Arthur grunted. "Since the Army of God, I am under the king's suspicion. All the rebel barons are."

"And Hugo has risen as a shining example of loyalty." Sour coated the back of his tongue. Hugo had played this well, the larcenous wretch, he stayed on the side most likely to pad his coffers. Supporting the late King John through the baron's uprising had played well for Calder when he was still alive, and it did now for his brother. Hugo enjoyed the favor of the boy King Henry.

"I did not see it." Sir Arthur shook his head. "I, who have always prided myself on my acuity in reading men, gave my daughter to that conniving pit of curs."

Anger curled low in Gregory's belly, demanding he tell the man the full truth of what he had given his daughter into. It was not his secret to tell, however, so he held his peace. Faye had sworn him to silence. He had failed her in so many other ways that he could, at least, keep his word.

Whining, the dog nudged his hand.

"Hugo was a master dissembler. I was fostered into Calder's household as a page and I did not see him for who he truly was until he was a grown man." To say more would be cruel. Sir Arthur's careworn visage rebuked his anger and he had not the heart to add another worry.

"But you are not her father. She was not entrusted into your care at birth." Sir Arthur brushed his hand across his face.

Nay, but she was entrusted into his care at her marriage. It had amused Calder to have Gregory stand as Faye's knight protector. Calder and Hugo had jeered at him and called him Father Piety and given into his care the most beautiful treasure of Calder Castle.

"I will do what I can." Sir Arthur leaned his elbows on his knees. "I have sent a message to Lady Mary's brothers. They are still in the new king's favor and will intercede on our behalf. The king is young and we can play on his youth to further the cause of the mother."

It was a fair plan. England still staggered under the weight of the dead King John's rule. Loyalties shifted like sea sand in the tide of power. The weight on Sir Arthur's shoulders might have crippled a lesser man.

Calder's, and now Hugo's, star had risen since King John's death and an act against the new guardian to the Earl of Calder could be construed as raising one's hand against the new king. After taking part in the Army of God against King John, Sir Arthur's every action fell under close scrutiny. As much as it chafed to admit it, the man trod a thin line between treason and loyalty to the family he had to protect.

Hugo would know it, too, which was why he acted now. There would not be much support for a rebel baron raising an army to take the heir to a powerful earldom from his demesne.

"And yet, one of us must act." Sir Arthur's stare glinted keen beneath his snarled brows.

The look crawled across Gregory's skin. Unspoken expectations hung heavy in the air between them.

"Faye is terrified for Simon." With awful precision, Sir Arthur hammered the blade home.

Gregory may be a postulant, but before that he was a man. A man who had held Simon since hours after his birth, told the boy stories to help him sleep, and placed him on his first horse. Simon and Arthur were grafted into his flesh as deeply as their mother.

Sir Arthur fixed a stare on him.

Choices, always choices. He scoffed at himself. He had made his choice when he got on that horse and followed Garrett. Strangely enough, he believed the Abbot would understand.

Iesus vero ait eis: Sinite parvulos, et nolite eos prohibere ad me venire: talium est enim regnum cÃfÂ|lorum.

Let the children come to Jesus. A just, Godly cause, and he could do this. It would be his one, final act as a man of the sword before he took his vows. He had waited years to enter his chosen vocation and a few days more could make little difference. He would do this, however, with Godliness in the forefront of his mind. He nodded and met Sir Arthur's steady gaze.

Relief loosened the tension around Sir Arthur's eyes and some of his habitual vitality returned to his face. "Simon was taken to Calder Castle," Sir Arthur said. "I need a pair of eyes close enough to watch that he is safe while I do what I can."

"I will be your eyes." Eyes, aye, and a pair of hands close enough to snatch the boy if the opportunity presented itself.

"Hugo bears you no love, Gregory."

True enough. Hugo knew who had aided his brother's wife and children in their escape. "I have friends close to the keep who believe I did right."

Sir Arthur grunted. "Still, best not to announce your arrival."

Christ had entered Jerusalem on an ass. The picture swelled in Gregory's mind as a plan formed. Not a noble or glorious plan, quite the opposite, and he chuckled softly. Humility, it was as good a practice as any with which to begin. God knew, he hadn't grasped obedience and chastity—

Best not to think on that too long.

Chapter Five

Faye blinked in the glare of sunlight streaming through the casement. She was in her bed. How long had she slept? The bed beside her was empty. Her pulse spiked as she sat up. "Arthur?"

"He is well." Ivy placed a cup on the oaken chest by the bed. "Tom is with him. He will not let the boy out of his sight."

If Tom watched Arthur, all should be well, but still unease churned in her middle. She would rise and find them to be certain. From the cup by her bedside rose a sharp scent. "What is it?"

"A little something Nurse thought would help." Ivy folded her hands together in front of her. "I sweetened it with lavender honey."

"And Nurse allowed that?" Beatrice heaved herself up from her seat by the casement. "She forces me to drink her potions as is."

Laughter lit Ivy's grave features from within, animating her pale face into an uncommonly lovely woman.

Faye took a tentative sip of the tisane. It wasn't too horrible. Bitter, aye, but softened by the fragrant sweetness of the lavender honey. It hit her empty belly. Hunger gnawed for the first time since Simon and been taken. The familiar dread weight settled over her chest. "Did I miss dinner?"

Beatrice pressed her fists into the small of her back and winced. "Aye and breaking the fast. You slept through the night well past noon."

Good Lord, she must get up, but the rest had helped clear her mind.

Ivy fetched a small salver and placed it beside her. The yeasty smell of fresh bread made her mouth water. Her stomach growled and Faye's face heated.

"Eat." Beatrice eyed the salver like a dog searching for scraps. "Or I might steal it from you."

"Shall I arrange some water for a bath?" Ivy flushed and her gaze strayed over Faye's gown.

With a start, Faye checked her appearance. She'd been wearing the same bliaut for three days, and it showed in the wrinkled, stained silk.

"I think that's a fine idea." Beatrice nodded and her braid bounced against her back.

Verily, it must be bad for Beatrice to be so eager she repair her costume. Faye touched her hair and encountered a matted snarl. Never had she allowed her appearance to disintegrate to this point. Gregory had seen her looking like this, a veritable hag. Gregory had come. The heavy press against her chest lightened and she breathed easier. Gregory would fix this. "I will eat and then bathe."

Ivy nodded and slipped out of the room.

Beatrice sat beside her and took a wedge of cheese. "Sorry." She pulled a face and popped it into her mouth. "I seem to be eating for an army."

The sharp bite of cheese and warm bread flooded her mouth. Faye almost snatched the wedge back from her sister. How long had it been since she had eaten?

"Faye." Loading her name with meaning, Beatrice picked at the bed furs.

Her sister wore her "oh, Beatrice" face. The one that came before Beatrice did something outrageous. Faye braced for the worst.

"I have questioned whether I should tell you." Beatrice shifted.

Belly too tight to eat, Faye lay down her bread. "What?"

Beatrice drew a long breath. "Sir Gregory was with Father and our brothers in the armory. They spoke well into the night."

"And?" *Say it.* She swallowed the building scream. Ladies never screamed or even raised their voices. Her heart pounded an uneven beat in her chest. It had to concern Simon.

Beatrice blushed. "And I happened to overhear what they were saying."

Overheard. Indeed. Beatrice's terrible habit of listening to conversations that didn't concern her was well known throughout Anglesea. She shouldn't encourage her, but she wanted to hear the rest of it. "What did they say?"

"Gregory goes to Calder Castle."

All the air rushed out of her lungs. "Why?"

Beatrice pulled a face. "I did not hear that part. Garrett caught me and pulled me away."

"Hugo will kill Gregory if he sees him."

"Then, he does not go to negotiate Simon's release." Beatrice chewed on her bottom lip.

"Parley with Hugo?" A bitter taste coated Faye's mouth. "Hugo does not parley and especially not when he has the upper hand. He has nothing to gain by releasing Simon."

Her brother-in-law would be relishing every moment of this. He enjoyed wielding his power over those in his control. Hugo didn't care for Simon and he, for certain, had no interest in raising a child.

Nay, this was Hugo's conceit. Without Simon, Hugo had no

power. He was merely the brother to a dead Earl. However, if he had control of the young earl, Hugo's ambitions could finally be realized.

And also revenge for her leaving Calder. She'd pricked the family's pride by leaving their beloved son. Blinded by her anguish, she'd been stupid to believe they would let her go and not care, be relieved even. Another had warmed Calder's bed before she'd even left, and she took that as sign he no longer wanted her. He hadn't wanted her, but Calder had always wanted to win.

Right down to the bottom of his rotten soul, she understood Hugo. Mother of Mercy, she had lived with the man for seven hateful years, seen the way he stared at her, caught the gleam in his eye. Hugo wanted the title, and he saw Simon as his path to ruling the earldom, but he had always coveted whatever and whoever his brother had. She shoved aside the bed linens and rose. Cold stones bit into her bare feet.

With a frown, Beatrice watched. "What are you doing?"

"Thinking." Faye paced over to the casement. Around them, the lands of Anglesea lay in a patchwork of fields. To the south whitecaps danced over the face of the sea. East of here lay Calder Castle and her son. If Gregory went to Calder Castle, he would go in secret.

Gregory acted, and she must wait, shut up in this room, staring out of this casement while Simon remained with a monster who would seek to control him. It was the way of the world. Men acted. Women waited and prayed they would not have to put the pieces back together again. A lifetime of waiting pressed down on her shoulders. Waiting for suitors, waiting for her wedding, waiting for her husband to drop dead.

The venom in her last thought shook her.

She might add years to her life if she tallied the time she had spent sitting idly by while others acted. Many of them spent waiting for Gregory to speak, act, do anything.

"Faye?" Beatrice's brow puckered into a frown as she touched her arm.

They were as different as two sisters could be. All her life, Faye had done the right thing, the correct thing, her behavior above reproach.

Beatrice tilled her own furrow. The adored youngest sibling, before young Mathew was born last year, Beatrice had been allowed free rein with her impetuous spirit. She had never meekly accepted her fate. Three arranged betrothals, but no marriage until Beatrice had chosen a man so unsuitable as to be laughable. And yet, here she stood, her belly large with that man's child, blissful in a marriage of her choosing.

"You have a peculiar look on your face." Beatrice cocked her head.

Aye, that would be because she was having a series of peculiar thoughts. Thoughts that caused her heart to hammer in her ears, wayward, wicked thoughts that had no business jangling around in the head of a dutiful woman. Years of serene obedience and she had naught to show for it but scars on her body and even deeper scars within.

So accustomed were they to biddable Faye, they didn't even share their plan. Scurrying around like rats hatching schemes that would change the course of *her* life. She was tired of blowing like a dead leaf in the wind, tired of letting other's whims send her drifting this way and that. Her father had sought a good marriage for her, and she had done as he wanted. Calder had near broken her in bending her to his will. Now Hugo thought he could take her child from her and she would allow it.

"Sod that." The forbidden words tasted like nectar on her tongue. Mayhap she should have taken up cursing before now.

Beatrice's gaped and took a step back.

In this keep she had been Sir Arthur's perfect daughter. She had been married from here and taken to Calder Castle to play the part of dutiful wife. She had done her duty, served her husband and her people, and this was the coin meted out to her. No more. Lady Faye was taking charge. She wrenched open the door and took the stairs at a run, dodging around a group of young boys playing stones.

"Faye?" Beatrice puffed along in her wake.

On a whim Beatrice had rushed off to London. This was no whim. This was her son. If anyone was going to Calder Castle, she was going with them. She knew the castle better than anyone. If her son was in danger, then that's where she must be.

A serving maid leaped out of her way as she stormed past.

The privacy curtain to the armory hung closed and she swept it aside. "I am going with Gregory."

As one, the occupants of the armory swung to look at her.

Faye sought the pair of dark eyes that mattered most to her.

Gregory frowned and shook his head. "What are you saying, my lady?"

Faye dug her nails into her palms. They needn't look at her as if she had lost what few wits she had left. "I am going with Gregory to Calder."

"Do not be ridiculous." Roger puffed up like a charging bull.

"It is not ridiculous." Her breathing came harsh and ragged and she fought to steady it.

Her father shook his head.

"He is my son." Nothing meant more to her father than his children. Sir Arthur had to understand that. "Simon is my child, and I am going to bring him home."

"Faye. You are upset and not thinking clearly." Henry stepped forward, spreading his hands before him like he was gentling a feral beast.

"Do not." Faye knocked his hands away. She would not tolerate one of Henry's lectures. He had no say here. "When you have held your child in your arms, then you can tell me how I should feel."

"Faye, sweeting, I am a father." Sir Arthur rose from his chair.

"And I do understand how you feel, but you cannot go with Gregory. If Hugo saw you—"

"Do you think I care what Hugo does to me?" Dear God, there could be nothing worse the man could do to her that Calder had not already done.

Roger cleared his throat and looked troubled. "You cannot mean it."

If only Roger knew how Calder had been. If only any of them knew. She had kept her silence to spare their anguish, but no more. "Calder was a vicious animal, and Hugo is worse."

Pain flared in Gregory's eyes before he dropped his gaze. He couldn't even look at her and acknowledge the truth between them. It was not good enough. Now he must stand with her. He couldn't run from this anymore.

Fine tremors shook her legs as she stared at his bent head. "Tell them."

"My lady." His head jerked up. She had sworn him to silence, forbad him from uttering her secrets.

Still as a predator, his face so cold she shivered, Sir Arthur turned to Gregory. "Tell us what?"

"I know Hugo from court." William leaned forward in his chair. "I heard things about him."

"You heard things?" Sir Arthur's voice rose with each word. "What things did you hear?"

Faye held Gregory's stare. All the evasions and half-truths hung toxic between them. Angry words never spoken, accusations never made, things known but never acknowledged.

Stripped bare of her pretense, she stood before him. Exposed in her shame in front of her family.

"What you heard of Hugo, was true for Calder." Gregory seemed to wrench the admission from the deepest part of him.

"Jesu." William leaped to his feet. "If he were alive, I would kill him."

"Someone tell me." Sir Arthur's voice thundered around the room.

"Calder beat her." As if he somehow stood aside from himself, Gregory's expression hardened into blankness. "He beat her often and so badly some days she could not rise from her bed. I would shield her from other people until the bruises faded. There is nothing Hugo can do to her his brother has not already done."

"Except to hurt my child."

They could not even look at her. Henry stared at his feet. Roger paced to the end of the armory, his boot heels ringing against the flags.

William had his back to her. "I heard the whispers and I did not ask. You always looked well enough when I saw you, and there were other matters. King John. The rebellion." He shook his head. "I should have asked."

"Faye." Her father's eyes gleamed damp as he moved to her, hands held before him to embrace her.

"I do not want your pity." If her father touched her, she would shatter. "I want you to do what you can to make sure we never have to go back there."

"You have my word." Sir Arthur dropped his hands. "But you ask me to allow you to put yourself in danger, and this I cannot do."

"Have I not earned the right?" She held her father's gaze.

Sir Arthur dropped his head. "Why did you say nothing? Why did you stay there? Why—"

"I don't know." Faye didn't have the answers to his questions. "At first, I stayed because I believed he would change. Then I stayed because I believed I deserved no better." There was so much to speak of, but now was not the time. "After I returned to Anglesea, I stayed silent because I didn't want you to blame yourself. I still don't." She pointed to Gregory. "Ask him. He will tell you how he begged me to leave, time and time again, but I would not."

Gregory's eyes blazed as they met hers. Shame was written in their midnight-dark depths.

She could not allow him to shoulder the blame for decisions she had made. "It was my choice, and you honored that choice. Now, I am making a different choice and I ask you to honor this one as well."

"This is madness." Roger paced back to them. "Now more than ever you cannot go. We will find another way, Faye. We will defy the king if we must, but I will not allow you anywhere near that whoreson's blood."

"I lived with that whoreson." Dizzy with the intensity of feeling rushing through her, Faye listed and caught her balance. "Every part of me needs to do this."

Sir Arthur stepped forward. "Faye—"

"She comes with me." Gregory's gaze found hers and locked.

"But—"

"He is right. We failed her, all of us, and we will make it right." William indicated the chair beside him. "Sit, Faye. If you are going with Gregory, we need to make sure you are not discovered."

"What of Arthur?" Expression thunderous, Henry crossed his arms over his chest. "Have you forgotten that you have two sons?"

Faye curled her hands into her palms. She would slap her brother silly if he said one more word.

"Arthur will be safe here." Her father gripped her arms. "If you must do this, Faye, know that we will care for the boy. Now," he turned to the others, "let us factor this new development into our plan."

* * *

Faye carefully shut her chamber door. She had made it out of the armory and down the endless passages of Anglesea without collapsing. The wood at her back kept her on her feet. Her legs shook so badly, she feared they would crumple beneath her.

The plan was simple. She and Gregory would travel in disguise to the Calder demesne. Once there they would seek out

Bess, the healer and midwife. Gregory felt sure they could trust her, and Faye agreed with him. A year ago, Bess had aided her escape and the midwife held no loyalty for Hugo. As village healer, Bess knew the family's brutality well.

"Faye?" Beatrice rapped on the door. "Let me in."

She couldn't face another person now. Not with the ugly, naked truth out there for all to see. "I must ready myself."

"Open the door." Beatrice pounded harder. "I am not going away until you do."

Beatrice was quite capable of standing outside her door all night and yelling, the determined little besom. Faye opened the door.

Beatrice dropped her hand raised to knock again. "Garrett says you are going with Gregory to Calder."

"Aye." Faye moved like an old woman into her chamber. She needed to get ready, but there was nothing here she needed.

"Have you gone mad?" Quite possibly. Faye choked back a bitter laugh. This from Beatrice, who never hesitated to tumble from one scrape into another.

Lady Mary swept into the chamber behind her daughter. "Hush, Bea, the decision has been made." Her mother held a bundle of clothing in her arms. "I brought these for you." Lady Mary lay a pair of chausses and a tunic on the bed. "I believe these are the same ones Beatrice wore."

They had agreed in the armory it would be best to disguise Faye as a young postulant. Traveling monks traveled where they desired and without question.

Lady Mary had procured boy's clothing for her. Her mother, the perfect lady, had agreed to be a party to his. "You are going to let me go with Gregory?"

Mother tilted her head. "Could I prevent you?"

"Nay." Nothing would stop her from getting to Simon. "I expected more of an argument."

"Aye." Resting her arms atop her belly, Beatrice nodded.

"I would do the same." Lady Mary's smile held a hint of

sadness. "We are mothers and we protect our own." As if preparing for battle, she drew a breath and straightened her shoulders. "I am not happy to see you do this, Faye. You are my child and putting yourself in danger cannot please me, but Gregory will protect you."

Aye, Gregory would protect her and he loved her boys.

"I cannot believe Father agreed to this." Beatrice shook her head. "He would never have agreed to me going to London."

"You never asked." Lady Mary sniffed. "Now, you must change. Gregory leaves within the hour."

The chausses clung to Faye's hips and legs. Her legs seemed naked and exposed without her skirts. They did free her to take longer steps, however, and she strode around the chamber, testing her new skill. It was little wonder men ran faster than women with their legs unencumbered by fabric. Lord, she hadn't run since she grew old enough to let down her skirts. Ladies did not run, they walked or glided.

Before she slipped the tunic over her head, Lady Mary helped her bind her breasts.

"Hmm." Beatrice and Mother stood back and surveyed their handiwork.

"A cap." Beatrice nodded. "She needs to cover her hair."

"Monks do not wear caps beneath their robes." Lady Mary frowned at the top of Faye's head.

"They do if it's cold." Beatrice glared out the window and sighed. The balmy summer night mocked her statement.

Faye snatched up her sewing shears from where they lay on her abandoned embroidery.

"Faye, what are you doing?" Hand held out for the shears, Beatrice took a step toward her,

At the barest touch of sharp shears, the first lock of hair dropped

"Faye." Beatrice shrieked and clapped her hands over her mouth.

"Oh, good Lord." Lady Mary paled.

Another golden lock dropped to the stone floor and lay like a gleaming skein of sunlight against the dark stone. Beatrice should know what she was doing. The idea had fermented in Beatrice's own mind a year ago. Except Beatrice stopped short of this point. With everything to lose, Faye could not afford to hesitate.

The shears slid through the braid at her nape. It slithered down her back to the floor. She shook her head, lighter without the heavy fall of hair.

Beatrice gaped at her over the hands clasped to her mouth. "What have you done?"

"What I must." She was going with Gregory. It was her only chance of getting her son back. Shorn curls tickled her fingertips. Around her feet lay the scattered remnants of a lifetime of nurtured hair. She'd cut her hair. Oh, dear Lord, she'd done it now.

"I see you are determined." Beatrice toed a shining lock.

"I have to, Bea, or I will go mad not knowing what happens to Simon. Hugo is cruel and he has a temper. He will stop at nothing to get Simon to bend to his will." It was the closest she could come to telling the full story.

Lady Mary stared at her for a long moment.

Suddenly self-conscious, Faye touched her shorn head. "What?"

"If you aimed to look like a boy, you have failed." Beatrice pursed her lips. "I think it becomes you. It makes you look younger."

"Like a young boy?"

Beatrice pulled a face. "A remarkably pretty boy." She grinned. "But then, people see what they want to see and dressed as a young postulant, you will pass inspection."

"Well." Mother took the shears from Faye's numb fingers. "Let me at least tidy the ends."

She was actually doing this. It made her head spin to think on it. Her baby would be without her. "Arthur?"

"We will watch over Arthur." Beatrice finger combed her hair.

"Promise me." Leaving her baby carved a deep, aching chasm inside her.

Beatrice touched her fingers to her swollen belly. "I swear it, Faye. I will watch him as if he were my own."

"And I." Lady Mary cupped her cheek. "But do take care of yourself, sweeting. And know we will not be idle at Anglesea."

The enormity of what she planned slammed into her and her shoulders slumped. "I have to get him back."

Beatrice's face softened. "You will get him back. I know you will." She enveloped Faye in a hug. "Let me see what I can do to help."

A knock came from the door and it opened to admit William. "It is time."

The time to act was upon her, and Faye wanted to run and hide behind her mother's skirts like a little girl.

William took in her boy's clothing with a nod. His gaze stopped at her head and he raised a brow. "You can still change your mind, Faye. We could send Henry with Gregory. Roger is needed here, but even I could go."

Doubt niggled at her. She could remain at Anglesea with her youngest son. Her brothers would do all in their power to get Simon for her and her father had sent word to her uncles already. "I am doing the right thing, am I not?"

"I do not know." With a groan Beatrice collapsed on her bed. "You could wait here for Henry or William to return. Or see what our uncles can do to help."

If she followed William out the door, she committed to this path. She wasn't daring like Beatrice or courageous like her mother. They would never have remained married to a man like Calder. She still couldn't fathom how she had borne it for so long. The truth was, she couldn't have, without Gregory. He had shared her shame and been her escape from it at the end, her salvation and her rescue.

Her family watched her and waited for her to make the decision. There was nobody telling her what she must do or how she must act. She was the sweet sister, the delicate lady who suffered her fate with grace and dignity. Except, she would not let her children share her fate. "I do not think I can do that. Not while Hugo has Simon."

Lady Mary pulled her into a fierce hug. "Then you are doing the only thing you can."

Chapter Six

Arthur slept so peacefully, Faye had not the heart to wake him and say goodbye. Little face flushed, limbs flung across the bedding as if she'd tossed him there. Deep into her mind, she pressed the image of him to carry with her. She replaced the covers and smoothed them over his chest. She trusted her mother with her son, but Faye needed to say it one more time. "Take care of him."

"As my own." Lady Mary touched her cheek.

At the entrance to the keep, she parted from Beatrice and her mother. Her back tingled with their stares on her as she walked to the cluster of men outside the stables. She ventured into a strange new land. Behind her lay all she knew and loved, and ahead were dragons.

Gregory stood taller than the men around him, her guide through this strange newness. At every major point in the last eight years, Gregory had been there. Standing beside Calder, his dark head averted, on her wedding day. Cradling her sons in his huge hands a few hours after their birth. Tending the wounds Calder had put on her. Racing through the darkness to bring her and the boys to the safety of Anglesea.

Outside the keep, William kept pace with her. Catching her

arm, he stopped her halfway to the men. "I beg your forgiveness, Faye. I am your brother and I should not have left the rumors I heard unchallenged."

Mayhap not, but she bore no anger toward William. "Calder was my husband. What could you have done?"

William's gaze slid away from hers and hardened as he stared at a point beyond her shoulder. "Faye, I wish you would let me go for you."

It was tempting to let him. People always *did* for Lady Faye. This time, however, she must battle her own demons and win. If William went, it would be as all the nights she had lain at Calder Castle, hurting inside and out, and condemning herself for not fighting back. The taint of her cowardice sank deeper into her bones each time Calder had visited her and left her crying and broken. Despite his constant entreaties, she had not allowed Gregory to take her from Calder, her fear of Calder, her shame and humiliation had been too deep. For all those times she needed to take action now.

"I know you would." She managed a wan smile. "But this is my battle." Pray God, she had the strength for it.

"I understand. They have your boy." William squeezed her hand before releasing it. "I may not have children of my own, but Simon is one of ours."

They walked on a few steps through the dimly lit bailey. The moon rode high in the sky, and the damp of first dew coated her skin.

"I know very little of what occurred during your marriage, Faye, but I was at court with Hugo for many months." William stopped her again.

She'd kept her secret for so long, his words jarred her. She would have to accustom herself to having her shame known throughout her family. Her father has asked her why she had stayed and let it continue, and she wished to God she knew.

William, eyes cold as the grave, looked at her. "If only half of what I heard at court was true, we will make them pay in blood."

William, her childhood defender and mischief-maker. How she thanked God for her brothers, even pompous Henry.

"Here." William opened her hand and pressed something into it. "If you get the chance, do not hesitate."

The dagger blade reflected the orange glow of the braziers. Against her palm it lay hard, cool, and deadly "I do not know how to use it."

"Slip it into your boot and keep it with you. Ask Gregory to show you how to use it on your journey." His handsome face broke into a familiar William grin. "You will not be traveling fast."

The cluster of men parted.

"Your carriage, my lady." William sketched a lavish bow.

Faye stared at it. "A bullock cart?"

"Poor monks do not travel by horse." Gregory made a jerky motion toward the cart.

"Aye." Her grand rescue had humble beginnings, and Faye chuckled. It felt like an age since she had done so.

The bullocks stood in the traces, their mouths working at the cud with no care for the responsibility resting on their powerful shoulders. One of them reminded her of Nurse and Faye laughed harder.

"She has lost her wits." Henry scowled at her. "We cannot let her go."

"Shut your cakehole." Cuffing Henry so hard he stumbled forward, Roger saved her the trouble of doing so. Roger sidled closer to her and lowered his voice. "You might want to stop laughing. Father is within a hair of locking you up in your chamber."

Faye stopped.

His mouth compressed in a grim line, Sir Arthur stepped into the pool of brazier light. "A sennight. I give you a sennight and if you are not back here with our boy, I will bring every man, woman, and child who can bear steel and fetch you."

"We will be back." Gregory's calm certainty spread around the waiting men.

Faye drew in a deep breath of his soothing presence. Her quest began.

Gregory held out his hand to assist her. "My lady."

Roger nodded at his outstretched hand. "You are going to have to stop that. A monk does not assist a boy into a cart."

"She is not a boy."

Like a caress, Gregory's laden words slid down her spine. For a brief flicker his gaze rested on her as a man views a woman, warm and wanting. Faye added the memory to her scant hoard of others like it.

"Enough." Sir Arthur grasped her by the waist and set her in the cart. "Go with God, Faye. Only do it fast, and before I change my mind."

* * *

Gregory flicked the reins and set the cart in motion. A waning moon lit the path from Anglesea castle to where it disappeared between the soaring beech trees. Beyond the thicket, the road took them down into the village. From here, they would travel east to Calder Castle. And Simon.

Lavender, the scent of Faye, twined through the calm night air. Many times, alone in his monastic cell, he'd sworn a hint of lavender lingered there. He'd had a dog as a boy, a scraggly beast that would find a scent it liked and roll in it. Legs waving in the air, the dog would press the smell deep into its coat. Dogs were clever beasts and not constrained by the tangles of mere men.

The danger on this journey increased tenfold with Faye's presence. It prickled beneath his skin like an army of ants. Hugo wouldn't get her. He swore it before God and before her father. Let Hugo try. Blood thrummed beneath his skin, warming him. In the bed of the cart rested his blade and it thirsted for vengeance. His score with Calder's blood was too many years in the settling. *Oculum pro oculo, dentem pro dente, manum pro manu, pedem pro pede.* An eye for an eye and no mercy given.

How would the Abbot judge his actions, a just cause or pure folly?

A lone dog announced their presence to the collection of sleepy cottages that made up Anglesea village.

Sir Arthur had set up sentries throughout his demesne following Simon's abduction. Too late. The sentry slid out of the dark to see who passed. He waved to Gregory before returning to his post.

Sir Arthur blamed himself, and the man did carry a portion of blame. The larger portion rested with him. He should have expected Hugo's ambition and pride would demand action. He had been too intent on gaining entrance to the Abbey and allowed himself to believe he left Faye safe at Anglesea. He had wanted to believe that, because then he could leave with a clear conscience. What a damned fool. Now she paid the price.

* * *

Faye rubbed her bruised elbow. Bullock carts were not made for comfort. With nothing to cushion her, she was tossed around like a loose apple.

The odd identifiable shape slid past in the shrouded landscape —a house, a low stone wall and even the occasional cottage, but for the most part there was nothing to see.

For a while, she had trod beside the cart. Until one too many bruising encounters with hidden obstacles on the road had sent her back to her perch. With the way the cart rattled about, sleep proved impossible.

Gregory sat stiff beside her. His long legs dangled over the edge, almost touching the ground. Rocks slid perilously close to the soles of his boots. She made a game of laying wagers on which ones would hit.

The boots were an oddity with the habit. She tried to picture his large feet in a pair of monk's sandals, and failed. Her Gregory wore boots and armor, and kept his hair cropped close to his head to allow for a helmet. Thankfully, he had not yet shaved his head in tonsure.

A monk? Gregory wanted to be a monk. The man beside her looked, moved, spoke, and even smelled like her Gregory, but he belonged to the church now. What would the church do with a man like Gregory? Put a rosary in those huge warrior hands and bend his strong back tilling rows of cabbages. He could have stayed with her and the boys at Anglesea as a household knight. Instead, he had taken Sir Arthur's offer of assistance and presented himself at the Abbey of St. Margaret as a postulant.

Unkind satisfaction they had not yet admitted him to novice nestled inside her. An unworthy thought and cruel to take joy in his failure to achieve his dearest wish. If he hadn't taken his vows, some part of him was still hers.

Dim moonlight glinted off the crucifix suspended from his rope belt.

Now she was being foolish. Aye, in the sense that he protected her and the boys while at Calder as her silent, faithful shadow he had been hers, but never in the have and hold sense. Even now, he came back, not for her, but to aid her in freeing Simon. There must be remnants of that foolish Fairest Faye still in her heart, because she still harbored her secret dream of Gregory riding through Anglesea's gates, laying his heart before her—

The cart wheel hit a rock, ramming her bruised elbow into the barrels at her back. Ha! Just punishment for pointless dreams laying fresh wounds on her sore heart. "What is in the barrels?"

"I do not know."

"Are they empty?

"Nay."

Verily, the Abbey had not improved his conversational skills any. When they traveled together in the past the boys had accompanied them, filling the long silences with their chatter and their needs. *Blast*! She had forgotten to tell Beatrice that Arthur liked honey and fruit in his morning pottage. Her youngest son woke grumpy and needed cajoling into the new day. Would he ask for her in the morn? "Arthur will expect to see me in the morning."

Gregory turned to her, his strong features indistinct in the gloom. "Aye, but he will be well cared for."

Faye knew as much but something about hearing Gregory confirm it gave her greater reassurance.

Above them, the sky remained inky black. "Will it be light soon?"

"In a short while."

How would Simon greet the new morn? Her boy woke full of energy and his lively chatter could drive a body out of their head. Dear God, Hugo had no patience with children. She prayed their old nurse was still at the castle. When they left, Faye had wanted her to come with them, but Ruth wanted to stay near her family. *Please let Ruth be with her boy now.* Ruth knew how to keep Simon occupied.

"Do you think Simon knows we are coming for him?"

"Aye."

"Hugo has no patience."

"Simon is a sharp lad. He will know to keep his head down." Gregory knew her boy as well as any. Simon was a smart boy, and he had steered clear of his father and his uncle.

The cart jolted over a rut and drove her elbow into the sideboard. Faye clenched her teeth and inched into the center of the cart. The distinctive melancholy yip of a fox made her shudder and she moved closer to Gregory's solid bulk. The safety of the castle walls lay behind them.

Only Gregory stood between her and the relentless, mysterious night. Dark nestled in loving shadows on his grave, handsome profile. People mistook his silence for lack of intelligence at their own peril. Many a time she had witnessed him shred the assumption with a few deliberate, considered words. Thank the Lord she had never been on the wrong end of one of Gregory's verbal tilts. Nay, but she had suffered enough under his unflagging silences.

She wanted to break his silence now. "I did not ask before. You have been well?"

He took a long moment before he answered. "Aye, my lady."

His lady. Never *his* lady. Not in any manner that mattered.

Another lurch rattled her bones, and she bit the inside of her mouth. Women taking charge of their lives did not complain of a few bruises. However, even take-charge women needed to relieve themselves and each jolt of the cart reminded her of that necessity. Surely Gregory would stop soon. Despite his near inhuman stoicism, he must be experiencing similar discomforts.

Faye scrunched her toes into her boots against the press of her bladder. She had sat for hours at Court beside Calder and controlled her need, because Calder had not liked her to draw attention to herself. She could suffer her discomfort in silence for a little while longer.

The cart pitched and she bit her lip to stop the whimper. Nay, she could not wait. "Gregory, I must, I need to—" A lady never said such a thing aloud. Her face heated and she pointed toward the bushes.

He stared at her, flushed with realization, and nodded.

Thank you, Father. He stopped the cart.

Faye slid from the cart, and stood with its solid bulk at her back. A lot of night lay between her and the shadowy outline of the nearest bush. Dear Lord, she would pee her braies if she didn't move, but there could be anything behind that bush. "Um...Gregory?"

"Aye."

"I find it rather dark."

Gregory dropped beside her. He stalked over to the bush, disappeared behind it, and a moment later, emerged. "It is clear."

Faye crept behind the bush. She kept Gregory in sight, tall and broad-shouldered, standing by the cart. She cursed her braies as she wrestled them down to her knees. Skirts were so much easier in these situations. Relief made her eyes water. She finished, retied her belt around the top of her chausses, tugged her tunic down, and ran smartly back to the cart.

Gregory handed her a water skin. "For your hands."

Her heart gave a small flutter. Gregory knew things about her like this. He knew she liked the white of the chicken and no fat on her meat. That she would eat apples but preferred peaches and grapes. He was aware she liked her hands kept clean. She washed her hands and dried them on her tunic.

She knew his quirks too. He kept his emotions even closer than his thoughts. You had to know the telltale signs, the clenched jaw and the muscle that jumped in his cheek. The one that had been working near constantly since they'd left Anglesea.

He rummaged through a bag and tossed her a dark piece of clothing. "Wear this; it will be light soon."

Faye spread it open. It was another habit like the one he wore. She slid it over her head. It swathed her in heavy dark wool and swallowed her feet. "Is this necessary?"

"You do not look like a boy." The muscle in his jaw worked like a mouse in a silk purse.

So, what did he see when he looked at her? She would give anything to have the courage to ask. As always, the air between them sat heavy with all they did not say.

She fumbled with her belt as she loosened it from her chausses. Belt fastened about her waist, she tugged robe fabric over the top of it to clear her feet. That was better. At least she could walk. Assisting her to her seat atop the cart, his hand warmed hers.

As he climbed aboard, the cart dipped under his weight. He shook the reins, and the bullocks lumbered into motion.

Faye twined her fingers together and settled into the silence between them.

Patience, Gregory spoke when he needed to and not before. He could go days without uttering a sound, a useful trick for a monk, but not much good in a traveling companion.

She hunted for a subject to break the silence and came up

empty-handed. Everything that came to mind was fraught with traps. It was no good, the silence was worse than an ill-fitting bliaut. "Are we going to travel the entire way without speaking?"

His smile warmed the cold place inside her. It always surprised her at its sweetness in his carved features. "I am often on my own at the Abbey."

At Calder Castle he was often on his own as well. She had never seen him with friends or a woman. She had watched particularly hard for a woman. For the most part, he was with her or the boys. Or in the practice yards. His shoulder pressed through the layers of wool, the heat of him comforting. "Why have you not taken your vows?"

His jaw clenched. "The Abbot judges me not ready."

Surprising. She'd never met a man more committed to the priesthood. Father Piety from the top of his dark head all the way to his huge boots. "Why?"

That infernal cheek muscle would jump right out of his face if he kept this up. "My lady, there are some things best left unsaid."

Fair point. This was the way between them. Questions not asked and answers not given. Things known, but never spoken. Tonight, in front of her family, she had ripped the scab off an old wound and it still smarted. She lacked Beatrice's courage to voice every thought or feeling.

The creak of the cart provided a rhythmic pattern underscored by the dull plod of the bullock's hooves on the road.

Perhaps the silence was not so bad.

* * *

Gregory's inner war had raged for many years; it was as an old enemy. Terrifying, but familiar, in its constancy.

His Lord or his lady. At the Abbey it was easy to forget how she tugged at every part of him. She was his test, his temptation in the desert. Christ had not faced a beautiful woman. He nearly snorted aloud. Now he added blasphemy to his sin tally.

He recited the Supplication to Mary over and over again in his head. Throughout her marriage he had resisted her and he would do so now. Once she and Simon were safe, he could return to his life as a monk.

Perhaps his battle was what the Abbott sensed in him. The secret place, the one he kept hidden from everyone. He tucked his sins and his forbidden thoughts into that hidden part of him, awash with color. *Purpure* for his lust; rich, dark and tempting. *Gules* was the shade of his pulsing anger. His need for vengeance pulsed a deep, bottomless *Sable*. And Faye was there. *Or*, a bright light in the darkness surrounding it.

Or, the same color as that glorious hair that had hung down her back in a gleaming rope all the way to the curve of her ass, and so thick he could wrap it thrice around his fist. He had only seen it unbound once or twice, curtaining her back in a silken fall.

Her shorn crop exposed the vulnerable arch of her nape. Her delicate neck, so fragile he could wrap his entire hand around her throat. For the life of him, he could not fathom what would make a man take such a precious gift as a woman and wreak damage. A gift like Faye should be cherished and protected with the God-given power of a man's body. He could have been that man if his life had taken a different course. His father had tried up until his death to make Gregory into his own brutish image. Gregory had vowed to his mother and his younger self that he would be a better man than his sire.

Nay, his decision was made. His life belonged to God. A decision unquestioned until eight years ago when he entered the bailey of Anglesea as part of an armed escort to fetch Calder's bride. He had looked up, spotted her in the casement and received a glancing blow from which he'd never recovered. He'd moved past that when he joined the Abbey.

Or had he?

God strike him for his lies, especially those he told himself. And while God was at it, could He grant a bit of strength. The cart threw her against him constantly. Gregory counted his breaths between contacts. His flesh reacted the way of all weak flesh and stayed with him despite the gnawing tedium of travel. Distance marked by wafts of lavender, brushes of heat and each press of her thigh.

* * *

Victory. Hugo smiled as they shoved the boy into his solar. Satisfaction had never tasted this sweet. It coated the back of his throat. His men had done well and would be rewarded.

By the door beside Sir John, cowered his reward. Simon, a weak name for a pathetic wretch. The boy looked just like his dead brother.

How that must gall the haughty cunt every time she looked at the boy. To see Calder's features stamped across her son's face as clear as a map. To know who had put that boy in her belly and whose seed she had birthed.

Jesu, he would love to see her now. Frightened, crying even. His shaft thickened in anticipation and he motioned the whore sidling in the corner beside his bed. "Come here."

Fear was better than a mouth on his tool. Tonight the whore would beg and plead. If he did not look too closely, he could pretend she was Faye. Faye on her knees before him, crying and begging. God's Bones, he would shoot his load if he carried on like this.

The boy wiped snot away with his tunic sleeve. This miserable, filthy little beggar who would carry forward the line of Calder. A proud line, dating back to well before William the Bastard put foot on these shores. A name too noble for a mewling, whining brat.

"Stop crying."

The boy ducked his head.

Coward. "Look me in the eye when I speak to you."

Up came the head, but his lips quivered.

Rage surged through Hugo. He blamed her for this, too.

Always coddling the boy. Did he have enough to eat? Was he well rested? Did he want a cup of hot milk before he slept?

Men were not stroked and soothed into manhood. They were wrenched up, tough and hard, like the wolf emblem of Calder. He stroked the Wolf Rampant emblazoned on his chest. Wolves ripped the throats out of those not strong enough to run with the pack. He would make a Calder of this weakling. "Get him away."

Sir John bent and wrapped his arm about the boy's feeble shoulder.

Jesu, they were all at it. They would learn differently. "When he stops crying he can eat."

"But my lord—"

"Not before then."

Sir John snapped his mouth shut and he led the whiner away. "Come along."

Calder grabbed the whore by her nape and tugged her to her knees before him.

Yellow hair obscured her face.

Good. He put his boot on her head and pressed down. If he drove her head into the ground hard enough, perhaps he could reshape her coarse features into Faye's.

Chapter Seven

The wool habit boiled her alive, but Faye blessed the extra padding beneath her bottom. Bliauts provided a bit more protection than chausses to a woman's nether regions. Ass. Not a word she used but she liked the sound of it. In the bright sunlight, her fears receded. Not for one moment did she forget her purpose, but out here, she was not Sir Arthur's daughter or Calder's widow, merely a nameless boy traveling beside a monk. Nameless boys didn't need to watch their words or keep their knees pressed together. They could slouch and fidget and scratch anything that itched.

Green farmland drifted slowly by the cart. They had left Anglesea demesne and traveled a small strip of land forming part of her dowry to Calder. It was good land, rich and fertile and fed by a large, looping river cutting straight through Anglesea on its path to the sea. The land had been well-tilled and the harvest waved in long ripples of golden wheat and barley over the fields.

She had not been this way since last summer. Gregory had been with her then too, taking her and the boys back to Anglesea. That night, she had asked much. Asked that he defy his liege lord and help her escape to her father's home. Gregory had turned to her, questions in his beautiful, dark eyes and nodded. Merely a nod. Through the night he had raced with her and the boys, never once voicing his questions or his doubts.

A lone farmer stood beside the stone wall to a wheat field. "Morning, Father."

Faye jumped and ducked her head.

Gregory nudged her knee. "Good morrow."

Please do not stop. Please do not stop. If the man saw through her disguise, they were doomed.

The farmer leaned his elbows on the wall and made himself comfortable. "That's a fine pair you have harnessed there."

Gregory halted the bullocks. "They are that. Sturdy."

Damn. Curses were so much more apt for these occasions. Faye shrunk into her habit.

The farmer's gaze swept her, Gregory and the cart, curiosity bright on his weathered face. "You traveling a ways?"

"Aye." Gregory's knee kept up a steady pressure.

Whether in warning or reassurance, she couldn't tell. She didn't feel any better, just like they should get moving and keep moving.

The farmer nodded and squinted up into the sun. "Fine day you have for it."

"Indeed," Gregory said. "The weather is fine this summer."

Most farmers she knew would talk about weather for days. She pressed his knee back.

The farmer sniffed and pulled down the sides of his mouth. "Would not turn away a spot of rain round about now."

The sun baked the black wool habit. Perspiration slid down Faye's sides.

"Who is that you have with you, Father?"

"Just a young boy." Gregory nudged her elbow. "Say hello, lad."

She lowered her voice to what she imagined a boy would sound like. "Good morrow."

Bending down, the farmer plucked a long stalk from his field. With weathered, dirt-encrusted fingers, he stripped the head and popped it between his teeth. "You on your way to the monastery up beyond Calder Castle?"

"Aye." Gregory motioned the barrels behind. "We bring some victuals from the Abbey of St Margaret."

"Right you are then." The farmer squinted at the barrels. The stalk poised between his teeth, as if testing the air like an insect.

"We best be on our way," Gregory said. "The monastery will not be best pleased if this lot spoils."

"Aye." The farmer straightened. "Best you do. Only, watch yourself on the road, Father. Been lots of comings and goings in the last little while."

"Busy you say?" Gregory squinted at the road ahead of them.

"Oh, aye." The farmer slapped his hand on the top of the wall. "We do not get much traffic hereabouts."

"Indeed?" Gregory grunted and glanced in both directions.

The farmer frowned at the road. "Men tearing along here on horseback like the devil himself was on their tails."

Faye's heart lodged in her throat.

"Indeed?" Gregory kept his tone light, but he tensed.

"Aye." The farmer's craggy face cracked into a smile. "Thought I saw his late lordship's brother not three nights ago."

Hugo. Faye's mouth dried. It galled her to be reliant on Gregory to ask the questions, but she didn't trust her disguise.

"Did you now?" Gregory's knee pressed hers, a silent warning.

Warning be damned. Faye returned the pressure, willing him to ask him about Simon.

"Cannot be sure." The farmer scratched his chest with a grubby hand. "Was late at night. Strange time for him to be out and about I thought."

Gregory grunted and shook his head.

"Was he alone?" The question escaped Faye before she could stop it.

Gregory stiffened, but Faye was glad she'd asked. The man might have proof of Simon.

"Sir Hugo?" The farmer snorted. "Nay, lad, when does he

ever travel without a bloody fuss and bother? Disturbed my best milk cows they did."

"Was there a little b—"

"You have the truth of it there." Gregory applied steady pressure with his knee. "Anyway, good day to you; best get these supplies out of the sun."

"Oh, aye." The farmer nodded. "No need to go and spoil good food over the likes of Sir Hugo."

Gregory slapped the reins, and the bullocks ambled forward.

"Why did you interrupt me?" Gregory had sat there and talked about the weather. Even had the gall to hush her while he passed up an excellent opportunity to gather more information.

"We are trying not to draw attention to ourselves." He glanced at her. "Asking about a boy with Hugo would have given the man fuel for gossip. You might have noticed he was a chatty sort. His speculation would not have stopped with us."

"Oh." Faye lapsed into a chastened silence. "At least he thought I was a boy."

"Lucky sod. He must be blind," Gregory muttered.

Faye's heart leaped. At times he looked at her like a man who wanted a woman, but he had never come close to voicing such a thing. "What do—"

"There is an inn a ways ahead." Gregory cleared his throat.

Faye's heart dropped again. And it appeared, he would not be voicing his thoughts now either.

"We will stop at the inn for the night."

"Why?" She had no knowledge of distance, but they had passed the tall, stone cairn that marked the border between Anglesea and Calder's demesne a ways back and it could not be much farther.

"Our arrival in Upper Mere must be timed to attract the least notice. Hugo has eyes in that town."

Hugo must be like Calder before him with eyes everywhere. Faye had learned that at her own peril once or twice. Calder had been harsh when she had returned to the keep and he had not approved of how she had spent her day. "Are you not afraid we will be recognized at the inn?"

"It is not the sort of inn I normally frequent" Color climbed his cheeks.

A hundred questions tumbled through her mind. "What sort of inn is it?"

He went redder and she laughed. He was so easy to tease at times. "The sort you should never enter."

"I see." That sounded interesting. The daughter of Sir Arthur of Anglesea was shielded from the common world, and Calder had kept her guarded and confined.

They stopped to break their fast beside a stream. It was a lovely spot, the trees providing cool shade and the stream whispering a happy gurgle over the rocks. The weight in her chest eased as she ate her bread and cheese.

Gregory gave her the largest portion of their meal. She pushed it back at him. A man his size needed a fair amount of feeding. He'd lost weight at the Abbey. His face was thinner, more defined, but the bulk of him beneath his robe was still impressive. He'd allowed his hair to grow, and it brushed his cowl in rich, sable curls. Who would have guessed Gregory to have curls? How they must gall him with their unruliness.

Faye tilted her face to catch the warmth of the sun.

As the day had worn on, Gregory's silence lost its edge. He had even unbent enough to have brief conversations with her. The ground between them became more familiar for the last few miles. It had always been thus. For the most part, she spoke and he listened. Or the boys were with them demanding all their attention.

His gravity lightened around the boys. He laughed more and told them wonderful stories. Gregory had endless patience with them. Answering questions, guiding their youthful exuberance, like a real father. What would her life have been like with Gregory as her husband and father to her sons? There had been times when she had pretended they were a family. The quiet caused her head to go places it had no place meandering. "Do you have a plan? When we get to Upper Mere."

"Aye." Of course he had a plan. Gregory did nothing without a plan.

A flock of sparrows argued noisily above their heads.

"We will need to be cautious." He rose and washed his hands in the stream. "Hugo is arrogant, but not stupid."

That was true. During her marriage, she had banged her head against the wall of Hugo's conceit and come away bloodied. "He must know my father will act."

"Aye." He bent to clear up their meal. "But he will be expecting an attack to come from Anglesea. We will sneak in beneath his nose and, if we are fortunate, be gone before he knows we were there."

"With Simon."

"Perhaps."

"Perhaps?" It took her a moment to register his meaning. There was no perhaps about it.

"We will see what we find."

Faye's belly tightened. Simon was in the hands of the devil himself. Every moment her son spent with Hugo was one moment too long. "I am not leaving without my son.

"My lady, first we survey the situation." He packed their provisions into the cart.

Faye gaped at his back. "What does that mean?"

"It means," he said without turning. "That first we must see how matters lie and then decide on the best course of action."

Getting Simon away from Hugo as soon as possible was the best course of action. "Simon is in danger."

"I realize that, my lady." He leaned down to check the bullocks. "But no good can come of rushing in unprepared."

His calm made her want to ruffle him. "This is my son we speak of."

He nodded. "We do not know what we will find at Calder Castle."

"Simon, we will find Simon."

He drew his words out as if he spoke to a child. "And Hugo will be expecting something."

"He won't be looking for us. You said as much."

His jaw clenched. "But he will be alert and I will not put you in danger."

Her angry pulse throbbed in her throat. Gregory planned to protect her when he needed to protect her son. The danger to her was meaningless. She cared only about her son. "I agree that we must reconnoiter first, but only to make a rescue plan." She took a calming breath. "I will have Simon back."

"If possible." He crossed his arms.

"I am getting my son back." She would countenance no other outcome.

"If I judge it prudent once we have assessed the danger." He spoke so evenly, dismissing her, making light of how vital it was to retrieve Simon. "If not, we will report back to your father. That is my mission."

Well, it wasn't her mission and he discounted this new Faye, the one in charge of her own fate. "I am not leaving without him."

"You may have to." He loomed above her a good foot, taut with suppressed emotion. He could tower and glower all he liked.

"You cannot stop me."

"I will if I must."

She could hardly credit her ears. Verily, their entire conversation was a cruel jest. Her mouth dropped open, and she snapped it shut again. "Let me explain this to you. I am here to rescue Simon, whether you will it or nay. It matters not what you and my father planned. There is a new plan now, and I will see this done."

He grunted and shoved a hand through his hair. "This is no place for a woman."

A lady does not show her temper. A lady does not screech like a hag. The trees dipped and swayed in her vision as she battled her temper. "I am his mother. Where else would I be?"

"Safe at Anglesea." Had be been merely mouthing words when he had supported her before her father and brothers at Anglesea? Here and now, when challenged, he took a different line.

"You said you understood."

"I do understand—"

"Nay, you do not. For you to even speak to me thus means you understand nothing of a mother's pain when her child is in the hands of a monster. You think you know how much of a monster, but you don't even know the half of it."

"My lady—"

"It was me who suffered every blow of Calder's hands. It was me Calder forced to submit to his will. Hugo enjoyed my suffering, encouraged Calder, even relished what he did to me. I bore it all to shield my children. Do not think you understand. Do not think you can stand between me and my God-given right to protect my child. You want to shield me." A broken laugh escaped her. "You cannot shield me from what is done. And you will not stop me now." Her breathing rasped in the sudden still. She could hardly credit what had come out of her mouth.

Stark anguish crossed his face. "I take your meaning, my lady."

What meaning had he taken? His words were laden with so much more. She'd wounded him in some way. Her newfound courage flickered and died. He cared for Simon and he'd demonstrated it in hundred different ways. She hadn't meant to speak all that, but she had opened her mouth and it had all poured out. "I beg your pardon."

"Nay." He hunched over the bed of the cart, his expression hidden from her. "It is I who must beg your pardon."

Chapter Eight

Faye's outburst exhausted all her words. She used the continuing journey to tuck away all the messy tendrils of emotion that swirled about her. Thank God, Gregory kept silent about her uncharacteristic behavior. She wanted to press Gregory about his upset, but that had never been their way, and she lacked the courage to change things now. She had little enough of him as it was, she dared not risk their friendship.

As the miles passed, the tension eased. She must keep a closer watch on her mouth and her emotions. God alone knew what could come out if she didn't.

Day bled into evening with a glorious display of red and orange flung across the sky in lavish abandon.

"The inn is a hard by." Gregory pointed to a small branch in the road. "We will stop for the night."

Faye nodded.

Gregory turned to her with his gentle smile. "You must be weary."

"I am." She returned his smile. "A bit."

His warm gaze roamed her face. "You are a woman of uncommon strength, my Lady Faye."

Faye didn't know about that. A woman of uncommon strength would not have remained with Calder as long as she had.

"Nay." Gregory shook his head, his eyes tender. "You bore what you believed was your lot, and you did so with grace."

He had often displayed an uncanny knack for reading her thoughts.

"I should have left the first time he raised his hand to me," Faye whispered, her shame tightening her throat.

Gregory looked away, his expression growing grim. "I should have insisted you did."

Tears threatened and she battled them away. Like she had so many times in the past, Faye slid her hand into Gregory's firm, steady grasp.

His fingers tightened around hers.

And like she had so many times in the past, Faye drew comfort from his touch.

Tomorrow they would arrive at Calder Castle and the greatest challenge of her life. There was no choice but to rise to the challenge. William's knife pressed against her ankle.

"We will sleep in the common room." Gregory cleared his throat. "It is not what I would like for you, but anything else will cause interest."

A night in a common inn, another new experience to tuck into her memory for when this was done. Beatrice had said something similar about her adventure. How she had discovered a world far removed from life within the keep walls.

The forest grew thick through this section of road. Tree limbs soared overhead and blocked the waning daylight. The reedy call of pipes twined with the rise of wood smoke in the evening air. The noise grew louder as the bullocks plodded forward. The hum of voices underscored the pipes as the tavern wove into view.

"Here?" Faye whispered. A drab, squat building huddled in a small clearing between the trees. People spilled out of the door and onto the benches set against the wall. A few heads turned their way as Gregory drew the cart to the side.

Gregory nodded. "Aye. It is a rough place, but frequented by honest folk."

Other carts littered the space to the side of the inn. A few horses sheltered beneath a makeshift barn. None of them had the look of a destrier, and Faye relaxed. A nobleman might mean recognition, but these were all mean beasts, meant more for plowing than riding.

"Do you know how to unharness a bullock?" Gregory kept his voice low.

"Nay." The Lady Faye in a bullock cart stretched credulity far enough. She'd like to see Anglesea's minstrel spin this tale into a ballad to her beauty.

"It will look strange if you do not help." Gregory grimaced as if it pained him to make such a suggestion.

"Indeed." She had never so much as saddled her own palfrey, but she was willing to learn. Copying Gregory, she hopped from the wagon.

"Good evening, Father." From behind a nearby cart a rough looking man appeared.

Gregory nodded in return. "My son."

Faye hastened to nod her greeting. She dropped her gaze to the ground. Hopefully she looked meek and obedient and not furtive. Excitement tiptoed up her spine. Her quest overshadowed everything, but this new adventure was so far removed from her life.

"Good, keep your head down," Gregory murmured as he loosened the traces.

Faye studied his actions and tried to, at least, appear as if she knew what she was doing.

Gregory removed the neck yoke. "See that they are watered."

The bullocks stood and looked at her, their tails swished back and forth. Goblets of saliva dangled from the their lips, mixed with green and brown bits that made her stomach churn. She shuddered and inched her hand forward, grabbed the head harness and led the beasts toward a water trough. The disgusting, sticky mess coated the back of her hand as they trundled along after her. She breathed through her mouth to lessen the stench.

Gregory tossed her a lightning-quick grin. Aye, he could well grin, he was not covered in cow spit.

Once the beasts were settled, Faye trailed Gregory into the inn.

The noise hit her like a wall. People filled the rough benches and tables and even crouched along the walls. All eating and drinking and bellowing at each other.

A portly man slammed his tankard on the table. "Watch yourselves, you blaspheming sons of whores. We have a good father with us."

Silent people turned in their direction. The stench of unwashed bodies pressed in proximity fought the ale's malty sweetness.

Gregory's broad shoulders made a good shield. "God bless all here."

The noise resumed.

"Here you are, Father." A thin woman, meanly dressed in rough wool, shoved her son from the bench. "You can sit here."

The boy leaped to his feet and dipped his head to Gregory.

"Finish your meal." Gregory's hand engulfed the boy's thin shoulder. "Go on, lad. My...the lad and I will find a corner and be content there."

The boy swallowed and edged back into his seat. "Thank you, Father."

"Would you bless us, Father?" The woman pressed her hands together in prayer.

Gregory crossed himself and the small family bowed their heads as he delivered the blessing. The Latin words rolled smooth and rich as velvet from his tongue. His conviction shone from his beautiful face like the church paintings of the martyrs. People stilled around him and listened. He would be a wonderful priest. The knowledge lodged like a thorn in Faye's chest. He was not hers, never hers. When would she get that into her dull head?

Gregory finished his prayer, took her elbow, and led her through the crowd. People shifted to make way, and they found a quiet spot near the wall beside an open window. Fresh air provided a brief reprieve from the heat and the oily tang of goat meat.

She sank to the ground beside him, relieved to be below the heavy cloud of taper smoke hanging above their heads.

"Are you well?" Gregory stretched his legs out.

Faye didn't want to risk tripping someone and kept her knees tight to her chest, her robe tucked beneath her toes. "Aye."

"I brought our food." His shoulder pressed against her as he rummaged in his sack.

"Is there enough?" The meat pie he held was only enough for one large man. Faye didn't fancy the pungent goat the inn offered.

"Oh, dear Lord, Father." On the bench nearest them a plump man turned and pointed to the pie. "You cannot starve a growing lad. That tidy little morsel will barely fill your belly. Great big man like you." He clicked his tongue and turned back to his table. "Mother, here, give us some of that nut loaf of yours for the good father and his boy."

The farmwife rose from the other side of the table. "Aye, indeed, Heart. And I have a peach tart to sweeten their journey." She beamed at Faye, her apple cheeks pink and shiny. "Oh, and look at the lad, Heart. Such a sweet-faced young thing."

Gregory shifted beside her.

The entire family stared at her and Faye reminded herself to act like a boy postulant traveling with a monk. She smiled and waggled her fingers.

A curvaceous young girl, a younger version of the woman, returned her smile with a wink. The brazen little strumpet.

Gregory would swallow his tongue if Faye winked at him like that. She ducked her head and hid her grin, her mind flooded with winking ladies and gaping knights.

"And so young." The woman bustled over and frowned into her face. "You are taking them into the monastery with their mother's milk still wet on their lips, Father. Such a shame. Why his mother must miss his pretty face every day of her life." The woman cupped Faye's face in plump, rough hands. "And his cheeks are still soft and smooth as a babe."

Oh, Good Lord. If her face grew any hotter it would explode. People did not cup the Lady Faye's chin. Most of them would hesitate to touch her mantle. Faye lifted her chin out of the woman's grasp. All the attention hung like a lead weight on her. She needed to do something fast.

"Step away from him, my good woman." Gregory pressed the woman's hand away. "His pretty face hides the soul of a very devil."

The woman jerked her hands back and clutched them to her bosom. "Nay."

"Aye." Gregory nodded. "His mother brought him to St. Margaret's herself. Three days she walked to bring him to us."

"What did he do?" The farmwife gaped and stepped away from Faye.

Faye dearly wanted to hear the answer to that question, too. She bowed her head penitently.

"I would not soil your ears with his misdeeds," Gregory said.

The woman's shoulders sagged and she sighed.

"Should we feed him?" The husband peered around his wife at Faye.

Faye's stomach clenched in objection as the nut loaf hovered out of her grasp.

"We are all God's creatures." Gregory clapped a hand on her shoulder. "Our Good Lord broke bread with saints and sinners alike."

"Aye, Father." The woman did not sound sure.

Faye would smack him if he talked their way out of that loaf. The smell of fresh baking and nuts tormented her tongue.

"Mother, feed the young knave." The husband clapped his hands together. "The good priest looks to be just the man to have him well in hand."

Skirting Faye, the woman handed the bread to Gregory. She added her peach tart and a large round of cheese. Her feet pattered beneath her skirt back to the table.

Faye pressed her lips together to stop her smile. "What were my sins?"

"Heinous." His eyes twinkled. "Debauchery is the very least of it."

Faye basked in his smile. It warmed the empty place inside her. They had not had many occasions for laughter betwixt them. She returned the smile. "You have been warned."

"Still." He glanced at the table. "It would be for the best if we stayed quiet until we depart."

"We will sleep here?" The wall pressed hard against her back. At Anglesea, she had a huge bed, draped in peacock-blue silk and embroidered with swathes of flowers. The same bed little Arthur would rest in tonight. She sent a quick prayer homeward to him.

"It will grow quieter." Gregory split the loaf and handed her half. "Once people have eaten, many will clear for the night and we can stretch out."

With her buttocks aching from the dirt floor, she could muster no enthusiasm for the idea. "Indeed."

* * *

Warm and soft, Faye rested against his side, the fragrance of her hair teasing him. She was awake. Lids lowered, peering at the inn about them.

As the evening settled into dark it grew quieter. Many of the occupants chose to sleep outside or to travel through the night.

Her delicate hands were tucked between her knees. He could hold both her hands in one of his. A fierce wave of protectiveness shook him. His to protect and cherish. Nay, she was not his. She had never been his and could never be. The knowledge gripped like a fist in his gut.

A group of men drank cup after cup of strong mead beside

the empty hearth. Gregory would wager they were not farmers. Their tunics were dirty, but finer than most of the folk in the tavern. Tradesmen or guildsmen were his best guess and getting drunker as the night drew on. They bore watching.

People spread on the benches throughout the tavern, soft grunts and snores rose in the air. A family, two parents and their five offspring, huddled closest to him and Faye. The children slept beside their mother, but the father stayed awake, his glower on the group by the hearth.

He nodded to Gregory. He watched the group, too.

The ground beneath his ass was cold and hard.

Faye shifted and settled. His lady was not accustomed to such rough treatment. If he could, he would see her resting on silk and velvet. He yanked his mind away from images of Faye spread over silk.

Laughter rose from the drinking men and Faye started. One of them stumbled to his feet and staggered toward them. His foot tangled in a sleeper in his path, he tripped, and cursed the air blue about him. The sleeper raised his head, grumbled and settled down again. The drunk wove with exaggerated care through the bodies littering the floor. "Need to piss."

He lurched to a stop beside Faye and pulled out his tool.

Dear God, Faye shouldn't see this.

Faye stiffened and pressed her face against his shoulder. Gregory tugged her closer as the man aimed a stream of piss through the window. Faye's trembling shook through him. A lady such as Faye was too delicate for a place like this.

A sparkling blue eye peeked up at him, alight with mischief. She was laughing.

The man put himself away and wiped his hands down his tunic.

A smile tugged at Gregory's mouth. He should have known better than to think she would wilt into a lump of matronly outrage. He forgot the spine of steel that ran through her.

Her hair tickled his chin. The color of clearest mead and

softer than silk, her new curls clustered about her face like a naughty cherubim. A delicious, tempting cherubim with the lush curves of a woman grown. Now he tortured himself and to no good purpose.

She raised her head from his shoulder, her blue eyes twinkled up at him. "At least his aim was straight.

Sweet Heaven, but her smile slayed him. The sedate loveliness of Faye's features warmed and sweetened, her full, red mouth invited him to join her. Gregory chuckled and turned his head away. Far safer not to get drawn into the magic of her. "The place is fairly basic."

She snorted and settled. "I wish the floor were not so hard."

A thankful streak of wisdom stopped him from offering her his lap. She was already too close for comfort. And the Lord only knew what the good tavern folk would make of a priest with a postulant cuddled in his arms. A pretend priest with no tonsure. Fuel for confession on his return to the Abbey.

A woman giggled to his left. Clothes rustled, more giggling and whispering. A sigh, a man's voice and an unmistakable grunt. The Lord had a perverse sense of humor at times. The corner of his eye twitched as his blood stirred in response to the rutting couple. Desire. Nay, he could not risk that with Faye right here. Priests did not rut. However much they wanted to.

Faye leaned forward and gasped. "Gregory." She tugged at his sleeve. "That couple...they are...Gregory!" Her face flamed as she stared, wide-eyed past him.

The grunting increased, interspersed with soft feminine moans.

Enough. He leaped to his feet and tugged Faye with him. A woman murmured in her sleep as he hauled Faye through the inn.

She tripped, her gaze still locked on the fornicating couple.

Gregory righted her and placed her in front of him. With a shove, he got her moving toward the door.

"Gregory." She gawked as she spun toward him. "They were—"

"Aye." He didn't need to hear it. His face burned, but his shaft reacted in a predictable and disgraceful manner. He marched Faye away from the door. "We will sleep beneath the cart."

"I—"

"These are common folk, my lady." He used her title as a deliberate reminder to his traitorous flesh that she was not to be considered in that manner. "They do not have the luxury of walls or doors."

"Good Lord." She choked and a small giggle escaped her.

He was behaving like the worst sort of prude. Father Piety was an apt name for him. Most priests understood the needs of their flock and turned a blind eye.

"Consider my eyes opened." She hugged her arms around her chest and grinned in delight.

He pulled on her arm. An answering smile spread across his face. "Come on."

* * *

Faye followed Gregory through the cool quiet to where their cart was pulled up inside the trees. It looked like any of the other carts and she wouldn't have known one from the other. Trees blocked the moonlight and all she could make out were the darker shapes of the penned beasts. "Why are we outside?"

Gregory tugged the sacking from the back of the cart. "We will sleep here."

"Outside." She didn't fancy that. The trees towered huge and gloomy all about her.

He disappeared beneath the cart and rustled around. "It is for the best."

"I would much rather sleep inside." The floor may be hard, but at least it was beneath a roof. There were creatures in the dark. Small noises came from the trees.

"We cannot sleep inside." Gregory reappeared and stood. "It is not suitable for you."

"Neither is sleeping outside." Anything could happen to her out here.

"My lady." He stopped in front of her, so large, it blocked her view of the trees. "You should not be exposed to what happens in there."

Faye laughed. "I'm no sheltered maiden, Gregory. I can tolerate a bit of—"

"You sleep there." He jabbed his finger at the cart. "I will sleep out here."

An owl hooted and she jumped.

"If you are making me sleep outside, you will sleep with me beneath the cart." Close enough to grab if something furry with large teeth came out of the trees.

"Faye." He dropped his chin to his chest. "It is not proper. I will sleep close enough to hear if anything is amiss."

"Nay." She glared at the shadowy shapes of the leaves against the gloom. "None of this is proper, and I am afeared to sleep alone."

He gestured to the ground. "I will be right here."

"It would be better if you were closer."

"Nay." He drew himself up to his full height and folded his arms.

Faye wanted to kick him. Gregory was being stubborn. "I shall not be able to close my eyes."

"Suit yourself." He bent and raked the undergrowth into a long shape. "I am tired and I shall sleep. Out here."

He lowered himself to his makeshift bed and turned his back.

Faye's foot itched to give his mulish head a prod. She stomped over to the cart and crawled beneath. She would never sleep with all this night around her. At least, inside, she'd not had to worry about being something's dinner. She glared at the dim, oblong shape of Gregory. A wolf could sneak under the cart and rip her throat out and he wouldn't know. Nay. Would not even care. He would be sleeping with his back to her.

There were spiders in forests. She examined the sacking for a stray lurking insect. Her nape prickled and she drew her knees beneath her chin. Great, hairy spiders that would crawl all over. She shuddered. Something brushed her arm and she shrieked.

Gregory shot up and spun around.

Faye scrambled out from under the cart. "There are spiders in there. And rats."

"My lady." He drew a careful breath. "There are no rats and no spiders."

"There are." Her skin crawled and she rubbed her arms briskly. "One touched me."

"A spider or a rat?" His voice quivered.

She glared up at him, not quite able to make out his face. Was the great lout laughing at her? "I do not know. I did not stop to ask."

"Fine." Over to the cart he strode and crawled beneath. He banged his fist against the sacking and rose. "If there were any spiders or rats, they are gone now."

"They could be hiding."

"Hiding?"

"Aye." Spiders crawled into the tiniest holes. She'd seen them. Rats were worse, sneaky and devious with their little red stares and big yellow teeth.

He bent and went through his banging again, a bit longer this time. "No more spiders."

She inched closer to the cart and crouched. "Are you sure?"

"Aye." He rested his forearms on his thighs. "Now, go to sleep. We have a long day on the morrow."

Scrutinizing the pools of shadow on the sacking, she crawled back beneath the cart.

He rose to go.

"You could tell me a story." That would work. "Like you tell the boys until they fall asleep."

He sighed and dropped on his seat.

At least he was a lot closer, and Faye lay down on her side. She rested her head against her arm.

Raising his face to the sky, Gregory leaned back on his hands.

"One story and I promise I shall sleep." It had always worked for Simon.

"One story." He sighed, lay down and propped his head on his hand.

If she stretched her toe out, she could brush against his chest. She settled herself for sleep. "No dragons."

He pursed his lips. "Indeed, I shall tell you a story I am transcribing at the Abbey."

"You transcribe?" To be a man of learning was rare enough, but doubly so in one who had, up until recently, made his living by the sword. "So, you can read and write?"

"Aye, my mother taught me." He gave her a wry smile. "It was her fondest wish that I joined the priesthood."

"But you did not? You earned your knighthood, instead." This was the most she'd ever heard him speak of himself. Faye hoarded up the tiny bubble of intimacy jealously. He knew almost every personal and humiliating detail of her life. Yet, she had only glimpses into his life.

"I am the only son of eleven children. My father is Calder's vassal. When one of my sisters did not catch his fancy, my father gave him a son instead."

Good Lord, ten sisters; it was no wonder the man had endless patience. She had an image of rather large, hearty girls. "Do your sisters resemble you?"

He laughed, his teeth white in the dark. "Nay, they are all small and dainty. A few of them are considered to be beautiful. I was a sickly babe and my father believed I would be small like my sisters. He allowed my mother to dream I would enter the priesthood."

"What happened?"

"I grew and kept growing."

"And now you are large enough to make any father glad, and you have entered the priesthood." His mother must be mad and, for certain, the only woman alive who would lock such a man away in a monastery.

He shrugged.

"What else do you do at the Abbey?" Faye had no clear idea of what monks did, but she had trouble picturing Gregory hunched over parchment. He had too much vigor.

He gave a short laugh. "I chop a lot of wood." He stared into the darkness. "Work in the fields, tend the animals, and transcribe."

At Calder, hours not spent with her had been used in the practice yards. There was no faster or more accurate sword than Gregory's and tales of his strength and stamina had provided chatter for many a winter evening. She had trouble picturing a monk's tamer existence. Perhaps because she did not want to see him thus. "Tell your story."

His head turned toward her. "This is the tale of the wolf in sheep's clothing."

It was a ridiculous beginning to a story. "How can a wolf wear wool?"

"If you listen, I will tell you." His deep voice held a trace of laughter. "And I promise, no dragons."

Happy to have him closer, she settled to listen.

"There was a wolf and he could not get enough to eat because the shepherd was so watchful of his flock."

"As he should be."

"Indeed." He nodded. "One night, the wolf found a sheep skin that had been cast aside and forgotten. The wolf dressed himself in the skin and strolled, easy as you please, right into the center of the flock. It was not long before a little lamb followed him about. The wolf led the lamb away from the flock and made a good dinner."

"This is a cruel story."

"You talk more than Simon."

"I beg your pardon."

"The following evening, Wolf again donned his sheep's

clothing and mingled with the flock. It so happened, that on this night, the shepherd had a taste for fine mutton stew. Looking through his sheep, he selected the very largest, picked up his knife and killed the wolf."

He fell silent.

"Is that the end?" She needn't have bothered getting comfortable.

"Aye." He shrugged. "It comes from a group of stories written by a slave. They are older even than Christ. All of them are short, for children to follow."

"And what is the meaning of this one? That you should not pretend to be that which you are not."

"That is one message, but more that those who do evil are trapped by their own deceit."

"It is a good message."

"There are many of them. I have only just begun my work with them."

Faye didn't want to hear any more words of wisdom. She would be awake all night if those were all the stories he had to offer. "I think you should tell me one of your dragon tales. Make it a long one."

She got lost in the soothing, dark treacle of his voice, as she had done some nights at Calder Castle. The words blurred into a comforting murmur. It was enough to know he was there.

* * *

Gregory woke just before sunrise. In the night, Faye had sought his warmth and lay curled against his side. Dear Lord, she was beautiful with her face relaxed in sleep. Her lashes made dark crescents against the rich creaminess of her skin. Her full mouth pursed as if silently begging to be kissed.

People moved about the clearing.

Gregory cursed and edged away from her. He could not be seen cuddling a young 'boy'. He should have moved away in the night, but after she had fallen asleep, he'd watched her for a long while. Free to look his fill while she was unaware. He must have fallen asleep. As quietly as he could, he grabbed a bucket from the cart. He took it to the well behind the beast pens and drew water.

Faye still slept.

He moved his bucket to the side of the cart facing away from the inn and stripped his habit. Garbed only in his braies, the morning air chilled his skin. He plunged his hands into the water, icy cold, straight from the earth. His muscles snapped and surged with energy. Waking up at the Abbey muted by comparison to the fresh bite of the air, the freedom of the forest about him.

His morning growth itched like the devil. He liked to be clean-shaven. He took a knife from his boot and tested the edge with his thumb. Next, he dug out a small pot of bathing soap from his pack and a washing cloth. Road dust coated him, and he needed to refresh himself before they traveled farther. When Faye woke, he would draw clean water for her.

Smoke drifted up from the inn's chimney. The smell of fresh baking bread made his mouth water. After he was clean, they would see to breaking their fast. He would need to buy some more food. He lathered his face. The blade rasped against his cheek.

At Anglesea, Sir Arthur would be busy this morning, the danger to Faye adding fuel to his fire. They were good people, Sir Arthur's family. Wily as a sack of fox cubs, but kind and well intentioned and their people prospered beneath their rule. He was glad Faye had returned to them. He would never have been able to leave her until he was assured of her safety. He wiped the blade clean and moved to his chin.

On the other side of the cart, a farmer sleepily harnessed a pair to his bullock cart. The cart was empty. He must be on his way back from market. Gregory would wager it would be well into morning before last night's carousers arose. They had made noise long into the night.

A woman appeared in the inn's doorway and tossed the contents of a bucket into the yard.

The well water stung his skin with cold. He hissed in a breath as he worked the frigid cloth over the skin of his chest and arms.

* * *

Faye lay dead still. If she so much as twitched, he might stop.

His limbs were all hewn strength. Darkened by the sun, his skin clung tight to the swells and ridges of muscle. Dark, coarse hair dusted the center of his chest, before marching in a straight line beneath his waistband.

Her fingers twitched to trace that path and beyond.

Calder had been a strong, well-proportioned man, but nothing to Gregory. His form thrillingly base and elemental, a beautiful male creature shaped for power and conquest.

Heat spread from her belly to between her thighs. Under her bindings, her nipples tingled.

He rubbed the cloth up his side and under his arm. His skin gleamed under a fine layer of water.

How would it be to take the cloth from his hand and stroke it over him? Follow the narrow indentation of his waist as it broadened into his shoulders, up and over and down the sinewy steel of his arms. Her skin prickled with heat. This was madness. She screwed her eyes shut, the image of him branded on her closed lids. She pressed her palms into her eyes to erase it.

"You are awake?" Gregory's voice startled her. "I will finish and fetch you some fresh water."

She nodded, not trusting her voice to speak or her gaze not to return right to the source of her discomfort. He would be shocked rigid if he so much as guessed the direction of her thoughts. She'd never seen him take a woman to his bed. At Calder she'd made it her business to know, half of her intrigued and the other terrified that he would. She had been married and had no claim on him yet, in her mind, he was hers.

In his mind, he was God's man.

She rolled on her front and crawled out from under the cart. The morning sun made scant inroads on the dense foliage. Long shadows stretched across the yard.

Gregory snatched up his robe and tugged it over his head.

She sighed. What a waste of male beauty.

Chapter Nine

Calder Castle soared against the moody gray sky casting grasping fingers of shadow over the deep green forest spread around it. It hit Faye like a fist in her belly. She had never wanted to see the place again. Over a year since she'd been here, and the familiar sense of being trapped fastened around her throat.

"There she is." Gregory halted the bullocks.

A solid red-stone structure atop a rise, built for defense, its front guarded by a large mere with only a single approach to the outer gatehouse. No one came in or out of Calder Castle without passing through the gatehouse. Hugo kept as tight a fist about his people as Calder had kept about his wife.

"The chance of recognition increases," Gregory said.

The road followed the river, down through the treed valley and past the hamlet of Lower Mere before it reached the outskirts of its bigger sister town, Upper Mere. Many knew her face in Lower and Upper Mere. As chatelaine of Calder Castle, she and Gregory had often ridden throughout the land on errands. In this, she had always tried to follow her mother's example. Gregory pointed to the pennants stirring in a soft breeze above the battlements. "Hugo is in residence."

A Wolf on Gules, Calder's colors. His family dated back to Aethelstan, as Calder had reminded her as often as he could. In the time before Calder had grown to despise her, they had spoken, shared their lives and she had been content. The change happened gradually. At first, she put it down to temper but her tame explanation paled against the onslaught of Calder's worsening behavior. The sudden, inexplicable rages, her failure to please him in any way, the ever-tightening grip on her freedom until even her thoughts were not her own. Then Calder had spent more time with King John at court. The deathblow to any chance of happiness, and a cold, angry stranger had replaced the man she married.

"What do you suggest?" She pushed those unhappy thoughts away. From here she could only just see the rooftops of Upper Mere clustered around Calder Castle like a lady's skirt.

"Your disguise should hold, if you keep the cowl over your face." Fine lines crinkled the corners of his eyes as he squinted against the fading day at the castle. "There is a man, more of a hermit, his name is Aldous."

Faye couldn't place the name.

"He lives half a day's ride north of here, at the edge of Calder's demesne, where it joins with the northern boundary of your father's land."

Faye had only been there once or twice. It was a barren, lonely place.

"If anything happens and for any reason you are unable to get home, I want you to head for Aldous."

Faye's mouth dried. If Gregory meant her to go alone, then... "I will never find him."

Gregory grasped her shoulders and turned her to face him. "My lady, heed me." The muscle bounced in his cheek. "Anglesea lies west of here, where the sun sets, remember that. But your way may be blocked and then you must go north. Keep the rising sun to your right and the setting to your left and you will be traveling north. Do you know where the old keep is, the one King Henry tore down?"

"Which King Henry?" He tossed information at her so fast it blurred in her head, the sun rising and setting, old keeps and kings.

"Henry Fitz Empress." Rigid with tension, onyx stare keen and piercing, he tightened his hold on his shoulders. "The old ruins, the ones they say are haunted."

"Aye." A glimmer of light through the fog. "I know them. William and Roger took me there once to see the ghost."

A small smile crossed his face. "Aye, well there is no ghost, but there is a man, Aldous. That is where you must go if all fails."

She would stumble around the hills like Ivo, the village simpleton at Anglesea, clothes torn, hair matted as the village dogs chased her. She gripped his wrist. "I cannot do this."

"Aye, you can." He bent his sable head, and pressed his mouth warm against her icy hand. "You have the heart of a lion, my lady, and the best reason in the world to use it."

More lamb than lion, staring up at the impenetrable square stone of Calder Castle. Simon was there. If only the wind could carry the knowledge to him that his mother had come. What fanciful and pointless whimsy on her part.

He rummaged behind them and drew forth an efficient-looking dagger. "Take this."

"I have my own." She dug in her boot and produced William's gift. The jewel in the hilt winked up at her.

"It is a pretty bauble." Gregory turned it in his hand. "Smaller and more suited to your hand. Can you use it?"

"Nay. William said you could teach me."

He shrugged. "When we get to Bess, we will have time before full dark. I can show you how not to lose a finger to that trinket."

"When we get to Bess?" Bess lived in Upper Mere, one of the best-known residents. Faye's flimsy disguise felt as insubstantial as air. There would be eyes in Upper Mere and tongues to tell what those eyes saw. A lump lodged like old bread in her throat. "Do we ride through the town?"

"Try not to look at anyone. We will stay cowled and keep to the back lanes."

And pray to God and all the saints nobody saw through them. It all rested on that slim hope. Last week's rain gathered in puddles by the road. She might be able to improve on her disguise a bit. She was a boy, was she not?

Faye hopped down from the cart. The puddle was nothing more than a large wheel rut of brackish water. Steeling herself, she thrust her hands into the muck. Wet clay oozed between her fingers. Faye dared not think what else was in there as she dragged her coated hands over her face.

Gregory coughed into his hand, but his eyes laughed. He knew her too well not to know how she hated being dirty.

Faye grabbed another handful of mud and, with a shudder, dragged it over her curls. Cold slime slid over her scalp. "You said I was a reprehensible lad."

Gregory gave her a huge grin. "Verily."

It was all very well for him to find this amusing. She dug out more mud and coated her habit. A few more swipes at her face and she'd had enough.

"Will this do?" She willed him to say aye because she didn't think she could stomach another basting in the filth.

"Aye." His lips twitched as he turned his gaze back to the road.

Faye alighted beside him. "Good."

Gregory flicked the traces and the cart moved forward. "If the sight of you is not enough, the smell ought to do the trick."

* * *

Faye shrunk closer to Gregory's hunched form, until she was nigh seated in his lap. She kept her head lowered, but her skin crawled that somebody would recognize her and call out.

Upper Mere bustled with daily life, shouts from merchants, young boys in apprentice tunics hurrying from one place to another. Women, children clinging to their skirts, stood in groups of two or three to while away the day in chat. A tanner's cart inched into the roadway, forcing them to stop beneath a low, stone arch. The death odor of the cured skins made her belly roil. The tanner's cart creaked to a halt.

Faye bent almost double. She barely dared breathe as people passed close to the bullock cart, so close they could touch her. A few nodded a greeting before they hurried on. John, the carpenter, stepped up to the tanner and berated him. Two summers ago she had helped his youngest son with the toothache.

"Easy." Gregory remained calm and impenetrable beside her.

The tanner's cart moved, and she breathed again.

Gregory left the main road and took them down a narrow lane. Although quieter here, she swore she could feel curious stares peering around shutters, marking her and Gregory, ready to run to the keep and tell Hugo. They crept through the winding lanes and out of the town, closer to the castle.

Her heart crashed in her chest. Above them, Calder Castle loomed over the town. Her prison for seven years, her personal hell. Light shone from the casements of the keep, braziers flickered with the movement of the guards on the walls.

Bess's cottage lay on the village outskirts, along the narrow road to the castle. Bess preferred her small piece of solitude and from here moved freely between keep and village. Many secrets, some of those Faye's, rested beneath the tidy thatch of Bess's cottage. Two well-behaved chickens pecked away in the immaculate yard.

Gregory drew rein and alighted. He raised his hand to assist her.

Faye shook her head and with a wry grin he dropped his hand. She followed, staying on the far side of the cart. Large tubs of herbs lined the front of the cottage in orderly rows. Even Bess's vegetable garden dared not grow unruly, but confined itself to the furrows and stakes.

The door opened and Bess appeared. A woman of middle years, her hair always neatly confined to her wimple and her large, white apron starched and white enough to make your eyes ache. Bess had attended both her births and left with that apron still as fresh as when she arrived.

"Sir Gregory." Bess peered at Gregory. "You had best come in and bring that boy with you. Only mind he takes off his boots."

Gregory followed Bess into the cottage.

Faye trundled on behind him. At the door, she removed her boots and slid into the cottage.

A large, scrubbed wooden table stood central to the hearth. Suspended above it, bunches of dried herbs perfumed the air with sage, lavender, and rosemary. A kettle hung over the fire and great swathes of fragrant steam rose from it. From the hearty smell, Bess must be making broth.

Faye's stomach grumbled. Bess's broth smelled rich and meaty. Their meal by the stream seemed hours ago.

A narrow cot rested against the far wall, the bedding folded and stacked on the end. Long rows of shelves adorned the wall on either side of the hearth. Casks, baskets, and jugs marched in order from tallest to shortest along their span. All sorts of miracles, large and small, resided in those jars.

"So." Bess glanced up from where she stirred the kettle. "You have taken vows."

"Not yet." Gregory's deep voice seemed strange in the precise, feminine order of the cottage.

Bess nodded. From a wooden cask by the hearth, she pulled a loaf of bread and placed it on the table. "Does Sir Hugo know you are here?"

"We passed through the village as you see us."

Bess nodded as she broke open the bread. "Then, he will know soon enough two priests traveled through. He has eyes everywhere right now."

Gregory grunted.

It was as they suspected, Hugo would be expecting some sort of retaliation. Even in peacetime, Calder had kept the village alert and ready to report anything new or unusual. Hugo must have followed the practice.

"Have you seen our lady?"

Faye started and edged behind Gregory.

"She is well." Gregory's voice rumbled from above her.

"Things have not been good since she left." Bess returned to the hearth.

Faye could see the other women's feet from where she cowered behind Gregory. She wanted Gregory to ask in what way. When he remained silent, she gave him a sharp prod in the back.

He tensed. "What do you mean?"

"Our lady took care of the village." Bess sighed. "The winter was long and many didn't make it."

Faye's heart sank. Some of her people had died. *Please Lord, not young Grace, the cobbler's daughter.* Her health had never been the best. Faye prodded Gregory again.

His hand snapped back, caught her fingers, and squeezed.

Faye accepted the warning with a return pressure. Gregory needed to understand these had been her people throughout her marriage. They still existed for her and she still cared what became of them. Even if by leaving she'd abandoned her duty to her people.

"I do what I can," Bess said. "And Father John is always about, but she was a fine lady, Lady Faye. The village misses her."

Faye's heart twisted. The villagers had been a glimmer of light in her marriage.

"I imagine you are hungry. I never met a man who was not." Bess ladled broth into bowls and set them on the table. "Wash up and we can eat."

Gregory steered her toward a bucket of water set on a stool inside the door.

The game would be up as soon as she washed her face. It amazed her Bess hadn't seen through her disguise the moment she entered the cottage. Beatrice was right. People saw what they wanted to see.

Gregory took up a small cake of soap and lathered his hands.

"I am sure you will want to wash the dirt off you." Bess stopped beside her. The woman's glare raked Faye from her filthy head to her soiled hem. She took a step back and folded her arms over the snowy white apron front.

The heat of her gaze prickled on Faye's skin and her cheeks heated.

Gregory accepted a drying cloth from Bess.

"Oh, my." Bess chuckled. "I did not think there were many things that could surprise me." She inspected Faye from head to toe. "I am sure you will want to bathe, my lady."

Gregory tensed. "I wanted to see if you would know her. If you did not, then we can be reasonably certain nobody from the village did either."

"Indeed." Bess jammed her fists on her hips. "I have seen you through two births, my lady. It would take more than a handful of mud to fool me. Still, you took a huge risk in coming here. That Hugo is a bad one, just like his older brother."

"I—"

"Not that I blame you." Bess jerked her head toward the castle. "Hugo will go spare if he knows you are here."

Everything within Faye froze, her mouth dried and she couldn't produce words. The marks of Calder's anger went deeper than her skin.

"Then, he must not find out she is here." Gregory's face grew cold and deadly serious.

Bess snorted. "As if I would tell him."

Faye's knees buckled. Bess had been her companion and helper through her marriage, the closest Faye had come to a confidant. Bess would not betray her.

Gregory clasped her elbow and steadied her.

"It is a good disguise. I would doubt anyone in the village saw through it. Wash that muck off your pretty face and come and eat." Bess stomped over to the table and drew a large bench from beneath it. "You are here for your boy."

"You have seen Simon?" She held her breath.

"I have seen him." Bess squeezed her hand. Her clasp was warm and dry. Healing hands that soothed and brought relief many a time. "He was letting his displeasure be known loud and wide."

That was her boy. Faye swelled with pride. The next moment, her heart skipped a beat. Dear Lord, Hugo would not tolerate opposition. Simon must not draw his uncle's anger down on his head.

"Hugo sent him away," Bess said.

Faye's legs refused to hold her and she dropped on the bench. Tears stung the back of her lids as she tried to keep the swell of hopelessness at bay.

"Calder has sent him to Brynn to be fostered," Bess said.

"Brynn?" Brynn was the keep of Calder's vassal, Sir Robert. Her head whirled. Simon was not with Hugo, which was good. On the other hand, Brynn lay another day's traveling away. Another day away from her child was a day too many.

"Aye." Bess took her hand. "Sir Robert is like Calder, but his lady is a good woman. Hugo sent Simon's nurse, too. Ruth will know how best to keep him out of harm."

"Then we go to Brynn," Gregory said.

Faye leaned into Gregory, solid and dependable beside her. Warmth flowed through her.

"Eat first." Bess pushed her bowl in front of Faye. "Then we will see if I can find something better than a grubby boy as a disguise." Bess touched Faye's hair and clucked her tongue. "All that beautiful hair."

"I will go up to the castle." Gregory picked up his spoon and ate.

Faye stared at him. Nothing could be gained by such a fool-hardy action.

"I want to see if there is aught of which we need to be aware." He took a mouthful of broth.

Faye clenched her hand around her spoon. It was that or hit

him with it. Blasted, stubborn man with his jaw set in that uncompromising line.

"It is a good idea." Bess touched her arm. "They will not see Gregory if he does not want to be seen. But I would suggest we find something other than that habit for him. If you rode through the village, you will have been noticed. I will put it about you came and left. You will want to draw your cart out of sight behind the cottage. I have a small animal pen within the forest."

Bess's calm good sense spread over her like a soothing balm. Her throat tightened. The best she could do was send Bess a look loaded with gratitude.

"Eat." Bess motioned her bowl.

After they'd eaten, Bess opened a large chest at the foot of her cot and rummaged within. She produced a tunic and a pair of braies large enough to cover Gregory's frame.

He took the clothing outside to change and draw the cart into the forest.

When he returned, Faye blinked at him in surprise. No more monk, but her Gregory stood there, the man she knew so well. Her stupid heart insisted on hankering after this man. The tunic fit tight across his broad shoulders, molding itself to the hard planes of his belly. She dragged her eyes away and helped Bess clean the dishes.

Gregory waited until moonrise and slipped into the night.

"He will be fine," Bess said as Faye helped her place a linen-lined bathing tub before the hearth.

The prospect of bathing was welcome indeed. The mud had dried on her face and hair and flaked off all over Bess's floor as she moved.

Bess heated water over the fire before pouring it into the tub. She added a few handfuls of dried lavender to the steaming water.

Heavenly. The hot water soothed Faye's tight muscles as the calming smell of lavender mixed with the steam. Bess helped her wash her hair and found a simple woman's bliaut and wimple for Faye to wear. The clothes were rough but clean.

They chatted about villagers. Not all the news was bad. Some had died, true, but babies had been born, couples courted and life went on. It helped distract her as time slowed to a crawl and Gregory still didn't appear. Their conversation drifted into desultory and then silence.

Bess busied herself with crushing herbs as they waited.

Gregory had been gone too long. He might have been captured, could be lying in Hugo's dungeon while she and Bess whiled away the time. Or worse, Hugo had him. She had to stop inventing one gruesome scenario after another or she would crawl out of her skin with nerves.

"Mistress Bess?" A young voice called from the other side of the door.

Faye jumped and caught the bench before it fell.

"Blast." Bess got to her feet. "Stay out of sight. It is young Tim. His mother is due at any moment."

"Tim from beneath the hill?" Tim was the oldest of eight, all within a short space of each other. Tim's mother was still a young woman, but when last Faye saw her, she had looked worn out by the constant childbearing.

"Aye." Bess clucked her tongue. "That man should try keeping his braies on. This babe is sitting heavy and she is going to need some help."

"You have to go." Faye slipped to the corner near the cot and crouched down behind the frame.

"Aye." Bess shook her head. "It will be remarked upon if I do not." She lifted the latch and peered into the night beyond the door.

"My mum sent me." A piping young voice sounded. "She says it is time."

"You run on home, lad." Bess shooed the boy with her hands. "Tell your mother I am on my way." She went to her jars of magic and gathered what she needed. "Stay here and do not open the door to anyone."

Faye hardly needed the warning, but she nodded to reassure Bess.

Bess's absence hung heavy. If she had embroidery with her, she could occupy her hands while she waited. The idea made her smile. When this was over perhaps she would not mind the stitchery as much anymore.

Outside the cottage, dim sounds carried on the night breeze from Upper Mere as people went about their business. She occupied her mind identifying the various voices. William, who kept a tavern and had always argued with Calder over his taxes, shouted at a barking dog. Black Thomas, named for his temper and not his hair, and his wife, Mary, passing by and arguing in full voice. It would end in things being thrown and, as it often did, a late visit from Bess.

The latch lifted and she scrambled for her corner, her heart pounded so violently it nigh left her chest.

Gregory slid into the room like a ghost.

"Where have you been?" Not the most auspicious of beginnings, but she had imagined him bleeding to death on Hugo's floor for the last hour.

He raised his eyebrow and bent to remove his boots. "Where is Bess?"

"Gone to a birthing." She drew deep breaths for calm.

Gregory frowned around the empty cottage. "You are here alone?"

"Aye." She needed to do something with her hands and she put the kettle on the hearth. Bess must be strong, because the water kettle weighed like a stone. "I did not see anyone and nobody came to the door."

He nodded and placed his boots together by the door.

"Well?" Faye couldn't wait any longer for news.

"Hugo is there." Gregory took a seat at the table. "So are many of his vassals."

That could mean many things, none of them good. Faye sank back into her chair. When he had wanted something from them, an army or money, Calder had tolerated his vassals in his keep. Mayhap Hugo preferred more company about him.

"It was easy to slip into the keep." Gregory placed his hands on the table, strong, capable and gentle, those hands. "There are a lot of men."

"Hugo is gathering an army." The blood drained from her head. Hugo armed for a battle.

"Aye." Gregory nodded, his face grim. "I stayed amongst the men-at-arms for a good while, but there were no details. I saw Robert of Brynn amongst them."

Finally, some good news. If Robert was not at Brynn, the castle could be poorly guarded. "We can get Simon." Faye stood. Hugo had made a mistake and they needed to move now.

"My lady." Gregory glanced at her from the table. "We do not know what we will find at Brynn."

Now was their chance, and they needed to act. "We will find my son there. We can rescue him."

"You are determined to do this?" Gregory rose.

"Aye." Nothing would stand in her way. If she had to take herself to Brynn, she would.

Gregory blew out a long breath. "Show me the knife William gave you. I will see what I can teach you while we wait for Bess."

"We have to go now."

"We cannot go now." Gregory held his hand out for the knife. "There are still too many people awake."

Gregory's thinking grew muddled. Half the village had been about and seen their arrival. "We traveled here in the middle of the day."

"Aye. And too many saw two monks enter the village in a bullock cart. It will be noted if a man and a woman leave in the same cart."

Indeed. She didn't like his reasoning, but couldn't fault it.

"Show me how you hold the knife."

Faye palmed the weapon. It lay heavy and strange in her hand.

"Not like that." Gregory opened her fingers to face upward.

"Like this." He repositioned the dagger. His chest pressed into her back as he took her wrist from behind and showed her. "You thrust up from here."

Faye struggled to listen to the words with his arms around her, the unique scent of him teasing her nose.

"Up." His voice rumbled through her back and sent tingles skittering across her skin. "This way you do not expose too much of yourself when you strike and you can put your strength behind the blow."

He stepped away and had her show him. She could pretend to misunderstand. Then, he would put his arms about her—

Concentrate, Faye.

"Good." He nodded. "But put your entire shoulder behind the blow. Chances are you will be fighting someone bigger and it takes strength to punch through muscle. Aim for a fleshy part. Here." He touched her belly, his strong fingers firm on her flesh. Her muscles tightened. "Or here." His pressed the base of her neck. Her pulse leaped in response. "Thrust forward and pull back when you disengage. You want the knife to do two things, cut on the thrust and cut deeper on the retreat."

She had gone mad. He spoke of rending the flesh of a real, living being and her thoughts drifted beneath his clothing.

Gregory made her repeat the action.

"A knife is a great weapon." He adjusted her grip. "But you have to be close to use it. Do not pull it out before you are close enough to do some damage. If your opponent sees it, he will attempt to disarm you."

She thrust the dagger into an imaginary foe.

"If it is Hugo, he will know how to disarm you before you can blink. Your best chance is in surprise. He will not expect you to fight back and, for certain, not with a knife."

Hugo. Faye went cold. The imaginary foe solidified into a tall man with flaxen hair and cruel eyes.

Nay, Hugo would not expect her to fight back. She never had

fought back against Calder. Not once in all the beatings she had taken from her husband.

"You have not even the pride to do anything but beg. You sicken me."

Instead, she had cowered behind furniture, raised her arms to shield her head and kept her cries soft so as not to anger him further.

"Beg me to stop."

Dear God, how weak and pathetic to let a man use her over and over again as the target for his rage.

"Crawl like the bitch you are."

The dagger clattered to the floor and she started. Her hands shook and perspiration coated her skin. She couldn't face Gregory.

"My lady." He nudged her chin upward. "Faye."

"I cannot—" Shame seared through her. She had to get away from his all-seeing gaze.

Gregory blocked her retreat.

Nay, he mustn't see. To see the truth in his expression would be the final humiliation. Faye shoved his chest. Dear God, for the ability to go back in time and raise that dagger. It lay on the floor at her feet and blinked up at her in condemnation. It took strength to punch through muscle. Aye, she had that strength now, when she didn't need it. It vibrated warmly through her muscles.

"My Lady Faye."

She reeled away from him. Nay, not his lady, not his anything but the pathetic girl he had stayed to rescue. It wasn't love that kept him by her side. He had pitied her.

"Cease." He grabbed her hands in one fist and held them. "What is it?"

"Loose me." Her shameful weakness before Calder taunted her. "I did not fight him. I never fought him."

Gregory made a soft noise in his throat as his big arms enfolded her. "Ah, my lady."

Faye struggled in his hold. She did not want his pity or deserve it. She was weak and pathetic. Yet, the heat from him stole through her muscles and robbed them of will. Her neck bent, of its own accord, to lay her head against him. She had no strength. Nothing. No resistance.

"The biggest part of being a warrior is to know when to fight and when not." Gregory's breath warmed the skin by her ear. "To know when you can win and when it is best to retreat."

It could not be that simple. She wished with all she had for it to be that simple. She shook her head.

His hands soothed her back. "Aye, my lady. There are times when we all, no matter how strong, need the wisdom to know it is better to live to fight another day."

"I let him do it."

"You survived." He rested his cheek atop her head. "You survived to protect your children and find a way to escape him. There is no weakness or shame in that. The shame lies with Calder."

She wished she could believe that. It would be much easier if she could. She must have done something to anger Calder. Perhaps if she'd been stronger or a better wife, Calder would never have done as he did. "Calder despised my weakness."

"Cowering in the corner like a cringing cur, this is the daughter of the mighty Sir Arthur of Anglesea."

Gregory tensed against her. "Only the worse kind of coward lifts his hand to one who is weaker."

Faye pressed closer. The closer she got to Gregory, the dimmer grew Calder's voice.

Gregory kissed the top of her head. "Your courage unmans me."

* * *

Helplessness clung like a chokehold at Gregory's throat. That Faye could carry the guilt of Calder's sin was unfathomable, horrible and wrong.

Dear Lord, his big, slow man mind had no words to take away her pain and her anguish. All he could do was hold her and try to tell her with his body she bore no shame. The shame belonged to Calder, and to him.

She stayed stiff with resistance in his arms.

He stroked her back, willing each brush of his hand to take away her hurt. The soft skin of her temple warmed his lips. He needed to see her and he put her away from him.

Tears welled in the haunted blue depths of her eyes and traced down her cheeks.

The need to comfort overwhelmed him and he put his mouth to her tears, kissing them away one by one.

Her breath hitched on a gentle sound so full of longing it tore through his resistance.

Her full, red mouth beckoned him. Kiss away the pain and the fear. Sweet Jesus, he could not. He must not. If he kissed her now, he had not the strength to draw away again. Wrenching up the will, he took a saving step away from her. He couldn't do this, couldn't be that man. Impotent fury clawed at him. He had no chance now to make Calder pay for what the sod had done to Faye. All he could do was make sure Hugo never got his hands on her, and that he took Simon back to Anglesea. And by God, he would see it done.

"Come." His breath sawed through his lungs. The ache to close the distance rampaged through every part of him. What he could do, was get her son for her and see them safe to Anglesea. "Rest and we will leave as soon as it is safe."

He led her, unresisting to the cot. She sat and he pressed her until she lay down. Her haunted visage twisted through his gut sharper than a sword. Carefully, he lifted her feet until she lay on the cot and pulled the covers over her. Uselessness writhed inside him. He needed to fix this. One way or another, he would fix this.

Chapter Ten

Faye wished for horses as the bullocks trundled north through the night. Brynn was a day's ride from Calder, but by bullock they would not reach it until the end of the following day. Dear Lord, she could run faster than this. Her weakness in the cottage sat like a third passenger between them.

He had nearly kissed her. Hot and dark, his eyes flashed his intent for a moment before it disappeared beneath painful kindness and consideration. Faye's lips throbbed from the kiss that never came. Perhaps the taint of her shame had repulsed him. She glared at the bullock's backs, willing them to grow wings.

"I must tell you something," Gregory said.

"About?"

"The Abbey." Gregory shifted. "The reason they will not admit me is because I have not released my former life. I am still clinging to something. Someone." He cleared his throat. "You. And the boys."

He could have knocked her off her perch with a wink. "Verily?"

"I wanted you to know."

His words warmed her chest like a mug of spiced wine on a

winter's evening. Faye's head whirled and she took a calming breath. "When this is over, you will return and take your vows?"

"Aye." He glanced her way and raised a brow.

And there it was. Foolish to even consider it might be otherwise. Her heart squeezed into a tight, bruised ball. It seemed she must say something. "You are here with me now and that is what is important."

He grunted. "I have been to Brynn a few times."

Subject slammed shut again. Not for her, though. She hugged his confession to her breast. It was all she had. He would leave her again, but he would carry a part of her with him. It wasn't enough. It could never be enough. Confusion dragged at her, sapping her strength. These last days with Gregory had her bouncing from hope to despair and back again. Simon. Better to concentrate on her son.

"There is a postern gate located near the stables. It will be the easiest way in," he said.

"Will it not be locked?"

"It could be." Gregory shrugged. "But Robert of Brynn is careless and we can hope it works in our favor. Also, Hugo is expecting the attack to come at his keep. It is probably why he moved Simon." He swept their surroundings with his gaze. "Also, he is probably considering your father's reputation, and believes the attack will come from an army."

Her father had garnered a reputation for his swift and ruthless retribution, but not for subterfuge.

Sneaking into Brynn and stealing Simon from beneath their noses had to work.

"Do you think Simon is frightened?" Faye shuddered. Asking the question aloud made it all the more real than in her mind.

"I am sure a part of him is scared." He took her hand.

She curled her fingers around his calloused palm, warm and dependable, her fixed point.

"But he has a cool head for such a young one."

Please God, let Gregory be right. Ruth would keep him

distracted and Hugo remained at Calder. It wasn't much, but she drew comfort from it. Such tiny scraps of nothing she gathered like a starving squirrel.

"Our safest chance is to steal him and leave before anyone is the wiser." Gregory released her hand.

She tucked her chilled fingers beneath her thigh. "I wish we had horses."

"Horses are easy to track." Gregory nodded to the bullocks. "This way, we may be slow, but we are one cart amongst many others. A man and a woman with their son."

Cruel. A sharp pain lanced through Faye. How she wanted Gregory's words to be true. He had been more of a father to her boys than Calder ever had.

Gregory cleared his throat and turned back to the road.

Did he ever wish it so? She couldn't keep tormenting herself in this manner. She allowed the motion of the cart to lull her. She swayed beside Gregory in a sort of half sleep as they traveled.

The road remained clear and empty throughout the last of the night. The sun rose on unfamiliar land. Faye rubbed her gritty eyes. Dense forest lined either side of the road. She shivered and rubbed her arms to dispel the chill of the shade.

"We need to rest." Gregory drew the cart off the road.

He was right, yet her heart ached to keep going, to get to Simon. They were close enough to touch, but her limbs creaked like an ancient as she staggered out of the cart. She needed sleep.

Gregory unyoked the bullocks inside the trees. "We will be concealed from the road." He drew the sacking from the cart and grabbed Bess's blankets. "We must sleep."

Faye staggered to where he lay the sheeting on the ground. She dropped on it and drew the blanket tight. Twigs and rocks poked into her flesh. She didn't care. The chill of the night lingered and her teeth chattered, keeping her awake.

Gregory lay down beside her and tugged her into the heat of his big chest. "Come."

Closing her eyes, Faye allowed herself a moment to dream.

* * *

"It is time."

Faye batted against the hand on her shoulder.

"My lady?"

She screwed her eyes tighter together.

"Faye?"

A harder shake forced her eyes open. She blinked against the bright light. "What time is it?"

"It is well past noon." Growth shadowed Gregory's chin.

So late. Precious time had sped by while she slept, time they could not afford to waste. She stumbled to her feet, light-headed.

Gregory steadied her. "We must go if we are to reach Brynn. We should get there after dark."

Faye nodded and helped him gather their blankets. Simon could be anywhere within Brynn. She had no idea how they would get to him. It made her head hurt to think of these things. Gregory would have a plan, he always did.

Gregory yoked the bullocks. He must have fed them, because he removed their feed sacks first.

"Did you sleep?"

"I rested." He shrugged and threaded the traces through the yoke.

Her chest warmed. He had stayed awake to make sure her sleep was undisturbed. No wonder she loved him. In a hundred small ways, he cared for her. "I will drive the cart and you can rest in the back."

He gaped at her.

"What?" Faye battled to hold his incredulous stare.

He shoved his hands into his belt and tilted his head. "You will drive a bullock cart?"

"I have driven horses." Her face heated. His incredulity had substance to it, given her life to this point. "How difficult can it be? It is not like they will take it into their heads to bolt." She motioned the phlegmatic beasts between the traces. Bolting might not be bad idea. At least that way, they could achieve some speed. She climbed aboard the cart and picked up the traces. "You need to rest."

Gregory shook his head and ambled over. "I am well."

He was such a good man. The sort of man a woman wanted to throw her arms about and show him her gratitude. It was not her right, however, and she tightened her hands on the traces. "I need you strong and rested or you will be no good to me."

He nodded.

At least, that he believed. Always duty with Gregory, before anything else. The cart dipped beneath his weight as he got into the back and lay down. Faye flicked the reins.

The right bullock raised its head and lowed.

Not a good start. She needed to get them moving but she didn't want to hurt the poor things. She flicked harder.

A foot stamp was all she got.

Flinching she gave them a good, sharp slap with the traces. Leather cracked through the air, the bullocks jerked and the cart jolted as the beasts lumbered forward.

"I am here if you have need of me." Gregory's voice came from the back.

Faye nodded. She would do her best not to have need of him. Maneuvering the cart onto the road, she blessed the empty path before her. The cart did not handle as a horse and she didn't trust her ability to turn the beasts. The bullocks plodded forward. They were not the brightest of God's creatures, but they seemed content to follow the road.

Gregory slept, his chest rising and falling in an easy rhythm. Faye wagered he would wake fast enough if she had need of him. She relaxed into the motion of the bullocks. A clear arc of uninterrupted blue stretched above her, the sun warm but not uncomfortable. She shifted position to shade Gregory from the glare. The crops would need rain if this dry spell continued. For now, she was glad of it. She adjusted the path of the right bullock. He showed too much interest in the grass along the verge. The trees thinned as she traveled. The forest broke into thickets and then meadows.

Large thickets used up good land that should be turned to crops to feed people, which would explain why there were only a handful of cottages scattered about the place. It was too late in the season for wildflowers, but the verdant swathes of green would be dotted with color in the spring. The faint toll of a bell signaled a monastery nearby. They must be sounding *Nonce*.

Gregory would know, but he slept deeply and she didn't want to disturb him.

The shadows lengthened on the road and her shoulders ached, but she let him sleep. It was the first time, in all the years they had known each other, she had done aught for Gregory. Always, he cared for her, soothed her hurts and cleared difficulties from her path. A bubble of satisfaction swelled in her chest. In some small way, it was good to be taking care of him.

The sun hung lower in the sky and a slight chill dampened the air when Gregory moved. Half in a stupor, Faye jumped.

He climbed forward and sat beside her. Sleep roughened his voice as he took the traces from her. "My thanks."

Faye rolled her aching shoulders.

His face looked more rested and the lines of exhaustion that bracketed his mouth had eased.

Faye offered him the water skin and he took it with a nod of thanks. The afternoon softened into evening.

"Brynn." Gregory pointed.

Faye squinted against the low sun. The battlements of the castle were visible on the horizon. The next step in their quest and nerves fluttered in her belly. She prayed they would find Simon and be able to free him.

They stopped before dark to water the bullocks and stretch their legs. The lights of Brynn grew stronger against the darkening sky. *Soon now*, she whispered to her son on the wings of the birds flying home to roost.

* * *

Faye tried not to fidget, but it was hard when she was moments away from having her son safe and with her again. They huddled together in their hiding place and watched and waited.

Brynn Castle settled for the night. Gregory had been right. Robert of Brynn was a careless lord. The single guard slumbered before a small fire in the gatehouse. It had been laughably easy to slip into the bailey.

Around the stone central keep, smaller, wooden buildings stood amongst large piles of unused stone, as if the building had stopped. One would pass a drafty, damp winter in Brynn. Noise from the keep filtered into the bailey. The kitchens stood outside and serving drudges dashed between the donjon and the kitchen, condemning Brynn's diners to an icy meal. Few torches lit the bailey. She and Gregory took advantage of the deep shadows and watched from a corner where the stable joined the curtain wall. Their view included the entire bailey, from the gatehouse to the keep door and the wide sweep before the stable to the kitchens.

Gregory's hand tightened on her arm.

Faye winced and glared at him.

He motioned with his head. "There."

A small figure trotted out of the keep and into the bailey. Faye's heart stopped. Her limbs froze. Simon walked with his head bowed toward the stables. Toward her. Faye lurched for him.

Gregory jerked her back.

Faye lashed out at him. That was her son and nothing would keep her from him.

"I will get him." Gregory caught her fists in his. "Stay hidden."

Thank you, God. Tears blurred Gregory's tall form as he strolled into the bailey. He slid in behind a small group of men headed for the keep. When he neared Simon, he stepped away from the group and ambled over to her boy.

Simon started and turned. A smile of recognition lit his face.

Do not shout out! Faye shot to her feet.

Gregory clapped his arm about the boy's shoulder and shook his head. He bent to whisper in his ear.

Simon nodded and turned with him.

She wiped the tears to clear her vision. She could barely contain herself in her hiding place. His face was dirty and he hadn't changed his tunic in days but he was hale and here.

Gregory reached her, and Simon was in her arms. Faye wrapped him close to her. His familiar weight, a sweet ache right through her. She ran her hands over him. Two legs, two arms, chest, back, neck, all accounted for and well.

Simon trembled and Faye tightened her hold.

"Mama." Simon wriggled free. He blinked rapidly and ducked his head to hide his tears.

Faye wanted to pick him up and cradle him to her. Simon was too old for that, so she spared his boyish dignity. Her mother's heart throbbed in protest. It seemed an age since she had held him.

"What are you doing here?" Simon spoke to Gregory.

Gregory cleared his throat. "We have come for you."

Simon's face crumpled and his lips trembled. He dropped his head and jammed it into Gregory's belly.

The big man wrapped his arms about Simon's slight shoulders.

Simon's shoulders shook as he buried his face deeper, clutching Gregory's waist.

Faye's tears ran fresh. Her son was small and fragile against the big man.

"Master Simon!" A plump young woman stepped into the bailey.

Faye's heart missed a beat.

Gregory tensed and swung his head toward her. "Who is it?"

"Brynn's nurse." The reply was muffled by Gregory's tunic. "She has come looking to put me to bed."

The woman's features were pinched, shrewish. Her son

should not be in the hands of a bad-tempered woman. "Where is Ruth?"

"At table." Simon shrugged. "She will come to me later."

"Master Simon." The shrew thrust her hands on her hips and glared about the bailey. She stopped a kitchen drudge. "Have you seen that boy?"

"We have little time." Gregory crouched in front of Simon. "You must listen and you must be very, very brave."

Simon blinked, his expression intent.

"No one can know we are here." Gregory gripped him by the shoulders.

Simon nodded.

Her son should not have to be brave. Already, he had weathered a large storm. If it were up to her, she would snatch him up, right this instant, and run with him until her legs could no longer carry her.

"You must go with her now." Gregory motioned the shrew with his head. "But we will come for you."

Simon's gaze seared into her. "Take me now."

Faye burned to do just that, but they must be careful. Leaving her son here went against all her instincts, but she had to let her head rule.

Simon glared at her, willing her to give him what he wanted. Her betrayal twisted sharp enough to catch her breath. There were things a mother had to do that made her heart ache. This was by far the worst and so much more important than denying him extra sweets because his belly might ache, or sending him to bed because he needed his rest. All their lives depended on her holding firm against the entreaty in Simon's face.

"We cannot." Gregory turned Simon to face him. "If we leave now, they will know you are gone too soon. We need time so we can put some distance behind us when we go."

She had not come this far to lose him in a mad, ill-judged escape.

"When will you come?" Simon's voice shook.

"Tonight." Faye cupped her son's cheek. Not one moment longer than that. "We will come tonight."

Gregory frowned and nodded. "Tonight."

Gaze glittering in the dark, Simon drew his shoulders back. "I can sneak out and meet you here. They never check on me once they think I am asleep."

Gregory pursed his lips. "After *Compline*, wait until all is quiet before you go. You must dissemble. Can you do that?"

"Aye." Simon's chest swelled. "Like Sir Gruff in the story about the fire dragon."

"Indeed." Gregory ruffled his hair. "Just like Sir Gruff. If the dragon knows what you are about, all could be lost."

Exasperation laced the nurse's tone. "Master Simon?"

"You must go before we are discovered." Gregory's hands tightened on Simon's shoulders. "But mark me well. Do not put yourself in danger. If you cannot escape tonight, we will find another way."

Simon shifted in his grasp. "But—"

"Mark me." Gregory gave him a small shake. "We will find another way. You must trust in your mother and me. Can you do that?"

"Aye." Simon gulped as he peeped at Faye. "You swear it?"

Her heart and soul if he asked. "I swear." Faye kissed his forehead and inhaled his little-boy scent, drew it deep, a tonic for her ache.

"Master Simon! This is no time for your mischief. Where are you?" Footsteps approached their hiding place.

"Go." Gregory gave Simon a small shove. "Go now and remember, tonight if you can, but do not put yourself in danger."

Simon backed away and his footsteps faltered as he stared at Gregory. "You swear."

"My solemn oath." Gregory put his hand over his heart. "You must be brave but not foolish. Now, you swear."

"I swear." Simon solemnly repeated Gregory's gesture.

A lump lodged in Faye's throat. Part of her walked away as

Simon dragged his steps into the light of the torches, dwarfed by the large, dim bailey.

"There you are." The nasty shrew grabbed his arm. "I have been looking everywhere for you. Where have you been, you naughty boy?"

Faye curled her hands into fists so hard her nails dug into her palms. Nobody grabbed her son like that. She wanted to dash out of her hiding place and cuff the woman.

"I was getting some air," Simon said.

"Getting some air?" The nurse snorted. "What will you say next? Come along now, it is time for your prayers and then bed."

"Aye, Nurse."

Faye hummed with the need to follow him, to snatch up her child and take him away.

Gregory's hand covered hers. One by one, he unclenched her fingers and laced them with his. Serious as the grave, he nodded. "Tonight."

Faye latched onto his strength and his certainty. "Tonight."

Chapter Eleven

Faye paced the patch of grass beside the wagon.

Gregory crouched beside the cart and dragged a whetstone against the side of his blade. The steady scrape had her near to screaming. "How much longer?"

"Not too much longer." Gregory kept his head bowed, his large hands working his blade. "We will hear the bells for *Compline* shortly."

She had no clue where he found his patience. It must stand him in good stead at the Abbey. He didn't look like a monk now with him dressed as a normal man, performing a task she had seen him do countless times before. Blade across his knees, whetstone in one large, scarred hand as he worked it over the edge. Gregory never liked to be still for long. Always, he had to keep his hands busy. He tested the edge of his sword against his thumb.

Faye braced for renewed scraping.

He slipped the sword into the scabbard and stood.

Thank you, Lord. "Now?"

"After *Compline*." Painfully slowly, he fastened the sword about his waist.

She would go mad. Her ears strained to catch the toll of the bells. The jagged scream of a vixen broke the still night, and Faye leaped.

"Soon now." Gregory perched on the edge of the cart and crossed his ankles.

Faye pressed her hand to her racing heart. "What if he has encountered difficulty?"

"We will find out soon."

A bullock lowed. They were yoked to the cart, their harness fastened to the trunk of a small tree. Everything stood in readiness for them to fetch Simon home.

Gregory adjusted his sword belt.

"How can you stand it?" It burst out of her. Any more waiting and she would snatch up his sword and charge into Brynn.

He shrugged. "I am accustomed to it."

The silence stretched between them. A nightjar sang, crickets chirped, the bullocks munched their cud, and still, no bell tolled.

"It is not much different from waiting for battle to join," he said.

Any conversation would be better than this strained, pressing silence. "Do you miss battle?"

"Nay." He shook his head. "I never craved battle as some men do. It was something I did because it was my duty. The violence is sickening." He tensed and cocked his head. "Listen."

"Wha—"

He held up his hand.

A gentle carol of bells rose from the valley.

"*Compline.*" Gregory stood.

Vigor surged through Faye. Perspiration broke over her and she wiped damp palms against her rough wool bliaut.

Gregory led the way deeper into the thicket, skirting the outer wall of Brynn. The postern gate lay hidden behind an outcropping of rock.

Jaw tensed, Gregory stopped. A guard's footfalls clipped on the stones. He turned and went back in the other direction.

On a nod, Gregory ran for the concealing rocks.

Panting, heart thundering, Faye followed.

The postern gate was still open, as they had left it when they departed earlier. It was shocking how easy it was to slip within Brynn. Her father would never have allowed a gate to go unguarded, never mind it remaining open hour after hour. The keep stood like a great, dark, silent sentinel.

Gregory returned to their former hiding place and crouched.

Faye stayed behind him and copied his movements.

In the deserted bailey, smoldering fires cast a faint orange glow outside the kitchens. One stray spark and the keep would be lost. Untended flames would devour the kitchen and find an easy meal of the wooden parts of the main structure. It was mete she get her son out of this place.

Gregory blended with the shadows.

Her breathing rasped louder than a file. She pressed her hand over her mouth to silence it. The air carried the stench of horse manure. Faye shuddered to think of the state of the stables in this place. Her knees grew stiff, and she stared so hard at the dark, still keep door, it blurred. Faye eased her knees to the damp ground.

Anything could be happening within that slovenly keep. Mayhap Simon had been stopped and confined. Or he waited, like her, for the chance to escape but couldn't. Had he fallen asleep from waiting for so long? He was only seven years and it was an awful lot to ask of a young boy. She should never have allowed him to return with that careless nurse. She should have grabbed him and run with him when she had the chance. "I—"

Gregory held up his hand.

She measured time by the tramp of the single guard's footsteps. At least this one was not dozing beside the fire, but walking the keep as he should. Simon was not coming. She was sure of it. Something had gone wrong. She would have to go and get him. She rose.

Gregory tugged her back down.

"He is not coming." Her whisper was like a shout.

Gregory pressed his finger to his lips.

Silence be damned. Her son could be in all manner of trouble. She had not come this far to skulk in the shadows until dawn and then make another of Gregory's infernal plans. She hated plans. She must be more like her father than she supposed. Sir Arthur was a man of action. Even so, her father did nothing to aid her. He, too, waited at Anglesea and made one plan after another. He would secure Simon's release through other means. Blast that to hell. The blasphemy soothed her ire a mite.

Gregory finally moved and her heart leaped. He motioned her deeper into the shadows.

She shook her head. From there, she would not be able to see if Simon had escaped. Her growing conviction he was not coming warred with her need to keep believing that he would.

Gregory gripped her arm and tugged, nearly unbalancing her as they crept away. "We will wait another hour and then I will go in and get him."

At last, some action "How will we know when the hour is up?"

He held up his hand. Faint moonlight outlined a long string with knots tied in it. An old soldier's trick for telling time in the dark. All three of her brothers had been taught how to do it. Gregory had his stupid knots to keep him distracted and calm.

They crawled back to their former lookout.

Now that he'd shown her the string, Faye watched how he did it. She tried to make some sense of the movements of his long fingers along the small piece of twine. Her gaze kept straying back to the keep door and she gave up. Dear Lord, let him come. Please, Heavenly Father, let her son come. Now. Was that movement in the shadow over the door? Faye held her breath. She strained to see in the dark. It was movement. Her heart leaped into her throat.

"Oh, God." It was a woman and not a small boy. She grabbed Gregory's hand and squeezed.

He returned the pressure, gentler but there.

Beside the woman, walked a smaller form.

Simon.

Her heart jammed in her throat as the two figures slid along the keep wall. They stayed within the shadows then stopped suddenly and waited.

The guard's footsteps passed near and then faded.

Faye's pulse drummed, drowning out other sound. Staying here, concealed, had to be the hardest thing she had ever done.

The two figures darted across the open stretch of bailey.

Faye had her arms out and snatched up Simon the moment he stepped within reach.

"My lady?" The woman stood beside Gregory.

"Ruth?" Faye held Simon tight to her.

"Aye, my lady." Ruth's voice wobbled. "I thank our Lord you are come."

Gregory patted her shoulder as Ruth buried her face in her apron and her shoulders shook in silent sobs.

"She caught me slipping out." Simon wrestled free of Faye's hold. "She wouldn't let me go until I told her I was coming to you. I know you said I was not to tell anyone—"

"You did well." Gregory ruffled his hair.

A smile split Simon's face. "I had to make a difficult decision."

"You did." Faye couldn't resist another hug. "And you did splendidly."

"You must go, my lady." Ruth lowered her apron from her face. "Sir Robert is due to return in the morn and Sir Hugo with him. I hear talk they have men all over the land between here and Anglesea."

Faye had hoped they would have a few more days to get Simon safe and guarded within Anglesea's walls. Then, Sir Arthur could make her ears bleed with his diplomacy nonsense for all she cared.

"I will do what I can to gain you some time," Ruth said. "I can say he is not well, but I will not be able to gain you much.

"Thank you, Ruth." Faye pulled the girl into a quick hug.

God only knew what would happen to Ruth when Hugo discovered what she'd done. Except, God and Faye knew exactly what might happen. "Do not risk yourself."

"It was wrong what Sir Hugo did." Ruth rubbed her nose on her apron. "I will be all right."

"Be careful." She was thoughtless, caring for naught else but getting her son to safety. Aye, but she would do what she must. "Come to Anglesea when you can. There will be a place for you there."

"My thanks, Lady Faye." Tears gathered as Ruth turned to Simon. "You be a good boy now, and mind your mother."

"God be with you, Ruth." Simon gave her a quick, hard hug. "You are the best nurse a boy could have."

"Indeed." Ruth gave a watery chuckle. "I will remind you of that when I get to Anglesea and find you not eating your greens." She spun away. "Take him, my lady, and may God speed your heels."

Faye floated back to the bullock cart, her heart full of love and her mind free of the gnawing worry. Of course, they had yet to get back to Anglesea, but all seemed suddenly within her grasp.

With Gregory carrying Simon on his shoulders, they covered the distance in no time.

Gregory moved with calm, deliberate expedience. He put Simon in the back of the cart and untied the beasts. He patted Simon on the shoulder. "If we come across anyone, hide. No need to draw anyone a map."

Faye's ebullient mood wavered. Hugo would arrive at Brynn to discover Simon missing. Anglesea would be his first guess as to where Simon had gone. "Should we not exchange the cart for horses?" She fiddled with Simon's cloak. It would be awful if the evening air gave him a chill.

Simon batted her hands away.

"We will change to horses as soon as we can." Gregory remained as calm as ever. "For now, I am taking bridle paths in the hope Hugo will stick to the main road. He will overtake us as he rides for Anglesea. That way, your father can honestly deny he has Simon. We will follow by a roundabout route."

It made sense, partly. "But if Hugo stays at Anglesea, how will we return?"

"We could fight." Simon stuck his head between them. "Nobody is better than Gregory with a sword."

"I appreciate that, lad, but my fighting days have passed."

Simon's face fell. His face creased in a mighty frown. "You could fight for the church."

"Fight for the church?"

Simon's face cleared into a grin. "They need fighting men, too."

"I shall think on it," Gregory said. "In the meanwhile, why do you not lay down and see if you can get some sleep."

"I could never sleep." Simon bounced on his knees.

Gregory's tone was steel in velvet. "Try."

Simon pulled a face, but settled in the cart bed. A loud sigh came from his direction and then another.

Faye worked hard not to laugh.

Beside her, the corner of Gregory's mouth twitched and he turned his head.

The cart moved into the still, dark night.

Simon fell silent.

Faye peeped over, and his eyes were shut. "How will we enter Anglesea?"

"You and Simon can remain with Aldous until I ascertain all is well at Anglesea. He will keep you safe until we can get you within Anglesea's walls." He had a beautiful smile. It softened the grave lines of his face and crinkled around the corners of his eyes and mouth. She didn't see it that often, but it always drew an answering smile from Faye.

He caught her staring. "What is it?"

Faye shook her head and leaned against his shoulder. Her

words would only make him uncomfortable. "I am glad you are with me."

He tensed, but stayed. "Likewise, my lady."

Chapter Twelve

Faye allowed hope to blossom inside her. Simon was with them and they were on their way home. She owed Gregory everything. Faye closed her eyes and snuggled closer to the husband of her heart.

Imagine if it had been him as her groom she had spied from her casement. How different her life would have been. The rumble of wheels against the dirt track vibrated through her. They might have been happy like Beatrice and Garrett, locked in an almost insufferable togetherness that barred the rest of the world. They could have had that, she and Gregory. This might have been their son sleeping behind them.

Gregory's rough tunic rubbed her cheek. Under the tunic, his arm was as forged steel. His large hands held the traces loosely. Power resided in those hands and yet, they could be gentle as a lady's maid. He always touched her with the utmost courtesy. How she longed for his touch to grow demanding, for him to caress her as a lover. Heat prickled over her skin and she lifted her head from his shoulder.

"My lady?" He searched her face for answers.

Her face heated and she turned and stared into the dark woods beside the cart. Always Gregory kept his composure, as

125

calm and still as deep running water. From his steadiness, she drew peace and comfort. It also made her want to scream.

He never lost control. Even in Bess's cottage, a part of him remained outside of himself, leading him away from temptation. Leading him away from her. Passion simmered beneath the surface like a banked inferno, flaring in his dark gaze, hot enough to scorch. Then his virtuous meddler would rise and extinguish it. Somehow, the meddler always won. She had wept like a babe when he left Anglesea to join the monks.

He had stoically bowed to her and left. You could have cut gems on his clenched jaw that day.

"Do you never doubt?"

He jerked his head toward her. "What do you mean?"

"About being a monk. Do you never have doubts?" *Do you never look at me and ponder the same questions that drive me out of my mind?* She couldn't say that, however.

"I have made my choice." Jaw set, he stared over the bullock's back.

"Aye, you have made your choice, but are you certain you have made the right choice?" She was mad to ask these questions. She wanted him to tell her he was mistaken. Even wavering would have been something.

"Nay."

Merely that, nay. A blow to her middle. Other men had found her beautiful and sung ballads to her beauty. Not Gregory, however. He was above such common, base sentiment.

"Nay, I suppose you are good for naught else." She shocked herself into a gasp. Those words had come from her mouth. Awful, cruel, ugly words, but they were out there and with enough truth for her to leave them there.

A muscle worked in his jaw.

"I mean, you have been living the life of a monk since I have known you. You may as well take your orders." She meant the words to soothe the sting of her last statement, but they sounded petulant and waspish. Calder had called him Father Piety, sneered it at him. Faye had seen how much Gregory hated that. She could apologize and tell him she was being a shrew. She folded her arms over her chest. A lady did not behave in such a manner. Fairest Faye. What a jest. So fair she sat beside a man who refused to want her and cast barbs at him. She shuddered to even think how the minstrels would put that to words. "I beg your pardon." She dragged the words out. "I should not have said any of that."

He nodded, but his face remained grim.

Simon slept on and the bullocks kept their slow, steady pace through the night.

He halted the bullocks and turned toward her. "What is it you would have me say?"

Faye stared at her lap. *Want me*, she screamed inside. *Love me and tell me you will stay with me always.* "Naught."

"Look at me." His voice vibrated with command.

Faye shook her head. She could not look at him and let him see her need writ clear on her face.

"Look at me." His fingers pressed firm beneath her chin. "You knew I would return to the Abbey."

She knew, but infernal hope kept at her to believe he might not take his vows. In the end, her foolish girl persisted—he might turn and see what he tossed away and throw his heart at her feet. Faye jerked her chin out of his grasp. "Aye."

"For as long as we have known each other, I have shared my desire with you. Why are you wroth?" He studied her face, but she looked away. He knew her too well. "Faye." He growled her name. "Do you think it was easy to leave you that first time?"

"Aye." Not once had he turned his head as he had ridden away. He had bid her God be with her, bowed and left. He had certainly done his best to appear as if it were easy to leave.

"Dear Lord." He leaped from the cart and strode into the night.

Faye checked on Simon, sleeping soundly. She slipped out of the cart and followed Gregory into the woods.

Beside a large tree, he rested one hand against the trunk, the other curled into a fist by his side. "And do you think I will stroll away, without a care, from you this time? From you and Simon and Arthur."

"Then why?" Faye wanted to touch him, but his manner forbade it. "Why do you leave us?"

"All I have ever wanted was to take my vows." He raised his head to the darkened canopy above them. "Since boyhood, I lived and dreamed it. I made my mother a sacred vow." He sighed. "Never did I have a moment's doubt. Until..."

"Until what?" She ached to hear what came next. Part of her knew, but she still craved hearing it like her next breath.

"Until I rode into Anglesea Keep and saw you standing at the casement." It robbed her of breath, the pain and the sweetness were that jagged. "You were standing at your casement, looking into the bailey. Calder had not noticed you yet, only I had. Dear God, you were beautiful. But it was more than that." He took a long, ragged breath. "I have seen many beautiful women. And some of them have even tried to turn my head, but you, Faye, without even trying you made me want things I never thought I would."

"What things?"

"Why must you do this to me?" He slammed his fist into the tree. "Why must you torment us both in this manner?"

"Because I need to know. I need to know when I have these impossible dreams that I am not the only one." And there it was, the truth, in all its stark and ruthless beauty.

"God's wounds, Faye." Striding to her, he stopped right before her. "These words should never be uttered. Once they are spoken, we cannot unspeak them and make them disappear."

"Please." The lump in her throat made it difficult to speak. The weariness went bone-deep and she had not the strength for it anymore.

"You were mine." His possessive stare glittered down at her. "From that moment on, you were mine. I knew I could not have

you, but here"—he covered her hand and pressed it to his heart—
"I knew you were mine."

She gripped his fingers until her knuckles turned bloodless.
Too long, she had waited to hear him say this.

"Faye." Against her cheek, his palm burned hot. Dark,
tortured thoughts flit across his face. "There is no point to this."

There was a point to this, a point to them. They could not
have all this between them and still be so far apart. How could
they love and be denied that love? She stood before him, raw and
exposed, an open wound.

Their breath mingled in the tiny space between them.

Faye throbbed with the need for his strong, hard form against
hers. In his arms she became the woman she hid deep within. She
shifted to press her head against his chest.

He tensed.

Nay, she couldn't let him pull away. She needed...so much,
and if all she could have was this, then she would take it. She
fastened her arms about his waist and breathed him in. Man,
leather, and earth wrapped around her. His chest, strong and
impenetrable, against her.

Slowly, his arms closed around her.

And she nearly wept. She could breathe when he held her. So
many times, in the past, she had ached to rest right here. In the
past two days, she had certainly availed herself of the opportunity.
More, whispered her heart, *take all he has.* "I never loved Calder."

"Faye." His voice broke.

"It was always you. You are my everything."

He jerked and staggered back. "Nay, you must not say it."

"It is the truth." She closed the distance between them. Her
heart thundered in her ears, but she stayed her course. "It has to
be said, because it is always there between us. I love you, Gregory.
I have loved you since the moment you entered Anglesea behind
Calder."

His huge chest rose and fell with shallow breaths, but he kept
his head bowed.

"And you have loved me." Fresh tears sprang up from the sweet ache that never went away.

At last, he raised his head and looked at her. The truth was writ across his face. "I cannot."

"But you do." His words caused fresh pain, but she steeled herself. This needed to be done. They could not go the rest of their lives trapped. "Tell me." The need ached within her. She danced close to danger and she couldn't pull back. The ache to hear him say it raged through her. She pressed her palms to his chest. "Tell me."

His skin was warm, his heartbeat strong. And then, his hoarse whisper, "I love you."

Dear Lord, sweet heat roared through her, swelled her breasts and pooled between her thighs. He loved her. For this one, tiny moment, he was hers without reality intruding. Faye raised herself to her toes and leaned toward him. Just one kiss and just this once, a memory to last the rest of her days.

Gregory stared at her lips. "Nay," he whispered, but his hot gaze said different.

Faye touched her mouth to the rigid line of his. Sweet and hot. The touch raged through her. She slid her hands around his neck and tugged him closer.

With a groan, he bent his head to hers.

Hers. Faye opened her mouth beneath his, sweeping her tongue across his closed lips. The taste of him, strong and male and precious. Her senses thrilled at the contact. His hair was silk between her fingers.

His mouth opened.

Boldly, she swept her tongue into his mouth. Too long denied, desire ripped through her.

He pressed her against him.

Faye molded her curves to his strength. The rightness of him made her weep. He was all she could ever want and more. She poured her need into the kiss.

His restraint broke. His kiss grew feverish as his lips bruised, his teeth caught her lips.

So much and not enough. More and more until she drowned. Faye burrowed her hands into his tunic. Hot, silken skin over hard muscle. She spread her fingers wide to soak up the sensation. The ties at the neck of his tunic loosened and she touched the entire width of his chest.

His heart pounded beneath her hands. At the juncture of her thighs pressed his arousal. She gloried in it, rubbing her mound against him. Her breasts were sensitive and ready for his touch. Against her breast, she placed his hand. Heat shot from her breast straight to her core. Her knees grew weak and she leaned into his strength. She yearned to get closer, to have all of him.

"Mama?"

Faye froze. Her pulse thrummed and her senses clamored, too full of Gregory. She dropped back on her heels.

Gregory's breathing came loud and harsh as he stepped away from her.

Faye shivered in the sudden chill, her pulse pounding in her ears.

"Where are you?" Simon's voice quavered.

Gregory spun and strode back toward the cart, his back rigid. "Here."

Legs trembling, Faye stood in the silence. She was mad. Her fantasies fell short of the magic of Gregory. She ached for more.

Simon perched on his knees in the bed of the cart. "Where were you?"

It had been careless to leave him alone. Oh, but what, dizzying, glorious insanity it had been. "Gregory saw something." It was the best she could do in the moment.

Simon bounced on his knees. "What?" Spare her from boys and their curiosity.

"A vixen and her litter." Gregory lied as smoothly as a court jester.

"Can I see?" Simon climbed out of the cart.

"Nay." Gregory caught his arm before he reached the ground. "It was naught." He'd loaded the words with meaning.

A piercing chill settled in Faye's middle.

Over Simon's head, Gregory's glare raked cold and accusing, his mouth grim.

Faye itched to ask Gregory what he meant.

In the cart, Gregory sat beside her, tense and distant. He glowered forward as a muscle moved in his jaw as if he clenched and unclenched his teeth. Gregory didn't rage or thunder in his ire; he remained frigid and contained. She wouldn't have thought it until right this moment, but Faye would rather deal with Calder's explosive anger than this distance she couldn't bridge.

They traveled in ponderous silence. His mood showed no sign of softening. Gone was her one, glorious moment, leaving her feeling soiled in its wake. His anger gnawed at her, sharpening the edge of her sorrow.

"I am hungry." Simon wedged his shoulders between them. "And I need to piss."

"Can we stop?" The first words she spoke to Gregory in what must have been hours.

He nodded. "There is a hamlet hard by. We will find something there."

"How far ahead?" Simon fidgeted with his chausses. "I do not believe I can wait."

Gregory threw him a quick smile and drew the cart up. "Then we will stop now."

For Simon he had a smile, but none for her.

Forest pressed dark and forbidding about them. Her son was very small to be venturing in there alone. "Do you need me to come with you?"

"Mama." Simon rolled his eyes. "A man cannot take a piss in front of his mother."

A retort rose on her lips, but she pressed them together. "Do not stray too far."

Simon was fiercely protective of his independence. He

muttered beneath his breath as he left the cart. Faye guessed his meaning well enough.

Simon slipped behind a large oak.

Faye kept her voice low. "Are we going to speak of it?"

"Nay." Gregory stared at the oak, the strong arch of his nose outlined against the night.

"Then you intend to travel all the way to Anglesea in this awful silence."

His jaw clenched and he shifted away from her. There was scant room in the cart, but he managed to put a wedge of air between them.

The urge to push him off the cart rose swift and fierce. Stubborn and set in his ways. She had no idea why she loved him as she did. Could she have not picked a more malleable man? One who was prepared to love her in return? And that was the heart of the matter. It lay between them like a large, rotting corpse. Faye was tired of this constant parry and retreat they played. "I have no regrets."

He jerked and his jaw worked like one possessed.

Let him keep ignoring her now.

"Simon!" His sudden shout startled her.

"In a bit," Simon bellowed back. "I think I have the runs."

"Why are you angry?" Some demon within demanded she make him respond. "It was merely a kiss." It had been much more than a kiss.

He swung toward her, blocking the moonlight. "Merely a kiss?"

Elation surged through Faye. There, she had got him to acknowledge her. Her triumph died in the face of the relentless, searing anger in his scowl.

"Merely a kiss?" He glowered. "It was a betrayal of all I hold sacred."

Breath left her in a rush. Hot words of denial clamored in her head, but refused any attempt to order them into a coherent response.

"You did it deliberately. You set out to tempt me from my vows. I know I must forgive you, but I am too wroth to speak with you. So, aye, we will travel all the way to Anglesea in silence. I will not give you the opportunity to spread your lures."

She opened her mouth and an inarticulate bark escaped her lips. The insufferable, bloated pig's bladder named her Jezebel and condemned her for it. He had been in those woods with her. It was his shaft pressed against her in silent demand and his mouth on hers like starving man. "You blame me?"

"How many times have I said there are some things that should never be spoken?"

"You craven churl." Dear God, she had never been this angry with anyone.

He jerked as if struck.

"You desire me and hate me because you do. You hide behind your robes and your vows and pretend you are not subject to the same desires as the rest of us."

He opened his mouth.

"You blame me for your own needs. You grow angry with me when it is with yourself you are wroth. You run away from us, everything we are, and hide in your Abbey."

"It is my vocation."

"Nonsense." If he mouthed his self-righteous idiocy one more time, she might smack him. "It is your stubbornness that insists there is no other course. You made a promise to your mother."

"I—"

"You set your heart on being a priest. That may have been true, but it is your obstinacy that insists it is the truth."

His face crumpled in a ferocious frown. His chest rose and fell rapidly with the harshness of his breath.

She had never dared speak so openly before. World bid welcome to a new Faye, standing proud and fierce and saying what needed to be said.

Simon reappeared through the trees. "All done."

Faye forced a smile.

Waves of fury throbbed from Gregory.

She didn't care. Let him be angry. She was angry, too. He had robbed her of her one beautiful memory of him as a lover. She wanted the sweetness back, but it was tainted by his condemnation.

The cart dipped under Simon's weight.

Gregory got the bullocks moving.

The air prickled and sparked around her. She was done with Gregory and his self-righteous obdurateness. He could rot in it for all she cared.

Her heart twisted. She did care. She would not be this angry if she did not. He was sunk into every part of her being like honey in bread. It was ruined. Tears threatened to spill over and she turned her head toward the forest. She could not cry before Simon and she refused to cry for the silent man beside her. It was pointless.

Dawn broke above the trees in a vivid mockery of her sore heart. Birdsong swelled, singing the day into being. Dew sparkled from the grass and leaves and chilled the damp air. The sky grew lighter, but not her mood. Weariness of this struggle seeped into the core of her. The years in Calder weighed around her neck. Years of concealing forbidden love, the impossible dreams and the unrequited desires. The way she clung to that slither of hope with everything in her.

In their stubbornness, she and Gregory were the same, would not be gainsaid. They turned their heads and would not hear or see any other course than the one they desired. They desired things in direct opposition to each other.

Faye gave up. This time for certain. She opened the casket within her and let her dreams and hopes pour into the new day. They were phantoms, nothing more. She could not constantly beat her head against her inflexible fate. Each time she came away more bloodied than before.

Chapter Thirteen

"Say again." Hugo stared at the girl, gaped at her, in truth. Such open defiance dumbfounded him. He almost admired the courage. Seasoned knights did not have the stones to dare what she had.

Ruth quaked like the palsied in front of him. "Simon is gone. His mother came for him."

Hard to believe that somehow, the stupid whore had found the courage to conceal the boy's absence from him. Jesu, she could have spun her tale for hours with nobody any the wiser. These stupid sods at Brynn nodded their limp heads and accepted her lie that the boy ailed. Except, she'd not taken him into account, and now she would have to pay.

Robert of Brynn had his uses, but he was a lazy, stupid dog and Hugo had needed to make sure the proper precautions were taken to keep Simon at the fool's castle. Years he had waited while his brother held the title. He would not lose what was his now. So, Hugo had arrived many hours ahead of when expected, hoping to catch the keep lax. His vigilance had been rewarded. Jesu, the place was looser than a cheap whore's cunt. It can't have taken much for Faye to get in here and take Simon.

Faye? He shook his head in amazement. He still couldn't get

his head around it. Sniveling, pathetic Lady Faye who wouldn't raise her voice if her ass was on fire. That Faye had traveled from Anglesea, discovered he was not at Calder and come here to get Simon.

She must have been close enough to Calder Castle for him to grab her. Jesus wept! He'd had her, right beneath his sodding nose. She wasn't alone. He would wager his head on it. Two monks had arrived in Upper Mere, one of them large and the other a grubby boy.

A man and his wife were observed on the road leading from Upper Mere to Brynn late that same night. The disjointed snippets of information fed to him throughout the day fell into place with a sickening click.

Damn her and Gregory. They'd made fools of him just as they had Calder. He'd seen them at Calder Castle, heads together, huddled in corners like thieves. God, how they had made him laugh with their secret longings, staring at each other like starving dogs. Father Piety had a limp rod and no ballocks. They had ridden into his town, in clear day. God, he could hear them laughing at him now.

"Get every man." If he looked at Robert of Brynn, he would rip the man's throat out. "Every single one who can sit a horse and get them out looking. They are traveling by bullock cart. They will not have gone far."

Ruth sobbed into her apron.

A shame really to stamp out her spirit. He admired it, up to a point. "Come here, girl."

Faye took in the entire place in a glance. Hamlet was a generous description of the three run-down cottages clustered around a mill. Mill sails flapped listlessly in the morning breeze.

A scraggly mongrel barked their arrival to anyone within earshot. He wasted his energy. The place looked abandoned. Not a soul appeared in the doorways. The bullocks flickered their ears at the dog and stopped.

Tense, Gregory turned a full arc, searching the hamlet.

"What is it?" The incessant barking wore on her nerves.

Gregory squinted. "Too quiet."

Faye listened. "I hear nothing but the dog."

"Exactly." Gregory pulled his sword out from behind him and motioned Simon. "Get down, lad and stay there until your mother or I tell you it's safe."

Simon's little voice quavered. "Mama?"

"Be still, sweeting."

His sweaty hand slipped into hers.

From around the mill, a man appeared wearing Brynn colors.

Faye whirled. Oh dear Lord, did Hugo know already that she had Simon? Surely not. She tightened her slick grip on Simon's hand. She wouldn't let them take her son.

A man slunk out of the nearest cottage. Behind him came a mounted man-at-arms.

"Take him and run." Gregory dropped to the ground in a fighting stance, his sword at the ready. "Do not look back for anything."

"But—"

"Do not let them take you, Faye. Run. I will find you."

Heavily armed men entered the clearing in front of the mill. Their gazes moved between her and Gregory.

Her chest tightened, and it grew difficult to breathe. She couldn't leave Gregory to fight this alone.

"Go." Gregory strode into the clearing. "I will cover your escape."

"I cannot—"

"Do it!"

She stumbled out of the cart, Simon's hand in hers.

With huge eyes, he stared from her to Gregory and then the strangers.

The lead man stepped ahead of his five fellows. "We want the boy."

Her boy, not theirs. She backed away with Simon tight by her side.

"I cannot give you the boy." Gregory sounded calm, but stood braced for a fight, between her and them like the archangel Michael. His sword caught the early morning sun.

The leader glanced toward her and he took a step nearer. "Do not move, my lady."

Gregory sprang to meet him. "Go, Faye."

The man hesitated, barely getting his sword up in time to meet Gregory's downward strike. "Get her," he yelled over his shoulder.

Tugging Simon behind her, she dashed into the forest.

The *clang* of steel followed her. She prayed as she ran. Prayed she would reach safety. Prayed Gregory left the clearing alive. Heartfelt pleas for the lives of those she held dearest.

Simon stumbled behind her, struggling to keep up with her.

A muted shout sounded behind her. It didn't sound like Gregory, but she dared not stop and see. Branches clawed at their clothing. Leaves muted the sound of their footfalls as Faye dodged trees. The further she ran, the quieter the battle grew behind her.

Simon tripped over a root and fell.

Faye stopped and righted him.

His knees were skinned through a tear in his chausses. She wanted to stop and tend his hurt, but they were still too close. She slowed to a fast walk.

Bless his heart, Simon tramped on beside her.

They reached a large stream too wide to jump over, so Faye turned to follow its path.

"Nay." Simon tugged on her hand. "We should cross."

"We will get wet." Water rushed past them, so deep in the middle, she couldn't see the bottom.

"They cannot track us through water." Simon's face gleamed pale as moonlight. "Gregory taught me."

Sweet Jesu, let Gregory be alive. The alternative clawed through her and near bent her in half. The last words they spoke had been angry.

"Here." Simon ripped off a section of his chausses and tied it to a branch. "This will tell him we crossed here." Not yet eight and he was better equipped to lead them through the woods than she.

"Are you sure?" The fluttering fragment of wool didn't mean anything to her.

"I am sure." Simon tugged her toward the stream. "I can take care of you, Mama." Her little man should not have to take care of her. He should be playing stones with the boys at Anglesea, or tormenting Arthur as was his wont.

Water flooded her rough work clogs and drenched her stockings. It rushed about Simon's knees as he waded ahead of her through the stream. Simon could swim, another thing to thank Gregory for. She had been angry with him and hurt. She had hurled her spite at him and now they might be the last words she spoke to him. If she saw him again, she swore before God, she would amend her angry words. It must not end thus between them.

* * *

Faye tugged her skirts free of a bramble patch. The day warmed as they struggled through thick undergrowth. Sweat stained her bodice and slithered down her back. She must smell rank. At least her shorn hair didn't lie heavy on her nape.

Simon battled on valiantly, but his legs dragged and he tripped over each small rock or crack in the path. He insisted on tearing off small pieces of his tunic and tying them to any available piece of foliage.

It gave both of them a small glimmer of hope, a connection to Gregory. Under the guise of her needing to rest, they stopped for longer and longer periods. Faye had no idea where they were or how much time had passed since they had run from the clearing. She kept her ears pricked for pursuit. Other than the occasional rustling of woodland creatures, the forest stayed silent.

Simon stumbled over a small rock.

"I need to rest." Faye motioned him to stop.

His legs buckled and he sank to the ground, his face strained and pale with exhaustion. It was so wrong for a child to suffer this.

The trees thinned in this part of the forest. She and Simon slaked their thirst with water from the stream. Faye didn't dare risk any of the berries gleaming ripe along their path despite their growing hunger. Neither of them could keep going indefinitely. She would need to find somewhere to rest and some food, but she had no money with her. "Did Gregory tell you aught about how to know where you were going?"

Simon blinked sleepily.

She toyed with letting him sleep for an hour or two, but they must find shelter first. She knew nothing of nature or any of the things that could aid them in their plight. Always, she traveled with a retinue of people who knew these things.

"Moss." Simon flashed a tired smile. "But I cannot remember what he said. The moss grows on one side of the tree more than the other, or something."

Not helpful. Faye gave him an encouraging smile anyway. There had to be something she could use. Why was she so useless? Nothing but a pretty ornament in a tower.

"The sun." Simon perked up. "We could use the sun."

Of course. Faye wanted to kick herself. "We could make a sundial." It would give her some idea of how long they had traveled and where they were. She hunted for a straight twig. The victory tasted sweet when she located a suitable stick, straight enough to make a good rod. Moving out of the shadow of the trees, she stuck it into the ground.

Simon stood beside her as they studied the wavy shadow of the twig.

"Well, we are past midday." Simon frowned.

Faye squinted up at the sun. "Which means, that direction must be west and we are heading south." Her brief moment of triumph dropped like a stone. South was no good. "Go north to Aldous," Gregory had told her. She should have asked more questions then, but she hadn't wanted to accept the possibility she might need the knowledge. She tucked the twig into her belt. At least they now had more idea of where they needed to go. The prick of the twig at her waist comforted her, a sort of talisman. Faye used it each time they stopped. The day marched forward relentlessly.

Surely Gregory would catch up with them any time now. Unless—

Nay, she couldn't think that. He was the best fighter at Calder Castle. He must have lost track of them, but he would find them. She had faith in him. Gregory had never failed her before. The strain of remaining alert bunched her shoulders and stretched her nerves to the point where each stray leaf flutter or scurry through the undergrowth had her jumping.

They stumbled across a small road early into the evening. Little more than a bridle path, it wound between a hedgerow guarding a barley field on one side and a tangled wood on the other. Shadows hung low over the road. It ran in roughly the right direction and Faye elected to follow it. It made walking easier and a road must lead somewhere people wanted to go. Fields indicated people nearby. They stuck to the verge, ready to slip into the hedgerow at the first sign of someone coming.

Simon held up his hand. "Listen."

The quick thud of hooves pounded the road.

Faye tugged Simon off the road and into a narrow drainage ditch. The water was fouled with roots and stank. Slimy mud oozed over her ankles and into her clogs. Disgusted, she clenched her teeth to stop the shudder.

"They might be help." Simon's gaze shone with new hope.

Or they could be Hugo. "We will see who they are first." She stroked a sweaty hank of hair off his forehead. He had been so brave through this day, more than she could ever ask of him. If the state of her belly was any indication, the lad must be nigh on starving.

Hooves clattered closer and Faye put her hand on Simon's head to keep him down. A rider wove into view, tall and dark.

Gregory. Her heart leaped into her throat. She stumbled partway out of the ditch and stopped. Not Gregory.

Back into the ditch Faye slid, her belly dropping right into her muddy clogs. Just a dark-haired messenger wearing colors she did not know. Past their hiding place went the hooves, growing fainter until the evening's silence descended once more.

Faye straightened and pulled her foot free of the mud.

"Well now, my lovelies, look what Odo has found."

Chapter Fourteen

Beside the hedgerow stood a man of middling height with his legs planted apart and fists on his hips. His broad chest stretched the thinning fabric of his dirty tunic. Long, scraggly hair hung on either side of a broad, flat face. His stare raked her from top to toe.

Faye's nape prickled as he wrapped a meaty paw around the hilt of a long dagger at his belt.

Three others slipped through a small gap in the hedgerow, equally filthy and ragged.

"Who are you?" Faye drew her shoulders back. She may be standing in a drainage ditch with mud fouling her up to the knees, but she was still the daughter of Sir Arthur of Anglesea. Men did not leer at Lady Faye.

"A lady?" The man's brows rose. "Lads we have found a lady in a ditch." His gaze crawled along her skin. "Forgive me, my lady." He grinned, revealing a gaping hole where his front teeth should be. "I am called Odo by my friends. And we are going to be good friends, my pretty lady."

Simon tugged at her skirt. "Mama."

Nay, she and Odo were not going to be any sort of friends. She had to get as far from Odo as she could.

There were five, now, all leering.

"My son and I are trying to reach the next village." She hauled herself out of the ditch, her heavy, muddy skirts hindering her. Faye kept Simon behind her as she stepped onto the road.

Two men slipped behind her.

She edged around to keep them in sight.

An immense man stepped into the gap beside Odo. His shaved head crowned a round face with an oddly boyish appearance. His wrists hung out of a tunic that strained to cover his breadth. Nasty, russet stains, which looked worryingly like dried blood, soiled the front of his tunic.

Beside them stood a wiry boy, who seemed to be no older than Simon until she looked at his face. The boy had the shrewd, sharp gaze of a child with experience well beyond his years.

Faye stepped to the left.

Odo blocked her.

The big one lunged, his gummy mouth open in a soundless grin.

Faye gathered Simon and backed away.

"Get them," Odo snapped.

Four men closed the gaps, cutting off any hope of escape.

Simon's grip pained her fingers.

The big man lunged for them, huge, hairy uncouth hands reaching for her boy.

"Nay." Faye fended them off. "Do not touch him."

"Settle down, Lady." Odo spread his arms wide. "We do not want to hurt the boy. We want to take him on a little adventure."

They were trapped, no way out through the closed circle. She doubted she could outrun them. Her best chance lay in going with them quietly, for now, and waiting for her chance to escape. "He will come quietly." Faye tucked Simon as close as she could. "Do not hurt him."

Perspiration coated her skin. Sweet Jesus, her mind fuddled in fear when she needed to think, protect her boy. *The knife!* She had William's knife in her boot.

There were five of them. She couldn't get them all. Sickening memories of Calder rose up before her. Calder's hard hands on her, Calder's face twisted in a mask of cruelty. Her cowardice as she remained quiet, anything to stop the anger and not worsen it. Know when to fight and when to retreat.

"Stay." Inspiration struck. "My father will pay a tidy ransom if we are returned unharmed."

"Lady." Odo's thick top lip curled in contempt. "If your father valued you, you and the boy would not be out here walking the road without an escort."

"Nay." Faye clawed at the hands reaching for Simon. She shifted to keep between the men and Simon's trembling form. "I have been separated from my escort, and he will pay handsomely to have me returned to him."

Odo's jeering laughter scraped along her nerves. "She lies."

Calm, she must remain calm.

"Who is your father?" The boy had a high, piping voice, its innocence at odds with his desperate appearance.

"Sir Arthur of Anglesa. I am the Lady Faye and my son is the new Earl of Calder. My father will not take kindly to seeing us harmed."

The men broke into laughter.

"What a fine jest, Lady." Odo's barrel chest heaved with laughter. "The Earl of Calder and his mammy are guttersnipes? You should provide fine entertainment for the lads and me."

"Nay, I speak true." Desperation made her tongue heavy and her voice strangled in her parched throat.

"Anglesea is a rich man." The boy pursed his lips. "He would, for certain, pay to have his daughter and her boy back."

Odo glared at the youngster. "Shut your face, boy!"

The thin man cuffed the boy, but the child ducked with eye blurring speed to evade the blow.

"The boy is right." A long, drawn-faced man spoke from beside Odo. "They say Anglesea has coffers of gold in his dungeon."

"In his armory." Faye's ears buzzed as the blood drained from her face. She clung to the tiny glimmer of hope. "My father keeps the gold in his armory. I have seen it. Piles of it."

"Enough." Odo wrenched her arm, as he hauled her from Simon.

"Leave my mother." Simon's lip trembled in his pale face, but his scowl blazed his defiance.

"They will not hurt me." She put as much reassurance in her tone as she could. "We are of too much value to them unharmed. Only a foolish man would ignore such a windfall."

Odo scowled, thinking. "Will!"

The big man grabbed Simon.

Her son writhed in his grasp. He cried out as Will twisted his arm up and above his head.

"Nay." Faye wrenched against Odo's hold.

"Use your head, Odo." The boy sneered. "She could be a lying whore, aye, but what if she is not?"

The other men looked between Odo and the boy.

"Calder died a few months back. Heard it myself." The boy hitched his sagging trousers.

Will shifted his feet. "The little turd makes a good point, Odo."

"Easier than this load of dog's ballocks." The boy hawked and spat.

Spittle hit the road near her skirt and Faye recoiled. She wanted to giggle hysterically. She might owe her salvation to a nasty, foulmouthed criminal.

"Heard a rumor all those armed men about are looking for a woman and a boy," he said.

Odo's brows furrowed as he stroked the hilt of his dagger.

Faye held her breath. She could see the ponderous movement of Odo's dull brain on his face.

The other men waited.

"Bring 'em." Odo jerked his head. "Do not fancy jawing this over in the middle of the road."

Relief brought tears to Faye's eyes. Reprieve.

Simon wriggled away from his captor and came to her side.

Will glared at her son and then shrugged.

"You try anything"—Odo turned back to her—"give me the smallest reason to regret your life and I'll end it." He meant every word. "And your son with you." Odo leaped the irrigation trench and ducked behind the hedgerow.

A jab in her back got Faye moving. Her legs were as water and she stumbled over the hem of her skirt. Her knees hit the road in a jarring thud. A sharp pain lanced up her leg. She righted herself on shaky legs.

Simon's face twisted in concern as he tried to help her to her feet.

Faye gave him a reassuring smile and wiped her hands on her bliaut. Rough wool scratched against her grazed hands. Simon needed her to be strong and she straightened her shoulders as she followed Odo through the hedgerow.

The camp was set not too far from the road. A tall row of trees hid it from view, but provided an excellent sighting of the road from leafy concealment. She and Simon had walked right into their view. These men had watched as she and Simon huddled in the ditch while the rider passed.

A circle of ashes in the center of a few stumps of wood comprised the entire camp. Dry bones, fruit peels and bread crusts covered the ground around the wood stumps. Fat, lazy flies swarmed about at one end of the camp. A midden, by the stench of it, and Faye pressed her hand to her mouth to stop her gorge.

A prod sent her stumbling into the center of the clearing. The prodder stank of onions and rank sweat. "What should we do with 'em?"

"Tie them." Odo pointed to the trunk of a large tree.

"What with?" Prodder sniffed. His voice had a nasal, whiny twang that made Faye want to box his ears.

Odo's look said he felt the same. "Find something, Ham."

"Aye, Odo." Ham skittered away.

The others feared Odo. Faye shivered as she studied his compact, strong body. He could wreak a lot of damage with such strength.

Will shambled over with a stout length of rope. "We have not enough for both of them, but we can bind them together to the tree."

"Nay." Faye's hopes of escape would mean naught if she were bound. "We will not run."

Odo laughed showing the gaps in his mouth. "Do you think I be stupid, Lady?" He sniffed and waved Will over. "Bind them tight. The lady fancies herself a clever wench."

"She be pretty." Will stroked her cheek. Her flesh crawled beneath his touch. Faye shuddered and shrank back from his fingers. Dear God, Will's leer augured ill for her.

"I have a fearful hunger," the boy said. "If you are going to tupp her, can we not eat first?"

"Mama?" Simon gulped.

Her belly churned inside her like a wild beast straining to be released. Faye drew a shaky breath. For her son, she kept her emotion confined. This would not be the first time her body had been taken against her will. There were four of them, not counting the boy. Bile rose in her throat as she thought of them on her, inside her. With Calder it had been best not to fight. If she lay limp and yielding, he would take what he wanted and leave her. The fight, he had enjoyed. It had fueled his desire and made him rougher with her than if she submitted to his will. Did she have the strength to submit? Four men. Her empty stomach heaved.

Simon pressed against her thigh. For him, she would have to. It was more important she live to protect her child. Dear God, what would they do to him if she was not about to see to her son?

"She is not going anywhere." Odo turned his back on her. "We eat first."

Will shoved her toward the tree. He turned her and her back

hit the hard bark. A flush stained his cheeks, his expression heavy with lust. His raised his filthy, huge hands to her breasts.

Simon glared at Will's hands. Big hands, coarse and blunt with dark hair across the knuckles, poised to touch her.

"Please." Faye managed past her parched throat. "Not in front of my son."

A struggle played across his thick features. Then, he dropped his hands and snatched up the rope.

Faye sank to the ground and tugged Simon as close to her as she could.

His small, solid weight warmed her side. Rope cut into her chest and stomach as Will bound them to the tree. Bark poked through her bliaut and dug into her back. Faye prayed silently. She prayed for Gregory to find them, for an act of Mercy to save them and, mostly, for the strength to endure.

Chapter Fifteen

Gregory took the horse from one of his attackers. Two of the three men he bested in moments. The third presented more of a challenge. Number four had real skill and set his head ringing with a lucky, blunt edge blow. Five he finished in moments. The sixth made a clever decision and ran.

Gregory silently wished him well. Five deaths hung over him as he tore into the forest with a prayer for their souls on his lips. The men had been determined to kill him. They feared Hugo's wrath more than they feared him, and he'd had no choice. Even knowing this did not alleviate the sticky mass of guilt in his gut. Another sin to confess when he returned to the Abbey, but not his most pressing concern.

He stopped and sifted through the sounds of the forest. The breeze whispered through the leaves. Chaffinches called and chuckled from above him. From deeper within the trees came the steady piping of a song thrush. He followed the low murmur of water to a stream.

Footprints in the muddy bank, a woman's and a smaller set—Faye and Simon. The tracks stopped at the stream and disappeared. Gregory set off through the trees. They must have stuck to the stream's course.

Hugo had men everywhere, more numerous than rats in the grain. They forced him to stop as he evaded group after group. Hugo must somehow know they had Simon and acted to retrieve the boy. The number of roving parties of men-at-arms also meant Hugo had called in Calder's vassals. The idea of Faye running into one of Hugo's hunting parties rode Gregory hard.

The pinch in his chest increased as the day waned into evening and he still hadn't found her. By now, she could be anywhere. Back at Calder. The flutter of blue caught his eye. He stared at it as if his mind wandered. A scrap of blue fabric tied to a gorse bush.

He dismounted and studied the scrap. Simon wore a blue tunic, this very blue. The fabric was knotted, not hanging there as if the wind had blown it. Somebody had secured it there, on purpose. Simon. Clever, clever lad and stupid Gregory. He could have passed countless of these throughout the day and not seen them.

He led the horse as he scoured the area for more signs.

* * *

Faye dared not sleep.

Simon had surrendered to exhaustion, his weight limp against her, his head drooping over his chest.

Full dark surrounded them, the trees too dense for her to see the night sky. The noise around the fire increased and drowned the sounds of the forest.

The boy had produced a flask of mead. Odo wrested it from him and now they passed the flask between them.

Will gripped his crotch and grinned at her, saliva gleaming on his thick lips. He sat with the others and shared the mead, but he waited, coiled and tense, for Odo to give him permission to do his worst. Every time she moved, Will's leer fastened on her. She rested her head against the tree trunk. Tiredness weighed at her limbs, but she must stay awake. Her prayer became a litany she said over and over in her mind. The fire blurred before her exhausted vision. She blinked and shook her head.

A shout from the fire and Faye started.

Simon stirred and wakened. "Mama?"

"Hush, sweeting."

Ham shook his head, staggered a few steps, and collapsed into a heap beside his rocky seat.

The others laughed at him.

Odo surged to his feet and kicked the man's boots. "Drunken sot."

Ham twitched and stilled.

Odo tipped the flask to his mouth and swigged.

"Odo." The thin man swayed in his seat. With a sigh, he dropped over backward. "My head. Dizzy."

Odo whirled and stared at the second fallen man. He stumbled and stood, swaying and blinking. "Not right," he said, his words thick and slurred. "Something not right."

Faye held her breath, not wanting to look away from Odo.

He shook his head and fell to his knees. "The mead." The earthen flask slipped from his grasp and shattered against a rock surrounding the fire. Mead hit the flame in a hiss and a flare.

"What did you do?" Odo glared at the boy. With a growl, Odo dropped face forward into the dirt. Close enough to be singed by the blaze. The reek of burning hair filled the clearing.

Will groaned, blinked and gripped his head between his hands. "What?"

"Dwale, you dumb ox." The boy grinned.

Faye's head felt woolen. Nurse sometimes used dwale to give relief from pain and help the suffering to sleep, but only as a desperate effort, for it killed the drinker as often as healed them. The boy had drugged his companions. If she could only think, she could make some sense of this.

Will went over like a tree, hitting the ground with a thud that shook the earth.

"Right you are then." The boy sprang to his feet and rubbed

his hands together. He tripped across the clearing from one man to the other.

"His hair." Faye jerked her head at the insensate Odo. Tendrils of smoke rose from his head.

"Let the sod burn." The boy lifted Will's head and dropped it to the ground with a *thump*.

"Please?" If Odo caught fire, Faye would be sick, for certain. Simon should not see something so horrible. "Could you move him?"

The boy snorted and shook his head. "Soft, you are, like the other one."

Her slow brain couldn't make sense of any of this.

The boy bent and heaved Odo a few inches from the fire. He peered up at her. "You know what he would have done to you."

"Aye." She struggled to form coherent words.

"So." The boy appeared before her. "You are Faye."

She didn't know this boy. "Aye."

From his tunic, he produced a wicked-looking dagger. The boy cut through their ropes.

Tiny needles jabbed at her extremities as Faye moved her hands first and then her arms. Her back shrieked in protest. Faye dug the knife out of her boot. She held it as Gregory had taught her. "Who are you?"

"What do you want with that?" The boy frowned at the dagger. "I am Newt."

"Newt?" Faye blinked at him. The whole of Anglesea had heard of Newt, the boy who had saved Beatrice in London. "Beatrice's Newt?" This was Faye's grubby answer to her prayer.

"Aye." He grinned and seemed more like a normal boy when he did. "And fortunate for you I was with this lot, or things would have gone awful for you." Newt studied Simon as her son stood. He turned that sharp stare on her. "You look like Lady Beatrice."

"We are sisters."

Newt sniffed and went back to studying Simon.

Simon raised his chin and glared back.

"What were you doing with them?" Faye dropped her dagger to her side.

"Heard there was some trouble up this way. Trouble for some means easy money for others. I drifted up here to see for myself and fell in with this lot." He gave Will a prod with his boot.

"Where did you...never mind." If but half Beatrice's Newt stories were true, Faye did not want to hear where he'd obtained dwale. "You have my thanks."

"Were not anything," said Newt. "This lot only share half a mind between them."

Despite his filth, Faye grabbed Newt and hugged him. His odor made her eyes water, but she didn't care. He stiffened, but Faye tightened her grip. He had saved her, this unlikely little hero. She released him and slipped the dagger into her boot. "Do you know the way to Anglesea?"

"For certain." Newt sprang back and eyed her as if afraid she might hug him again. "But you don't want to go that way. Busier than the road to London that way is. Lots of men are looking for you."

Gregory had told her to find Aldous. He would look for her there. She knew he would. "Newt." Tired and hungry as she was, new hope surged within her and gave her strength. "Can you take me north?"

"Ay, my lady." He held up a grubby finger. "But then you will be in my debt."

Probably for the rest of her life. "Indeed."

Newt grinned and spat. She might see if she could cure him of that disgusting habit on the way to Aldous.

"Let me see what we have here." Newt rifled through the fallen men and took what he needed. Odo's body relinquished a purse. Coins clinked from within and Newt grinned. "Knew the cur had some coin on him." Newt found a dagger on Will. He turned to Simon. "You know how to use this?"

"Aye." Simon took it from him.

Faye battled not to ask and then shrugged it off. It didn't

matter at this point whom had been teaching her young son to fight with a knife. She would guess Gregory in any case. Gregory. She had no time to think of him now.

Newt finished with his last body and trotted over to them. "Best get going. Odo will come looking for me when he wakes up."

If he wakes. Faye had no compassion to spare on the brute as she and Simon followed Newt into the darkness.

Simon heaved an enormous sigh. "More walking."

"Aye, sweeting, a little farther."

"Will Gregory come?"

"Aye." If he was alive, Gregory would come. The weight of "if" pressed on her shoulders. They had been going the wrong way all day. God knew how far out of their path they'd traveled. And there had been six men in the hamlet. Six were steep odds for any single swordsman, no matter how skilled. She couldn't think on it now, or she would lose what little remained of her mind. First, she needed to get her and Simon to safety. And Newt.

* * *

Gregory's horse went lame around sunset. He'd ridden the poor beast hard all day and it was not the finest of animals. He halted the horse and dropped to the ground. Running his hand over the fetlock, he encountered a swelling on the joint.

"Damn." Possibly a strain or worse, either way he did not have time to nurse the beast or take it to safety. Unharnessing the animal, he took what he needed from the saddlebags and slapped the horse on the rump. It hobbled a few paces forward and turned to stare at him reproachfully.

"Find yourself a nice warm barn." He was talking to a horse. He'd lost his mind.

Gregory set off at a run. He'd tracked the bits of tunic back to the stream, hard by where he'd first lost the trail. Faye and Simon moved in an erratic pattern. Gregory could follow the most basic trail, but several times, he lost their tracks and had to retrace his steps.

Night closed in. Faye and Simon were out there, somewhere, without the knowledge or the skills to survive. Faye's angry words pounded in his brain throughout the day. The Abbot had said something similar about Gregory listening with his heart and not his hard head.

As the hours passed with still no Faye, his mind played a new game with him, one that scared him to the depths of his being. What if he didn't find her? Ever. Him at the Abbey and Faye at Anglesea was one form of torture. A world without Faye in it was so much worse.

What a dolt. It staggered him he hadn't seen any of this before. As long as Faye lived, tucked away at Anglesea, the chance for them remained. He got to cling to some misty dream of them together. Stupid sod. He believed the choice was his to make. His lady or his Lord. Even the agony of that choice gave him a twisted sense of being in command of his fate.

Fate must be laughing at him now. What if the choice was not his to make anymore?

A lifetime without Faye sliced him to the raw and left him bleeding. A lifetime with not even the chance of Faye in his life. Eight years, he'd known her and loved her. Played her paladin and her partner, her champion and her protector and with one touch of her mouth to his, it had all become hollow and lacking. Indeed, he'd lusted for her until his ballocks ached, but it had no substance until he cupped the sweet weight of her breast in his palm. Reality was infinitely more torturous than fantasy.

Dear Lord, what a sodding mess of contradictions and jumbled loyalties. Fate had played her boldest stroke. Jeering the question in his mind. *What if she is lost to you forever?*

Hooves thudded on the earth.

Gregory ducked behind a tree and waited.

The men passed at a fast trot. Wolf Rampant on Gules emblazoned across their surcoats.

The patrols grew more frequent as Hugo's net tightened.

* * *

Faye called a halt to their march. Simon had no more strength in his young legs and she fared not much better. They needed to find a safe place to rest.

In addition to the men out searching, Newt told her Hugo had offered a reward for any free man or woman who would lead him to her and Simon. He had set the entire of Calder's demesne against them. Several times, they stopped and retraced their footsteps to avoid people. They were still on Calder land and Faye trusted nobody.

The farther north they traveled, the more infrequent the patrols. Hugo must have trained most of his resources on the western path between Calder and Anglesea. Newt had proved right about that.

The night stayed clear and balmy. They took shelter beneath a narrow rocky ledge and made a meager meal of what Newt had scrounged from Odo's men.

Simon curled up beside her, his head in her lap and dropped into a deep sleep. His jaw hung slack in his dirty face. A little boy should not be this exhausted or go to sleep with only stale bread to fill his belly.

She teetered on the edge of disaster, alone, hungry and frightened with two young boys as an entire army ran them to ground. Surely things could not get much worse. Unless Gregory didn't find them. Faye shoved the fear away. She had enough trouble on her shoulders without borrowing more.

What a fool she'd been to think she could do this, any of it. Nothing in her life had prepared her for the rigors of her journey. She must have been mad to even contemplate it. Now she had two young boys to get to safety. Not that Newt seemed to need any help. Indeed, she would be in worse trouble without him. She'd thought only of getting Simon back. For that alone, it had been worth it.

Faye brushed a sweep of hair off Simon's face. He had the look of his father. Calder had been a fine-looking man, tall and powerfully built with wheaten hair and dark eyes. Simon's face still bore the softness of youth and not the sharp, square lines of his sire. She vowed her son's looks would not be the same handsome mask that hid a dark soul that his sire's had been. Calder didn't deserve the title of father. Gregory had always been so much more of a father to her boys. Dear Lord, she hoped she saw him again.

Their rocky shelter stood inside the straggling edge of the forest. Trees had been her constant on this journey; trees, trees, and more bloody trees. She might wake in the morning to find herself half wood sprite.

Calder drew wood from these mighty forests. A large part of the wealth of the demesne lay in these endless trees. Coming to Calder as a young bride, she had found the trees oppressive and imagined them encroaching on her in a slow, steady march. She'd grown up with the unobstructed, endless sweeps of ocean from Anglesea's casements.

"You should sleep, Lady." Newt's voice came out of the darkness. "Nothing will come that I do not hear."

Faye shook her head. She was too stirred up inside to sleep. Gregory would have known how to set her right. He had a way of clearing through the debris in her mind and bringing clarity.

Newt shrugged, rolled into a tight ball, and fell instantly asleep.

Faye envied him the ability. It must come from a life growing up hard. You snatched what you could when you could, including sleep. She would let the boys sleep for a while before they must be on their way again.

The trees rustled and sighed. A handful of nights past, her greatest fear had been spiders. There were far more terrifying hunters in the night. Her escape earlier had been near miraculous. She might not be so lucky again. Reaching Anglesea unscathed was a frighteningly slim possibility. She had not Newt's boyish ebullience to keep her spirits up.

* * *

Newt's voice ripped Faye out of sleep. "Wake up, Lady."

"What is it?"

Shadows covered Newt's face, but he was tense as a bowstring. "Someone comes."

"Mama?" Simon stirred.

"Hush." She lay her fingers over his lips and strained to separate the sounds of the night.

Silence greeted her. Not the silence of earlier, filled with the rustle of night creatures and insects, but this silence was absolute. Faye grabbed William's knife, its weight rested unfamiliar, but reassuring, in her hand.

Simon's determined stare glittered up at her. He had his knife in his hand, too.

Crouched, Newt cocked his head and motioned them back.

Faye and Simon edged deeper into the shadows. Their pitiful shelter offered scant concealment. The sky stretched a streaked indigo above the trees, no longer the deep black of before and with fewer stars littering its canopy. Dawn must be approaching.

A shadow flickered over by the trees.

Faye tensed and strained to see past the gloom.

"I swear there is someone there," Newt said. "It is too quiet."

A tall form loomed out the dark. "Thank you, Lord."

Chapter Sixteen

Strong arms snatched Faye up and enfolded her. "Thank the Lord, I have found you."

Gregory. She drew the unique scent of him deep into her being until she grew light-headed. The world dipped and reeled around her as she clutched his shoulders. Safe.

"Gregory, you are come." Simon tugged at her skirts.

Gregory's voice vibrated against her ear as his arms tightened. "Aye, lad."

"You came." Faye's throat constricted into a whisper.

"Never again." Gregory rested his cheek against the top of her head. "I can never let you out of my sight again."

Her heart thrilled, even as tears leaked out and over her cheeks, and she tightened her arms around him.

"I knew you would come," Simon said.

"Always." Gregory tugged Simon against his side and wrapped an arm about the boy's shoulders.

Confident in his strength, Faye gave him her weight. He was alive and well and here.

"Hush now," he said into her hair, but his voice shook. It made her cry harder to know he was similarly affected.

"We were accosted on the road and tied to a tree." Simon wriggled free of their huddle.

Gregory stiffened and put her away from him. Gaze alive with questions, he stared down at her.

"I am well. We both are." Faye wiped her sodden cheeks. She motioned to Newt who stood to one side, poised as if on the edge of flight. "We had some assistance."

"I will hear the whole tale, but first let me get you to safety." Gregory cupped her cheek with a large, roughened palm. "It is prodigious good to see you, my lady." More silly tears pricked her lids when she swore she had not one left. "My horse went lame. We are going to have to walk. Can you do it?" His glance moved from one to the other.

Newt snorted.

Simon shifted and dropped his head.

"Shall I put you on my shoulders?" Gregory kept his voice for Simon's ears alone.

Simon hesitated, the inner battle clear on his features. "Nay." He lifted his chin. "I have two feet, do I not?" So brave. Faye resisted the urge to coddle him and insist he take Gregory's offer.

Gregory nodded and clasped Simon's shoulder. "Good lad, if you should change your mind, there is no shame in being a tired knight." *Blast*, fresh tears threatened. Gregory turned back to her with a small smile. "Or a tired lady."

"Watch yourself, or I might accept your kind offer."

He grinned and the severe lines of his face softened and tugged deep inside Faye.

Gregory took the lead. Newt and Simon followed as Faye walked beside him. "Where will we go?"

"We are near to Aldous." Gregory pulled a wry face. "He is not one for people, and I am not sure he will welcome our intrusion. In truth, he will resent it, but he will offer us safety until we can plan how to get to Anglesea."

"Hugo has men looking for us."

"Aye." He gave a grim nod. "I have been dodging them

constantly. It appears Hugo returned to Brynn long before expected."

Hugo would not give up easily, especially not when they had Simon. A cold shiver slid down her spine. However, with Gregory by her side, they would find a way. Somehow. Pitching her voice for his ears only, she said, "I was concerned you might be hurt."

"Not I." The grin he gave her was unabashedly sure. "Who is the gutter rat?"

"A friend of Beatrice's." Faye threw a quick glance at Newt. The lad bounced along as if he were enjoying his adventure.

Gregory raised an eyebrow, but he knew Beatrice well enough not to remark. He set a manageable and steady pace. Once, they spotted a group of men in the distance, and stopped within the trees to wait until they passed. As the sky changed from indigo to a deep, pearlescent gray, Gregory led them forward.

"Those men." Gregory broke the comfortable silence between them. His stare roved the area around them, checking for Calder's men, his jaw tight. "They did not harm you?"

"Nay." Faye touched his arm. It was hard and warm beneath her fingers. "As I said, Newt saved us before they could do their worst."

He grasped her hand and raised it to his lips. Bending his dark head, he planted a kiss in her palm. "I am here, now." If she could hold him here forever, her life would be complete. Faye shook her head at herself. Such useless thoughts and when she'd promised herself and God she would do better.

Simon succumbed to his tired legs and allowed Gregory to bear him on his shoulders.

Newt amazed her. He kept to the same jaunty walk all the way. Life had forged a toughness in the lad that had no place in one so young.

Her belly reminded her it had been many hours since they had eaten. The few crusts Newt had scrounged had long since worn off. "How much farther?"

"Just beyond that rise." A small hillock sat proud of the

surrounding trees and Gregory pointed to it before touching her cheek. "I admire your courage, my Lady Faye."

The touch startled her. Gregory barely ever touched her and especially not without purpose. My Lady Faye. He called her that so rarely and it thrilled her every single time. The first time had been the day after Simon was born. Gregory had cradled the tiny baby in his huge hands and smiled. "Well done, my Lady Faye," he'd said. He'd put a slightest stress on the "my" when he said it. He took her hand. "You are lost in thought."

"Merely tired." She expected him to drop her hand, but he kept hold. A perfect fit. She had not the strength to tease out every subtle shade of meaning. It may mean everything or nothing at all. For now, he held her hand and her horrible night was over.

Sure and confident in his direction, Gregory led them away from the road. When this was over, she might ask him how he knew such things. There were several areas in a girl's education sadly lacking. Weapons, for instance. She had never learned. Something she intended to remedy. The world, dark and forbidding mere hours ago, opened to all manner of possibilities.

They crested the rise and Faye stumbled to a halt. There was naught here but a few broken down walls of what had once been a keep. For the boys, she kept the dismay out of her voice. "It seems your friend is no longer here."

"He is here." Gregory smiled and kept walking. He pointed to a thin tendril of smoke drifting up through the morning air. "The keep was destroyed many years ago. King Henry had it razed, but the dungeons remain."

"You friend lives in a dungeon?" It seemed to be a strange manner of man who would live in such a way.

A breeze ruffled his dark hair and gave him a boyish cast. "Aye."

"He lives under the ground?" Simon leaned over from his perch.

"Indeed." Gregory grinned up at him. "Like a mole."

Faye could not imagine such a thing. "How do you know him?"

"I came upon him one day when I was not long knighted. I forget what I was doing this far north. Hunting perhaps." He squeezed her hand.

"And?" Simon tugged on Gregory's ear making him laugh. Such a deep, full sound she heard so seldom. Faye wished she could stop time and watch him be happy for as long as it lasted.

Gregory tugged her forward. "Aldous had been injured by a fall. I offered to take him back to the keep, but he directed me here. Aldous lives here and takes everything he needs from the land."

Smoke rose straight out of the ground. "Is he a hermit?"

Gregory shrugged. "In a manner. He has an interesting way of looking at things. I stayed with him a few days and he told me many things. Some of them strange, most of them near blasphemous, but he intrigued me. I come back every now and then to check on him." Another little treasure she gathered up and kept. He peeled off one golden leaf of information after another on this journey, showing her parts of him she'd not seen in the seven years they'd spent together at Calder. Perhaps she had not really known him at all.

Gregory stopped and tensed. His gaze sharpened on the wall nearest them. "I can hear you, old man."

A man's form materialized out of the honey-hued rock. Faye would swear there had been no one there. Yet here he stood, easily the same height as Gregory, but spare and ropey as a stray wolf. His hair hung well past his shoulders in a tangle of gray and a beard covered most of his face.

"Who are you calling old?" He croaked like one unaccustomed to using his voice. "And what manner of trouble have you brought to my door?" He stopped well short of them and assessed Faye with the brightest blue eyes she had ever seen. Their color was nigh otherworldly and shone with a strange light. He might be addled. She inched closer to Gregory. "Is this your woman?" Aldous nodded at her.

"She is my Lady Faye." Gregory stepped forward and held out his hand. "It is good to see you."

Aldous clasped his hand. Over Gregory's shoulder that stare was back on her. Faye shifted beneath his steady regard. "Why does your lady carry such a deep sadness within?"

Faye blinked at Aldous. Not two minutes and he'd read that in her. Dear Lord, they had not even been properly introduced. If she spent more time here, he might have her every secret spread out before them. She looked at her feet, unable to hold that piercing stare. He saw too much, this odd man.

"That is part of the story I would tell you," Gregory said. "But we have walked through the night to get here. We were hoping you could rest us and give us something to eat."

Faye perked at the idea of a meal.

Newt stood behind Aldous and studied him with a frown. He looked up at Faye, crossed his eyes, stuck his tongue out the side and waggled his head. Faye looked away before she laughed. She didn't disagree, but it would be rude to say so.

"Come." Aldous turned and strode away.

Gregory took her hand. "He is a gentle soul. He lives away from others because he cannot condone any form of killing."

The opening to the old dungeons rested within a small section of the original wall still standing. A dark, dank hole that didn't seem to lead anywhere, and Faye didn't fancy going in there.

Ducking his head to clear the lintel, Aldous disappeared into the maw.

Gregory motioned her to precede him.

"Is it safe?" She could barely make out the stairs leading down.

"Trust me, my lady." And there it was, all he need say. Faye entered with Simon's hand clasped firmly in hers.

The staircase took a sharp twist to the left after only a handful of steps. The dark melted away under the warm glow of light from a brazier set high in the wall. From here, it was easier to see the steps as they wound round and round and took them deeper into the earth. The woody scent of sage grew stronger as she descended. Reaching the bottom, Faye gaped like a toddler at a fair.

Aldous had transformed the grim reality of the dungeon into a warm and welcoming burrow. Beeswax candles lit the stone in a golden glow. In the central area, where guards would have sat, thick braided rugs lay across the hard floor and walls. A rough bench nestled beneath a table of unplaned wood. As if Aldous had dragged the tree into his hole in the ground and put it on a set of cross braces. Only the top had been planed and leveled. Faye's feet throbbed in anticipation of a time when they could rest.

Aldous motioned her over to the bench.

She sat.

To one side an old cell faced the central space, the door gone. Inside, a large pallet, piled high with blankets and cushions, spread over the floor. He must sleep there. An adjacent cell held shelves like Bess's cottage, lined with a haphazard array of basket and crates. The hearth chimney disappeared into the roof above them. She wanted to examine how Aldous had achieved such a thing. A kettle hung over it and exuded a smell of something that made her stomach growl.

"Wash." Aldous carried a pail of water into a third cell.

Delighted to oblige, Faye followed with Simon. Aldous had set this space up for bathing, with another of his rough tables and a series of buckets lined across the wall. The scent of sage grew heavier in this room. She sank her hands into the cool, silky water. More sage. Clearly, a herb he favored.

Aldous dropped a pile of washing cloths beside her and fetched another pail of water.

Faye wet a cloth and tended to Simon first. As she worked off some of the accumulated grime, he pulled a face, but stood mostly still. "See there." She gave him a final swipe with the cloth. "I knew there was a handsome boy beneath there somewhere."

Simon rolled his eyes, but gave her a small grin.

Leaning against the empty doorjamb, Newt watched with his lips curled up in distaste. Faye crooked her finger at him. It would take more than a quick wipe with a cloth to get that face clean.

A look of unadulterated horror crossed Newt's thin features and he straightened. He licked his palms and scrubbed them down his cheeks. "There."

Mother of two boys, and no stranger to their antics, Faye knew the amount of steel required in her tone. "Come here, Newt."

"I do not bathe." Newt crossed his arms over his chest.

Faye leveled a stare at him. "You do if you want to eat."

Newt gave it a valiant effort before he scowled at the ground and dragged his feet toward her.

Faye dipped a fresh cloth into the water.

He grabbed it from her hand.

Boys! All the same. Scared of a drop of soap and water. She snatched the cloth back. If she let him have it, he would do a rough job at best.

Newt glared at her, but dropped his hands.

Faye did not spare the water on his filthy face and neck. A boy this dirty must have been years in the making.

He writhed and squirmed beneath her, but Faye kept at it.

With a nod of encouragement, Aldous brought her a fresh bucket of water.

"There." Faye stepped back to examine the fruits of her labors. She had done Nurse proud with her work.

Newt was not a comely child, with a large nose and wide mouth in his too thin face. His small, dark gaze darted around like a rodent.

"Much better." She smiled at him. Without his years of grime, she could actually see the color climb his cheeks. Food. The idea had never appealed more and Faye trailed the boys back to the central area.

With too many to squash around the table, Gregory and Aldous ate standing.

Faye ate with an appetite she had never known she had. Savory stew exploded in a blend of carrot, celery, onion, and parsnip across her tongue. Exotic spices defied her attempts to name them. She had not the heart to admonish Simon for shoveling it down his throat. There was enough for all to fill their bellies, and for the boys to take a second helping, almost as if Aldous had known and prepared for their coming.

"He appears prepared for us." Faye restrained herself from wiping her fingers around her bowl as Newt did.

"Aldous is a strange one." Gregory smiled and put his bowl aside. "He keeps many secrets, eats no meat, and has ways of knowing things beyond understanding."

There was something more to this old man. His beard and gray hair gave him the appearance of advanced age, yet he moved as spryly as Newt and his face was smooth and unmarred by time. His eyes were his most striking feature, bluer than any she had seen, they seemed deeper than the ocean.

Aldous raised his brow in question.

Faye's face heated as she looked away. It was unbearably rude to stare. Yet, her gaze drifted back to him as if drawn that way.

"We should sleep." Gregory rose and took her bowl. "We need to rest and then decide the best way forward."

Chapter Seventeen

Faye woke to find Gregory's gaze on her. "Simon?" She bolted up right. He had gone to sleep beside her on a makeshift pallet beside the hearth.

"Aldous has him." Elbows resting on his knees, Gregory sat at the table.

"Where are they?"

"Gone foraging for food." Gregory smiled. "They will be safe with Aldous."

"You are sure?"

"Aye." He cleared his throat. "I would not have let them go if I were not. Aldous can disappear like smoke if the need arises." Gregory loved Simon like his own. He would not have let him go if there was danger.

"You are certain they will be safe?" She was a mother, after all.

"I am certain." He nodded. "I have been waiting for you to wake."

"Indeed." Gregory seemed different this morning. She could not put her finger on how.

"There are things I need to say." Gregory wanting to speak without prompting was one glaring difference.

"Things that should not be spoken?"

"Nay." He dropped his gaze to his hands. "Things that, indeed, should be spoken." He pushed to his feet. Gregory's strange behavior unsettled her and she took a moment to compose her thoughts as she tidied her bliaut about her knees.

He paced to the hearth. "Are you hungry?"

"Aye."

"There is pottage, still warm."

"Indeed." She rose.

Gregory ladled oat pottage into a small wooden bowl. A basin of honey rested on the table beside a jug of rich, fresh cream.

Faye approached the table cautiously. She tried to read Gregory's masked face as she took a seat. She should know better by now. Gregory could draw a blanket over his features that she could not penetrate. The blanket was in place, but that muscle worked in his jaw. Faye ate her pottage. It might have been earth for all she tasted. "Have you eaten?"

"Aye." He scraped his fingers through his hair. "I am confused, my Lady Faye."

Another, *my Lady Faye*. Giddy bounty, indeed. Faye held her breath and waited. For what, she had no idea, but his mood seemed to demand her silence.

"Yesterday, when I couldn't find you, I was more afraid than I have ever been in my life." He sat opposite her and laid his hands on the table between them.

"But you did find me." Faye stretched out her hand to touch her fingertips to his.

He captured her hand. "I thought I had lost you."

It made no sense. He had walked away from her. Time and time again. "Gregory—"

"Let me finish." He pressed a kiss into her palm. "Only be patient with me because I am not a man of words."

Indeed. Her hand tingled from the hot press of his mouth. Faye curled her fingers around the spot protectively.

"You were right when you told me my own stubbornness is what ails me."

She shouldn't have said that. Shouldn't have said any of it. He was not the only one with confession on his mind. She had sworn to make this right. "I should not have said what I said."

"Aye, you should. I deserved no less."

"Indeed." She couldn't fathom him. He didn't want her apology or her regrets.

Color climbed his cheeks. "What I said before, about the...um..."

"The kiss?" His embarrassment might have been amusing if it did not concern her. *We kissed.* She wanted to bellow what Gregory could not even bring himself to say.

He cleared his throat. "What I said about it being your fault. I was wrong and I humbly beg your pardon. It was poor of me to do so." This huge, strong man with his head bowed in penitence, humbled himself before her. Her heart ached to make it right again. The distance between them was too far.

"Nay." Faye stood. "I kissed you and I should not have."

He rounded the table to her. Before her transfixed gaze, his chest expanded. "I was not wroth about the kiss, my lady. I was wroth the kiss ended and I did not want it to."

A heavy pulse pounded in her middle. Her limbs threatened to melt into the floor. She needed to touch him. Faye raised her hand to the warmth of the skin above his heart. There did not seem to be words to explain the clamor through every part of her. "Gregory."

He pressed her palm closer to his skin. Larger and darker, the nails blunt and short, his hand engulfed hers. "My desire for you maddens me." His voice hoarsened. "For as long as I can remember, I have wanted to join the priesthood and yet there is always you."

"Aye." She understood only too well. The longing weakened her knees. His flesh scalded her palm.

"I know not what to do with it." He stepped closer until there was barely a heartbeat between them. "Aldous believes the bond between a man and a woman to be sacred."

"What do you believe?" There was something different about Gregory. His face, looking down at her, bore an expression he always hid from her. Desire. She spread her fingers beneath his. The beat of his heart pulsed through the small connection.

"I know not what I believe." He smiled ruefully. "I know only when I could not find you yesterday, there could be nothing worse."

"Aye." Countless questions bickered in the back of her mind, but they fell silent under his dark, tender gaze. Faye rose to her toes. She moved slowly, her heart pounded at her own daring, as she closed the distance between them.

His head lowered and he met her halfway.

Aye. The first touch of his lips scored through her. She leaned into his strength to keep her balance.

His arm fastened about her waist and pulled her to him. With a low rumble, he opened his mouth over hers, his tongue seeking entry.

Faye trembled under the assaulting sweetness. The kiss warmed every part of her, spreading to her extremities. Everything melted away under the gentle tangle of his tongue with hers, his arm about her waist, her only anchor to the earth.

He cupped her face in his palms and eased her away.

Faye wanted to stay near him. She craved the closeness he offered.

"I know not what the future holds." He stroked the swell of her cheek with his thumb.

"Nor I." How could such a thing as love feel sweet and tragic all at once? Faye's breath caught on a sob.

"No tears." He pressed his forehead to hers. "There have been enough tears betwixt us."

All she could think to do was kiss him, and Faye did. The tangle of emotions between them flared into life and the kiss grew hungry. Faye clung to his broad shoulders. Her nails dug into the muscle. *More.*

He fastened his hand on her breast.

Faye froze. Images battered at her and her eyes popped open to halt them. It was Gregory's face above hers. Gregory's hand on her breast and the spike of fear lessened.

"Forgive me. I hurt you." He dropped his hand. "I have not lain with a woman before." His cheeks reddened at the admission.

Any traces of fear disappeared and Faye smiled. This was not Calder who touched her. Gregory's confession gave her a new boldness. Grasping his hand, she put it to her breast. "You did not hurt me." She pressed his hand over her flesh to show him how she wanted to be touched. "It feels wondrous."

A shy smile split his face. His gaze dropped to watch his large hand span her breast. Heat throbbed between her thighs as he stroked the bud of her nipple. He brought his other hand up to caress her.

Faye grabbed his arms to steady herself. The pleasure surged wanton and liberating through her. Against her belly, his shaft pressed hard. She wanted to touch. Seven years of marriage and she had never contemplated such a thing with Calder. His shaft had repelled her as she understood what Calder would demand. With Gregory, she touched the evidence of his desire. She slid her hands down the fascinating indents of his belly. Lines of muscle marched in a ladder over his ribs.

He hissed in a breath. A muscle tensed beneath her touch. A thin line of hair disappeared beneath his braies and Faye slid her fingers along it. He was warm and heavy to the touch, the skin over his shaft surprisingly soft, silken. He pulsed in her hand, and she closed her fingers around him.

"Faye." His jaw clenched. His breath came harsh as he watched her hand through hooded lids.

"Let me." She moved her hand over him.

He made a strangled sound and dropped his head forward. She was doing this to him. The knowledge was as heady as mead. A fine tremor shook him as she stroked him. Gregory groaned, his hand clasped her wrist to stop her. "I will spill."

"Let me." She rose on her toes.

His mouth descended on hers as he loosened his hold on her hand.

Between her thighs, she grew heavy and damp. Their mouths mated in time to her strokes on his shaft.

With a garbled shout, he tensed and sticky wetness covered her hand. He pressed his head into the crook of her shoulder. "Dear God."

Faye throbbed unfulfilled, but she reveled in the knowledge of what she had given him. No other woman had touched him thus and rendered him helpless with a few strokes of her hand.

Gregory raised his head. Color rode high on his cheeks. He kissed her as if she were the most precious thing on earth. "You are, indeed, a sorceress."

Feet scuffed the stairs. Faye leaped away from Gregory. They could have been interrupted at any point. She had allowed herself to be swept away in the madness. She had no regrets, but guilty heat flooded her face.

Gregory handed her a washing cloth and she wiped her hand.

She dared not look at him or she would give the game away. Faye dropped the cloth back into the bucket as Simon rounded the staircase at a run.

"Mother." He greeted her with a small bow. "Are you well rested?"

His little-boy dignity made her want to clasp him to her and cover his face with kisses. Matching his formality, she inclined her head. "I am well thank you, son."

"Plants." Newt curled his lip up in disgust as he hefted a large sack at her. Grime and fresh dirt once more covered his face. All her cleaning undone in a morning. It would take an entire army to keep that boy clean. "Aldous says we are to eat these."

"You dare not tarry here." Aldous entered the burrow carrying a sack like Newt's, only this one bulging. "The men draw closer."

Chapter Eighteen

Reality crashed over Faye in a sickening wave. Hugo's men drew closer. She had almost forgotten in those precious, stolen moments with Gregory. Many miles lay between them and Anglesea's safety, and countless foes along the way.

Gregory narrowed his gaze to Aldous. "Did they see you?"

Aldous snorted and dumped his sack on the table. "Do not be daft. The danger is not immediate, but they are combing the land hereabouts. It will not be long before they find my home."

"We must leave." She turned to Gregory.

"Nay." Aldous upended his sack, dumping an assortment of tubers, plants, and nuts on the table. "They are too close and you will run right into them. Best to remain here, hidden, until they pass and then make for Anglesea."

Gregory nodded. "We will hear them coming and stay hidden. Then, we will go aloft and I will scout which road would be best to take."

Faye's belly clenched. Every instinct yelled to run and not stop until she reached safety, but Aldous and Gregory made sense.

"These passages from the dungeon run for miles." Aldous sorted through his bounty with long, elegant fingers.

Newt cleared his throat. "I could make it to Anglesea." He vibrated with enthusiasm. "I could tell them where you are and they will send aid to see you safely home."

"Nay." Faye's answer was immediate. She would not put another boy in danger.

Gregory frowned and waved Newt to sit. "You will be captured."

"Nay, I will not." Newt bounced on his toes. "Nobody catches Newt when Newt does not want to be caught."

A thoughtful look flit across Gregory's face.

Faye didn't like that look and she shook her head at him.

"Just ask Beatrice." Newt puffed up his scrawny chest. "I can make myself a shadow."

Faye needed to stop this. "Na—"

"They are not looking for such as he." Aldous snatched up an empty bucket and walked to the stairs. Aldous disappeared up the stairs on silent feet. His voice drifted down the stairwell. "And he is a sly one."

Indecision weighed on Gregory's face as his gaze met hers. They needed the help, this much was clear. Yet a small boy against Hugo's extensive army did not sit right.

"We cannot risk him being caught." Faye spoke to Gregory.

He nodded.

Newt huffed and folded his arms. "I will not be caught. And like the addled man says, they are not looking for a gutter brat. I could walk right past them and they would not stop me."

"What about Odo?" Faye stared at Newt. They could not place such a burden on a child, even an extraordinary sort of child like Newt.

"Odo will not be a problem." Gregory grimaced. "I found his camp before I found you."

Oh, Lord, she had, unwittingly contributed toward Odo's death.

"There." Newt sniffed, unabashed by the notion he had killed a man. "And the rest of them do not have a thought between them without Odo."

"We have no horse for you," Gregory said.

Newt blew a raspberry. "I cannot ride, in any case. Alls I have ever done is sit on one as someone else did the other bits." He skipped over to Gregory. "You tell me how to get to Anglesea from here, and Newt will be there before you can blink."

Hugo's trap fastened about Faye. Newt and Simon stood near shoulder to shoulder in height, Newt the slighter of the two. There were not many years between them. Yet those years weighed heavy on Newt. He was more able and crafty than she, by far. Her resistance wavered.

"I will pack some provisions." Aldous returned with his water, put the bucket on the table and dropped the tubers and plants into it.

Irked by the man's ridiculous assumptions, Faye crossed her arms over her chest. "Nothing has been decided."

"Hasn't it?" Aldous quirked a brow at her.

Wanting to utter a hot denial, but knowing it might be a lie, kept Faye silent.

Gregory studied Newt. "He has a better chance than any of us."

"Aye." Newt nodded vigorously. "Although I would be faster if I had some meat in my belly."

"I eat no flesh of beast." From beneath his gray, shaggy brows, Aldous glowered at him.

Newt pulled a face and turned back to Gregory. "While we fuss and fume, they get closer. I could be at Anglesea by now."

"Not quite." Gregory gave a small smile. "I do not like it, but we have not many alternatives." He looked at Faye.

"I'll do this." Newt grinned at her. "And then you'll owe me."

He had tracked Beatrice through London and gotten her to Westminster. If it hadn't been for Newt, she and Simon might still be in Odo's clutches. Hesitantly, Faye nodded.

"Come." Gregory motioned Newt to the table. "I will show you where we are."

What a sorry state. Reliant on a child for rescue.

Gregory used the nuts to make a map on the table for Newt.

Faye clasped Simon close to her side, his slight weight a comfort against her.

Gregory finished his explanations and made Newt repeat them. He broke up his makeshift map. "Now you make it."

Heaving a huge sigh, Newt remade the map.

"Good." Gregory nodded. "Again."

"God's Bo—"

"Again."

Newt repeated it three more times before Gregory looked up and nodded. "He has the way."

More out of necessity than hunger, Faye ate the meal Aldous prepared.

Newt chattered away as if he had not a care through the meal. The boy possessed not an ounce of fear. Faye envied him that. For her part, her heart beat erratically and she froze at any small sound from above.

Gregory appeared at ease, but she read the tension in the taut way he held himself.

All too soon, the meal was done and Newt ready to depart. Aldous supplied a skin of water and some nuts and tubers in a small sack.

"You must make sure you follow the same path on your return." Gregory held Newt's shoulder in a firm grasp. "If aught happens, we will travel that same path."

"Once I am done, I will add this favor to the three Beatrice owes me." Newt rubbed his hands together. On that, he disappeared up the stairs.

Faye sent a swift prayer after his scurrying form.

"Now we wait." Gregory answered her unspoken question.

"Come." Aldous drew a small leather sack from beside the hearth. "You can try to best me at stones."

The sack hit the table with a rattle. Faye nearly leaped out of her skin.

"Aye, but you cheat." Gregory took the bench opposite Aldous with a grin.

Playing a game at a time like this. Faye didn't know how they managed it.

Simon drew closer to the table and took a seat beside Gregory. He soon lost himself in the play. Well, it distracted Simon, which she supposed made it useful. Faye wandered over to the pallet and sat. What she wouldn't give to have her hands on her sewing now.

* * *

Tension built like a bloated bladder in Gregory. Aldous accepted his pretense of playing the game, but still took enough advantage to trounce him. The waiting gnawed at him. Waiting for what, exactly? Newt to return with a rescue party? Or Calder to stumble upon them?

Too young to be cooped up beneath the earth, Simon grew restless. Faye bore the brunt of the boy's frustration. He admired her calm and infinite patience as she invented distraction after distraction to keep the youngster content.

"Perhaps you should go above and scout?" Aldous took pity on him. "I will remain here and see to the boy and your lady."

His lady. Even as he surged to his feet, the phrase jangled in his brain. He didn't know if he even had the right to call her that. Things shifted between them daily. Her touch on his male flesh had been wondrous. Even now, he swelled recalling their encounter. He wanted more than that and the knowledge sat ill. He didn't know where that would leave them when this was over. Once the danger passed, life would continue much as it had before. That idea didn't sit right either. What if the danger didn't pass? What if this was the only time they had?

"Can I come?" Simon pleaded with him.

"Nay, lad." Gregory suppressed a shudder at the idea of taking the lad anywhere close to danger, or trying to amuse a whining seven-year-old as he scouted. "Your task is to stay here and care for your mother."

Perhaps some time away from Faye would help clear his head. As if his time at the monastery had helped exorcise her from his being. How thick could one man be? This snarl pulled tighter by the hour.

"Be careful." Faye touched his arm. The simple contact crept across his skin like the sun's rays. Would there ever come a time when a touch from her remained a brief, impersonal contact?

She gazed up at him. A man could see his entire future in those blue eyes. She had been a beautiful girl. As a woman she was breathtaking. Life had carved maturity into her features and a compassion to her that had not been part of the girl. He placed his hand over hers, relishing the brief connection. "Always."

Aldous accompanied him outside the dungeon to see him off.

Concealed by the broken walls of the former keep, they took a moment to check for unwelcome visitors. The gently undulating hilltop remained clear as far as he could see. Once he cleared the walls, he would have to find cover as soon as possible.

"Why do you fight so hard?" Aldous scoured the countryside. His sharp gaze would see forms where others couldn't. The man had an almost ungodly ability to spot intruders.

Aldous had no patience with dissembling and Gregory didn't bother. "I have lived my life to join the Holy Fathers."

Aldous shrugged. "Fate does not always take note of these decisions we make."

As if he didn't know that. Gregory bit back a sharp retort. "I do not think she is for me."

"Why?" Aldous cocked his head and examined him as he would a new type of insect.

Aldous considered the idea of a man dedicating his entire life to God ridiculous. Any argument on that basis would only end in frustration.

Gregory couldn't hold his piercing gaze. "She could look to the highest families in the kingdom for her next husband."

Aldous grunted. "Always with the fences you put around yourselves. Your kind are like sheep, herding yourselves into pens and then wondering why the wolf comes calling." Damned if Gregory knew what that meant. Aldous spoke of "his kind" as if the old hermit considered himself not a part of the rest of God's creation.

"Listen to me, sword wielder." Aldous grew stern, a fine furrow between his brows. "I had hoped you would find this truth within you, but my time grows short. There is no test to decide if you are worthy of love or happiness. They are yours, simply by virtue of your state as a man." That couldn't be right. Everything within Gregory rebelled at the notion. The old man spoke heresy.

Aldous growled and thumped him on the chest. "Our hearts are our best ears, not the ones balancing the side of your head." Aldous and Father Abbot must be exchanging confidences. "Go." Aldous jerked his head. "I grow weary of talking to you."

* * *

"Come." Aldous waved Simon closer.

Faye bristled at the old man beckoning her son forward in that imperious manner. She was not entirely sure she liked the old man at all. He made her twitch when he stared at her with those strange, unfathomable eyes that hid secrets and knowledge at which she could only guess. What did he see when he watched her thus?

Simon had no such hesitation and plonked himself at the table across from Aldous.

"I will teach you something useful." Aldous snatched up a small log from the hearth. "What do you see here?"

"Wood?" Simon frowned.

"Wrong," he said. "Look closer and tell me what you see."

Faye wandered over to where they sat, intrigued. She saw nothing more than a log of wood.

"A piece of firewood." Simon twisted his face in thought.

"Wrong. Look closer."

The log lay on the table between Simon and Aldous. "Fire," she said. Good Lord, she sounded foolish.

Aldous pulled a face. "Better, but look closer."

She tilted her head to study the wood from a different side. "It partly resembles a rabbit." She flushed. Next she would see faeries in the stone walls.

Aldous beamed at her. "Show me."

"Here." Absurdly gratified to have pleased him, she pointed to a slight protuberance. "There are his ears and this is his body."

"What do you see?" Aldous turned back to Simon.

"A wolf." Simon grinned at him.

Aldous raised an eyebrow. "Have you ever seen a wolf?"

"Nay, but I have seen a picture."

"Pictures are not wolves. You will know the difference if you are ever fortunate enough to see a wolf."

Faye hardly believed seeing a wolf in the flesh would be fortunate at all. Indeed, it could prove most uncomfortable.

Simon looked crestfallen. "A rabbit, then."

"Nay." Aldous thumped his hand on the table. "Your mother saw a rabbit. What do you see?"

Simon frowned at the wood in concentration. He screwed up his face and held his breath. He released it in a loud whoosh. "I see a badger. And, aye, I have seen a real badger."

"Good." Aldous nodded. "Now show me the badger."

"Well...." Simon tugged the wood closer to him. "Here are his ears and this patch is darker—"

"Nay." Aldous dropped a short, curved knife on the table. "You have looked at the wood and asked it to show you its true spirit. Now, honor the gift."

Simon's small fingers near the wicked blade frightened Faye. "I do not think—"

"You think too much," Aldous said. Nay, she did not like the old man. He grinned at her as if he could read her thoughts "He will not cut himself. I am here to guide his hand. Did you not give him a dagger to defend himself when the need arose?"

"Aye." That was entirely different and she had not been happy to do so.

Aldous tapped his temple. "Thinking again, woman. Your thoughts will make cold bedfellows." Aldous turned his back on her building tirade and pushed the knife toward Simon. "Earth Mother has gifted you with this badger and the king of trees has shown you the form within this limb. As a part of this bounty, you will use your gifts to bring forth the form."

Faye's ire banked to a simmer as she concentrated on his words.

"But it's only a piece of wood." Simon lunged for the knife.

"Then you are not fit to carve it." Aldous covered the knife with his hand. "You are not the master of all you see about you, but a part of it. As a part, you must respect the other parts."

It made an odd sort of sense to Faye. There seemed to be truth in the hermit's words, despite going against most of what she had learned in church.

"We are born and we die as part of all we see about us. We take from it and we give to it. An ebb and flow, like the ocean."

"Does God not teach us we have dominion over beasts and creation?" He had the oddest way of looking at things, but beautiful in its simplicity.

"Whose god, woman?" Aldous adjusted Simon's grip on the knife.

"Is there not only one God?"

Aldous sat back and crossed his arms. "Is there?"

The conversation made her uncomfortable. "I do not suppose you have a piece of wood for me to carve?"

"Nay." Aldous stood. "But we could bake nut bread."

Faye despised baking, but the only alternative was to sit and wait while Simon carved. "Where do you—"

"Hush." Aldous tilted his head, his hand raised to silence her. The man was beyond rude. She had only meant to ask where he kept the flour.

Simon stopped carving and looked up.

"Riders are coming," Aldous said. Less of a distinct sound than a rumble, hooves pounded the earth. "Five." Aldous nodded. "Perhaps more. Come, we must hide you."

Simon slid from the table and Faye grabbed his hand.

Aldous led the way beyond his pallet and out into what must have formed the main corridor to the original dungeon. "I can give you no light, but you must stay in these tunnels until Gregory or I come for you. Fear not, woman, we will find you."

The rumble grew louder. Loose earth and stones tumbled down the entrance stairs. Faye gripped Simon's hand tighter as she ventured into the total dark beyond the light cast by Aldous's candles. Anglesea had an entire rabbit warren of tunnels leading to and from the dungeons. They ran the length of the keep beneath the ground all the way to the ocean. It was easy to get lost in those dark, winding tunnels. If they got lost down here, Gregory might never find them. She kept her free hand to the wall at her left. Her fingertips skimmed past slimy, unknown shapes in the dark, and she shuddered. Her flesh crawled. She hated spiders.

The muted growl of male voices reached them, and she froze. She still had William's knife.

Aldous replied, the words inaudible, but the timbre of his voice recognizable.

Simon pressed to her side, and she dropped her hand to soothe his back. Beneath her touch, his heart thudded. He was scared, as was she.

More voices, one raised in anger.

Faye's heart thumped an unsteady rhythm. Aldous might give them away for the reward. Nay, she did not believe he would do that. Aldous was a strange, brusque old man but he had no use for coin. Gregory trusted him. Gregory was out there. Pray Gregory would see the horses and know better than to stumble into a trap. Of course he would, her fears got the better of her.

A crash resounded down the passage and the splinter of breaking wood. Simon jumped beneath her hand, and she resumed her soothing motion.

Please God, let them not have hurt Aldous. They could have no argument with a harmless looking old hermit. The minutes dragged past as Faye strained to hear. Silence fell. Beneath her skirts, her legs shook. The dead black all around offered no clue as to what happened.

Simon shifted. She winced at the loud scuff of his feet.

Faye counted her heartbeats to mark the passage of time. She gave up and concentrated on keeping Simon still. A scrape. Faye tensed.

"Woman?" Aldous's voice. "Woman, I can hear you and it is safe to come out now."

Keeping her right hand to the wall, Faye edged through the gloom. Simon clung to her side, the poor lad. So much fear and running in the past few days could not be good for a young boy. Faye had sought to protect him, but this was not safety.

"Are they gone?" Simon whispered.

"Aye." Aldous appeared as a dim shape before them. "But we will speak when Gregory returns. You cannot stay here. Their leader knew too much. He asked if I had seen Gregory, so he knows of our friendship."

"Faye," Gregory called, his voice rough and urgent.

"She is well, sword wielder." Aldous shambled down the passage ahead of them, his bare feet near silent on the floor.

"I saw Hugo's man, Royce." Gregory's voice came closer. "He and his men were here. I waited in the trees until they left."

"Gregory," Simon called. "We were hiding in the dark and there were spiders. I am sure of it." God, to be so young and resilient. Faye envied her son his indefatigable spirit. For her part, weariness settled into her bones.

"Did you scream when you saw the spiders?" Gregory asked from up ahead.

"Nay." Simon snorted. "And one ran over my foot, or it was a rat."

Faye shivered, relieved nothing had run across her feet. She stepped into the soft light of the burrow and Gregory stood there, large and impregnable. His hand rested on Simon's shoulder. Whatever the way to safety, he would find it for them. His stare met hers over Simon's head and she nodded in response to his silent question. All was well, for now.

"We cannot stay here and we will need horses," he said. "We are too slow on foot. This way, we can meet Newt along the route he followed to Anglesea."

If Newt reached Anglesea.

Faye nodded. They had enough to contend with already. "Where will we get horses?"

A boyish grin split Gregory's face. "I will steal my Lady Faye a horse."

"You should not steal." Simon scowled up at him.

"Nay, you should not." Gregory grinned back. "I would only so do for my lady." It was the most romantic utterance he had ever made. Didn't that make her the most pathetic sort of fool.

Faye climbed with Gregory to the entrance of the dungeons. He surveyed the area before he let her come into the open. Blue sky soared above them, a glorious clear day. Aldous's little burrow could have been an entirely different world.

"You are not really going to steal a horse?" She kept her tone light, while a weight pressed at her chest. She did not want him to go. Without him, danger seemed to crowd about her and overwhelmed her. Countless times, she had watched him leave Calder Castle on some armed foray for Calder. Then she could not put her arms about him and hold him to her as she wished him well. She could now, and she pressed her cheek against his collar, her head beneath his chin.

He held her.

Faye breathed him in, as she shut her eyes and pretended for the smallest moment.

"I am going to borrow a horse," he said against her hair. "I promise, on my honor, to return it when I have you safe at Anglesea."

"Simon is right, you should not steal." She wanted to keep him here for a few more precious moments.

"I would do anything for you, my lady." *Except stay with me forever.* Faye pressed her face into his neck. Her selfishness sickened her.

"Be safe." Her chest ached, not wanting to let him go.

"Always." He put her away from him. "I may be some time. I have to wait until nightfall before I can do my borrowing. I will be back for you."

"I know."

As if he sensed something amiss with her, a small frown creased his brow. She managed a smile.

He lowered his head and touched his mouth to hers.

Faye opened for him. The kiss ran sweet through her. The first one he had ever given her that she did not seek first. Desire lay banked beneath it. How sad that this was a kiss of parting.

He stepped away and cleared his throat. "I will return."

Chapter Nineteen

L ong after Gregory disappeared beneath the trees, Faye lingered above ground. He took her heart and her hopes with him, and she sent a quick prayer after him. When she could delay no longer, she descended the stone stairs into the dungeons. Already her feet stepped surer on the treads. Aldous was certain to have some more of his strangeness to fill the passing hours.

Simon sat at the table, busy with his carving. The wood resembled a misshapen animal of some sort. Tongue trapped between his teeth, Simon worked away. Little Arthur shared the same habit. Arthur remained safe at Anglesea, with Lady Mary and Nurse caring for him and Beatrice distracting him with her dear silliness. This time tomorrow, God willing, she and Simon would be home. Gregory would find them horses and they would travel swiftly to Anglesea. She leaned against the wall close to the hearth. More waiting. How much of her life did she spend waiting?

Aldous stirred his stew over the fire. The rich aroma tantalized her nostrils and made her mouth water. He may eat no meat, but Aldous worked miracles with herbs and tubers.

A footstep grated against the stairs.

Aldous cocked his head and tensed. He swung about, his face set in a rigid mask.

"Hide." Aldous pointed to the dark passages.

"Do not move, my lady."

Faye sprung around as a man filled the entrance. Royce. Always in the thick of it with Hugo and ready to dirty his rough hands with whatever Hugo asked. For a moment, she remained frozen, shocked by his sudden appearance.

Simon. He sat at the table, vulnerable. Faye dashed for her son.

Royce got there before her and plucked Simon from the bench by the back of his tunic.

Faye slid to a halt.

Simon cried out and struck with his carving knife. Royce grabbed his wrist and shook it, until Simon dropped the knife

"Do not hurt him." Faye froze at the sword near Simon's neck.

"That is up to you, Lady Faye." Royce's teeth flashed white through his shaggy, russet beard. He was of middling height, but built broad and powerful like a small bull.

Four other men crowded in behind Royce and blocked the stairs.

"Do not look for your precious Gregory." Royce sneered at her. "He is long gone. We waited until he left. This will be a lot easier without him."

Royce swung his gaze behind her. "Do not move, old man. I knew you were lying. Where else would the blasted monk go but here?"

Aldous stood at her back.

Royce gave a short bark of laughter as his gaze raked her from top to bottom. "Sir Hugo will be powerful glad to see you. Take the boy." Royce shoved Simon toward one of his men. "She will give us no more trouble if we have him."

"Please." It was hopeless to plead, but she could not help

herself. "Just give me my son and leave. I cannot return to Calder."

"Aye, you can." Royce grinned at her. "And I aim to see you do. Take her." He motioned a second man. The man laid hold of her arm in a firm clasp.

"All will be well, woman." Aldous stood silent and still, his face beautiful in its serenity.

Royce stalked toward Aldous, his sword raised. "You lied to me."

"Nay. I made him lie." Faye wrenched at her captor's hold. The steel of Royce's sword glowed orange in the candlelight "He had no choice but to shelter us."

"Hugo does not tolerate betrayal." Royce pressed the sword tip into Aldous's neck. Blood swelled around the blade and dribbled down from the wound.

"Nay." Faye lurched toward Aldous. The grip on her arm tightened and snatched her back. Pain shot through her from the cruel grip, and she kicked out against her captor.

Her captor grunted and pinned both her arms behind her.

The wrench of her muscles throbbed from her shoulder to her wrist. It didn't matter, and she grit her teeth as she struggled for freedom.

"I know." Inevitability writ on his smooth features, Aldous glanced toward her and smiled. "I am ready."

"Nay." Faye sobbed. Why did he not pick up a log and fight?

A flash of steel and Royce pierced Aldous through the gut. "Miserable cur."

Aldous crumpled to the floor. Over his homespun tunic, blood bloomed with sickening speed. It pooled scarlet around him and stained his beautifully woven rugs.

The burrow grew hazy. Sounds muted. Aldous stabbed, Simon captured. Rough hands on her arm. Voices spoke, a gruff exchange of meaningless words.

Aldous kept his blue, blue gaze locked on her. "Courage," he seemed to say, "have courage, woman."

They dragged her up the stairs. Faye went with them, limp and broken in the man's hold. Dear God, Aldous gravely wounded, it could not be possible.

Simon sat before the man who had taken him, his face pinched in terror.

Faye locked her gaze on Simon. "All will be well."

Tears filled his eyes.

"Your mother speaks true." Royce came up behind her. "Once you are back where you belong, all will be well."

Back where they belonged? Back to Calder. Nothing would be well again, ever. *Calm. Think.* Fear, dark and bitter, spread through her mind. She beat it back. Five mounted men, strong and battled hardened. Their chance of making a run for it was nonexistent. She would bide her time until she found a way out of this nightmare. William's knife pressed against her ankle. Somehow, there was a way out.

Faye did as she was bid. Her mind drummed in time to the horses' hooves. *Back to Calder. Back to Calder. Back to Calder.*

The journey blurred. The landscape flashed past with barely a halt. Fields, dwellings, forests. The sun moved toward the west and dark clouds spread across the sky. Places she had passed with Gregory. Through Upper Mere. The clatter of the drawbridge beneath hooves. The walls of Calder Castle closed around her as Royce forced her to dismount in the inner bailey. The soaring red stone battlement stood stark against the deep pewter of the sky. Much needed rain hung heavy in the clouds. It seemed curiously apt the storm brewing above matched her storm within.

"You are to wait for Hugo." Royce grabbed hold of her arm and tugged.

Faye dug her heels in. "Release me. I am able to walk without assistance."

Royce dropped her arm. She almost laughed at the way he still obeyed her commands, as if she were not his captive. It was nothing more than false bravado on her part, he had her trapped.

Simon stayed close by her side as they strode into the keep.

Faye refused to hide her face as she marched before Royce. Glances swung in her direction, some of them surprised, others frightened. For the most part she read compassion on their faces. They had been her people. Some knew—most had guessed—how unhappy her time as chatelaine had been. The daughter of Sir Arthur and Lady Mary of Anglesea would not be dragged home like a whipped dog.

The rushes in the hall needed changing. Beside the hearth, a pack of dogs snarled and snapped over some discarded treasure buried beneath them. The stench turned her stomach. Hugo had allowed the keep to degenerate into a filthy hovel. "Why have the rushes not been changed?"

"My lady." Betsy, the upper serving maid, bowed her head.

Faye stopped. Royce growled beneath his breath as he near trod on her heels. Faye forced her rigid face into a smile. A lady never let her pain or her fear show. "How are you, Betsy? And your mother, has she recovered from her fall?"

"Aye, my lady." Betsy bobbed her head. "That liniment you sent worked wonders."

"I am glad to hear it." Faye raised her chin and commenced her march. This must be how a condemned man felt being taken to his death. She refused to die like this. She had survived worse.

"I will see to the rushes, my lady." A kitchen drudge bowed his head and scurried out of the hall.

Simon straightened his shoulders beside her. Proud blood ran in her son's veins. The blood of warriors and survivors, and blood would tell now. Simon still had the misshapen wooden carving of a badger clutched to his chest. Dear Lord, Aldous might be dead. Killed for aiding her. Surely, God would not forgive such a terrible injustice.

Gregory would find him and guess what had occurred. Faye grabbed the tiny glimmer of hope. *Please God, speed his return to Aldous's burrow and comfort him through his loss of a dear friend.*

"My lady." One of the castle pages bowed low before her.

"It is good to see you, Peter." Faye stopped once more. "How fares your training?"

"Good, my lady." The boy flushed and his gaze slid away from her. "It is good to see you, my lady."

Royce prodded her. "Move."

"Take your hands off me." Faye stared the misbegotten dog down. His gaze dropped. *Remember with whom you deal, villein.*

Outside the keep, thunder rumbled.

"It seems we are in for a storm." Faye commented to the keep at large as they climbed the stairs. "We need the rain."

"Aye, my lady. Welcome home, my lady."

Faye smiled in the direction of the speaker. *Home.* The word reverberated in her head like a clarion bell.

Royce marched them to the lord's solar and motioned them inside. "You are to wait here."

"We require refreshment." She met Royce's bold gaze without flinching. If he hoped to see her cowering and whimpering for mercy, he would be disappointed.

"Sir Hugo never gave instructions for anything like that." He stuck his chin out like a sulky boy.

"Indeed." Faye met his reaction with the disdain it deserved. "Is the intent to see us perish from thirst and hunger?"

Above his russet beard, Royce flushed. He glared at her, trying to menace her down.

Miserable churl. Faye held her ground until the man spun and stomped from the room.

The room had changed. Finely embroidered silks she had placed there hung, dull with dirt, about the large bed. Pillows she had sewn to match had been cast on the floor in a pile. Bed linens tangled in a rumpled, stained mound. A fire screen she had embroidered in deep shades of blue and yellow stood before the hearth. The ashes looked not to have been swept since she left. Dust covered the clothes chest at the foot of the bed. Grime lined the ewer and basin standing on a table by the casement. She would never have allowed that had she been here.

Faye waited for the door to shut. The bar dropped into place on the other side and her shoulders slumped.

Pale and frightened, Simon stood in the middle of the solar.

She gathered him in her arms. In this place, she had first learned fear and come to understand her helplessness. Memories clustered around the edges of the room and jeered at her She didn't have to listen to them. In the past few days, she had lived a lifetime. She was not the frightened, broken bride who had run for her life a year ago. She snatched up two pillows and beat them together to rid them of dust. "Let us make ourselves more comfortable."

Hooves clattered into the bailey below, and Faye ran to the casement.

Hugo dismounted and tossed his reins to a stable hand.

* * *

Gregory found his horses and an army to go with them. His luck finally turned when he met with the men of Anglesea on his way. He almost wept with relief.

Newt had intercepted them as they traveled to Calder.

"Told you I would do it." Newt hawked and spat.

Gregory abandoned any idea of hugging the filthy child in gratitude.

Newt waited only long enough to be sure Garrett understood exactly how in his debt they were. Then, he turned and disappeared. Gone wherever with a large purse of coins in his pocket.

Sir Arthur carried a writ from King Henry to assume guardianship of Simon. He and Lady Mary's brothers marched to Calder to deliver it. The larger party had split and now William, Roger, and a strong escort rode hard for Aldous's hideout.

The party drew rein atop the rise. Too quiet and no smoke from below. Gregory's nape prickled as he dismounted. Aldous had not come to meet them.

William and Roger kept pace with him as he descended into the old dungeon.

"Sweet Christ," William said.

Aldous's home had been destroyed. The table lay in splinters, linens and pillows ripped, the straw stuffing of the pallet scattered over the floor. The upturned kettle dripped its contents into the dead hearth.

Amongst the carnage lay Aldous in a large, glistening pool of red. Blood crept along the floor out of Aldous. It edged over the pallet straw and mixed with the overturned stew. Gregory's belly clenched and heaved.

Roger crouched beside Aldous. "He breathes."

Aldous might yet live. Any wound bled prolifically. So much blood. Gregory crouched beside Roger.

Roger glanced at him and shook his head. Roger lied. Gregory wanted to pound his fists against Roger and force him to recant.

A gaping hole winked its seeping maw at him from an inch below Aldous's ribs—a gut wound, agonizing and fatal. How could God have let this happen? God could not be this cruel and unjust.

Aldous's breath rattled in his throat. "Sword wielder."

"Old man." Gregory's tongue swelled thick and dry.

Aldous watched him.

Gregory clasped the man's bloody hand in his. He had strength in his limbs, enough to spare, enough to fill Aldous. God, the pain must be nigh unbearable. How had Aldous clung to life this long?

"They took her." Aldous raised barely a whisper. "They took her and the boy."

"Hugo?"

"Aye."

Roger shot to his feet. "Whoreson!"

Feebly, Aldous tugged on his hand until Gregory lowered his head closer to his mouth. "Listen with your heart, warrior,"

Aldous whispered. A sweet smile spread over his face as his eyes dimmed.

Gregory closed the old man's eyelids. Aldous looked as if he merely slept, peaceful and serene. *Nay.* The word built in Gregory's chest wilder than the summer storm outside. He threw back his head and roared it to the heavens.

He bellowed until his throat burned raw, but still it grew within him in wave after wave. His voice failed him before he was spent. He clutched his friend's hand in his. Aldous had been a good man, one of the best he had ever met. His beliefs may have been strange to Gregory, but his deep-seated respect for all things living came as close to God as Gregory had ever known.

"We need to ride for Calder." William touched him on the shoulder.

Not trusting himself to speak, Gregory nodded. Carefully, he slid his hands beneath the old man. He hefted him into his arms and cradled him to his chest. Without his formidable spirit, Aldous weighed nothing in his arms.

"Shall we bury him?" William followed him into the brewing storm. Wind whipped across the knoll and battered them with the moist scent of coming rain.

"Nay." Gregory placed the man on the ground beside the entrance to his lair. "He would desire to be burned."

Roger looked startled, but instructed his men to gather wood.

Gregory returned underground and hunted through the debris until he located the old man's staff. He wiped it free of blood and carried it out. Hugo had Faye, but Gregory refused to leave Aldous for the crows and carrion eaters.

They built a pyre and placed Aldous on it.

Aldous had spoken of this, and Gregory would see him honored thus. Carefully Gregory laid Aldous's hands by his sides, straightened his legs, and smoothed his robe over his ankles.

Gregory removed Aldous's battered sandals and put them beside him. Finally, he placed the staff close to the body and stepped back. Just as Aldous had desired.

Roger stepped forward with a lit brand and thrust it deep within the pyre.

As the wood caught flame, Gregory had no words for a prayer. Aldous would not have recognized their sanctity in any case. Thick, oily smoke and flames oozed around the old man, and engulfed him.

They rode out with the flames burning behind them.

* * *

Faye turned to greet her dead husband's brother. They so closely resembled each other, it was like looking at a ghost.

Hugo stood in the doorway. A triumphant smile spread in a flash of white teeth across his handsome face. He opened his arms wide as he strolled into the room. "Welcome home, my lady." His movements contained as he walked forward, the anger in him leashed but pulsing beneath the surface. He had her and they both knew it.

Faye backed away as she inclined her head in greeting.

"No words of welcome, my lady?" Hugo cocked his head. "No tears for how bereft you are without my brother?" He stopped right before her, towering above her by several inches. His shoulders crowded the room from view.

She caught the scent of mint on his breath, the sickly-sweet smell of the oils he used for his beard. A tremor began in her belly and spread to her legs.

Hugo lifted his hand.

Faye tensed for the blow.

He grinned and slid his hand past her ear.

Faye breathed out, softly so as not to provoke him further. She had lived with a brutish bully, she had seen the same evil in Hugo as she had survived in Calder.

"What have you done to your hair?" He toyed with the shorn ends of her hair. "I do not like it. You will grow it back."

Like Calder, Hugo ordered, and she obeyed. Faye nodded and

dropped her gaze to the floor. He did not like her hair. He would punish her for certain.

His hand, hard beneath her chin, forced her face upward. "This rebellion of yours is done, my lady. You belong here with your son, and we will be wed." His gaze burned into her, implacable and cold. Ice crept over her skin. Hugo's fingers tightened on her chin. She would be bruised come morning. His boots barked against her bare toes and pressed. "I want to hear you say it."

She knew better than to cry out and she curled her nails into her palms. Faye opened her mouth to give him what he wanted, anything to spare herself the harshness of his hand. Her racing mind slowed. Her breath drew in and out of her chest. The steady thump of her heart sounded loud in her ears.

Hugo's face loomed in front of her, brown eyes, pale hair, square jaw, bold nose and chin, a man like any other. His mint breath wafted hot and moist on her face. She had thought him taller, larger. A man, vicious and twisted, but still just a man. Faye probed at the new place within her. Fear, aye, and near to overwhelming, but beneath that, a woman of strength and courage. A woman Faye had faith in. "You will not keep me here."

Hugo's face tightened in anger. "Aye, I will. You will become my wife before man and God." He dug his fingers into her jaw until she cried out in pain. His delight in her pain spread over his face. "Simon will remain my ward, and I will have what is mine. With you as my wife, nobody will question me."

"You are hurting me." His hand over her jaw made it difficult to speak. "Release me."

Hugo jerked his head back. Surprise bloomed over his features for a moment before he threw back his head and laughed. The sound echoed against the stone walls and battered against her ears. Hugo flung her away from him. "How Calder would have loved your defiance."

She tripped over the hem of her gown and tumbled to the floor. Her palms slapped against the stone floor and stung. Her knee went numb on impact. The steel tang of blood filled her mouth from where she bit her tongue as she fell. *Whoreson.* Faye eased onto her haunches.

"You have grown a spirit." Hugo crossed his arms over his chest and chuckled. "I like it."

A blur out of the corner of her eye as Simon darted to her. He shook as he pressed his weight into her.

She managed a smile for him. "Are you all right?"

"Come here, boy." Hugo loomed over Simon.

Simon paled. His hands gripped hers as he shook his head.

Never. Faye crawled to block Simon from Hugo's view.

"Do not make me ask you again." Hugo's voice purred with menace as he took a step toward them. His shadow fell over her. "I will not take a light hand with you as my brother did."

"Leave him be." Faye inched her hand into her boot. Her fingers touched sharp steel. She drew it into her palm, hiding her hands in her skirts as she struggled to her feet.

Simon clutched the back of her skirts.

Faye raised her chin and met Hugo's stare. "Your anger is with me."

Hugo's glare glittered almost black. Color stained his cheeks as he advanced. His breath rasped loud in the still room. "I have not forgotten you. I will deal with you once I have seen to my ward."

She circled to keep Hugo in sight. The jewel on the dagger's guard dug into the soft flesh between her thumb and her fingers as she tightened her grip around the knife.

Hugo stopped. He clenched his hand into a fist and raised it. Slowly, he taunted her.

"Do not." The blow snapped her head to the side and set her ears to ringing. Sweet Jesus, the man did not spare his strength when he struck. Miserable, cowardly swine.

Simon cried out and Faye grabbed his shoulder to keep him where he was. She spat blood at Hugo's feet. "Sodd—"

Heat exploded across her cheek with Hugo's next blow, and

she staggered to stay upright. The blade cut into the tender flesh of her palm.

"Do you see?" Spittle flecked the side of Hugo's mouth. Rage contorted his features. "Do you see what you have made me do?"

Faye pressed Simon behind her and away.

Hugo lunged, and his arm lashed through the air. His fist caught the side of her head and took her right off her feet. Her hip cracked against the floor. Black spots danced in her vision and blood filled her mouth.

Simon was exposed, so slight and young as Hugo stalked the distance between himself and her child. Faye grabbed the bed linens and scrambled to her feet. The whoreson would not touch her child. She lurched for Simon.

Simon stood frozen to the spot. His mouth worked soundlessly.

Faye flung herself between them.

"Nay," Hugo roared. Cruel fingers fastened around her neck and jerked her to halt. Her head twisted, pain seared through her muscles, and she grabbed for the hands.

The clatter of metal hitting the ground echoed through the chamber.

Hugo stilled. His gaze flew to the knife.

It lay against the stone, the gem in the hilt blinking at them.

"Was that for me?" Hugo inclined his head, his hand tightened against her throat. "Did you think to stab me?"

Faye flailed as his grip tightened on her throat. Her vision blackened at the edges. She gasped for air past the constriction in her throat, but it would not come. Hugo's face blurred before her.

He lifted her onto her toes. She clawed at his hand to get free, struck out with her legs.

He held her at arm's length, his powerful shoulders bunched beneath his tunic.

She could not get air into her starved chest.

Hugo laughed, cruel, jarring, as she dangled in his grasp like a poppet.

God, Simon watched this. Her boy stood there, face ashen and watched his uncle strangle his mother. Twisting against the hold, she lashed out with her legs. Air, she needed air or she would black out.

"Stop it." Simon's voice, tear logged and shrieking. "Let her go."

Simon hurled himself at Hugo, who jerked back a step

"Nay." The word couldn't escape past Hugo's fingers. Simon would be hurt. He must stop.

Hugo dropped her. Her legs gave way beneath her and she fell to her knees. The dagger lay inches from her and she crawled for it.

Hugo had Simon by the nape and shook him like a terrier with a rat. The man was so much bigger than the boy. Simon barely reached Hugo's waist. His thin chest worked like a bellows as he sobbed at his uncle to release him.

"Stop it." Her scream was nothing more than a rasp. She scrambled toward her son, the knife in her hand. "Stop it."

"You dare defy me." Hugo released Simon and spun toward her.

Simon froze.

"Run!" Faye forced the words past her damaged throat. "For God's sake, Simon—"

Hugo backhanded Simon.

The blow caught Simon on the side of his head and lifted him off his feet. He twisted through the air. Faye scrabbled forward to catch him. His cry filled her ears and then a sickening *thump* as he crumpled to the ground.

"You need to learn some manners, boy." Hugo stalked to her child. "You need to learn how things will be here."

Faye got there first. She wrapped herself around Simon, her back to Hugo. Simon whimpered in her arms, and she tightened her hold.

Hugo grabbed her wrist, bone crunched as he forced her to open her hand. The knife fell out of her hand.

Faye tucked her head into Simon and braced for the next blow.

"You sicken me." Hugo hawked.

Wetness hit her nape. Faye shuddered and curled about Simon. The boy shook so hard, her entire form shuddered with it.

Hugo stalked to the hearth.

The spittle slid down her spine and she retched. She could not let go of Simon.

Hearth flames flared. Simon sobbed as his wooden badger smoked and then caught fire.

"Let me show you what to do with a knife." Malice lit Hugo's face as he bent to scoop up the knife. He raised it and tested the edge with his thumb, hissing as a small bright red dot of blood blossomed on his thumb. "Sharp, too. What a pity you will never use it."

Hugo twirled the dagger in his grip and held it as Gregory had taught her, underhand to deliver the most damage.

A sharp rapping at the door. "Sir Hugo?"

Simon burrowed deeper.

Hugo wrenched open the door. "What?"

"You had better come," Royce said.

"Now?"

"Right away, Sir Hugo."

The door slammed shut and the bolt slid into place on the other side. Their footsteps receded, growing fainter and fainter.

Faye dragged in a deep breath. She had no time to weep and bemoan her fate. Hiding her winces, she uncoiled from Simon. Faye ran her fingers over his beloved, sweet face. She traced the angry red mark on his cheek. He had harmed her child. Her vision blurred and Faye shook as if she had the ague. The miserable whoreson had marked her precious child.

"You are bleeding?" Simon touched the corner of her mouth. "He hurt you."

Faye wiped her mouth with the back of her hand, the aches from Hugo's blows making themselves known. Knees shaking, she struggled to her feet. Her voice rasped from her raw throat. "I am fine."

They couldn't wait for Hugo's next brutal act. Like Calder, he would tolerate no defiance. The chamber offered no hope. The casement stood open, but it sat high above the bailey. That way would bring certain death. They were locked in. Hugo had her knife.

Her hip ached as she stumbled toward the food tray from earlier. She dipped a cloth napkin into the wine and motioned Simon over. Water would be better, but this was all they had.

Simon stood for her while she bathed the mark on his cheek. It would bruise for sure. Her hand shook and wine slopped over the table onto the floor. Faye drank straight from the flagon. Wine stung her broken lip and spilled down her chin. The inside of her bruised throat screamed in protest.

The stench of Hugo's power crept into the room. It seeped into the furnishings and hangings and hung in the air over her head. Faye kissed Simon on the forehead. It could not end like this. She would not allow it.

The tray held the remains of their meal. Some meat, bread, and fruit. No knife or anything else of use.

Simon trembled and she clutched him close to her, running her hands in soothing motions over his back. She needed to think. There must be something in the chamber she could use as a weapon. Hugo would not lay another hand on her child. The chest at the end of the bed held linens. All weapons were secured in the armory. There had to be something, "Search." She squeezed Simon's shoulder. "Search for anything we can use to defend ourselves."

Chapter Twenty

Gregory rode with Sir Arthur and Roger at the head of the army.

Calder Castle rose from the forest in all her majesty, a beautiful keep of massive proportions standing guard over the land for miles. What a pity she housed such a craven dog. Faye and Simon were in that keep. Gregory would take it down stone by stone, with his bare hands if he must, but he would get them back.

The army passed through the eerily still town of Upper Mere. Doors remained shut fast, windows shuttered. They traveled with colors flying in full view of the battlements. *See us,* the pageantry of the army yelled. *See us and tremble before this might.* Only Bess stood in her tidy yard and waved.

Gregory nodded to her as they passed.

"Set up the camp." Sir Arthur spoke to Roger. "They know we are here."

Sir Arthur's men moved out of the forest like wolves, wary and alert to the possibility of archers. They stopped outside of bow length, but these men took nothing for granted.

"What is your plan?" Sir Arthur's gray destrier shifted beneath him.

Gregory turned to stare at the older man. "My plan?"

"Your plan." Sir Arthur swung his head back to the keep. "How are you going to get my daughter and her son out of there?"

"We need to present the writ." Hugo wouldn't honor the writ. Gregory's blood surged in imminent victory. And when he didn't, Gregory intended to relish every moment of exacting the king's justice. "When that fails, we attack."

Sir Arthur grunted and crossed his arms over his pommel. "Ever attacked a heavily fortified keep before?"

"Nay."

"I have. A time or two." Sir Arthur leaned forward on his arms. "It is going to be a sod to get in there."

"Aye."

"So be it." Sir Arthur nodded and straightened. "And then what, Sir Monk?"

"Eh?"

"After we get my daughter free and make that sod sorry he ever laid a hand on my grandson, what then?"

"We free Faye and Simon and return them to Anglesea."

"And then what?" Sir Arthur posed the question that had haunted Gregory since he'd first laid eyes on Faye. The answer rang clear in his brain. So clear it almost unseated him. He would not be returning to the Abbey. Sometime in his frantic search through the night, or even before then, something had changed for him. Leaving Faye at Anglesea a year ago paled before a life in which Faye no longer existed. Aldous's last words to him made a ringing sort of sense. His heart might have known all along what his head refused to accept.

Sir Arthur's glare bored straight to the heart of him, the eyes of a father demanding answers.

"Faye is mine." The admission resonated through Gregory. It fit. The old, familiar battle stilled inside him.

"Make sure of it." Sir Arthur clucked to his horse. "Because that is my daughter in there, and she deserves all I would wish for her. I gave her to a man who did not cherish her before, and I will not do so again." He moved off to join Roger.

William nudged his mount into place beside him. "My father makes a good point."

"He often does."

The red battlements of Calder soared between Gregory and the closest thing he had to a family. He had walked away from Faye before, and it had nearly killed him. Never again. She was his. "I have been a knight and a monk. What now?" He hadn't meant to say the words out loud. Now they were said, he was glad of it.

William nodded. "It is no easy thing to change course midstream."

"I should never have left her with Aldous. Every time I leave her something bad happens."

"Then make sure you do not leave her again." William tilted his head and appraised him. "Have you not had a surfeit of guilt, Sir Gregory?"

It hit Gregory like a blow to the middle, and he gaped at William.

"Our father should never have married her to Calder. I should have checked when I heard those things at court. You should have made her leave Calder sooner. None of us should have let her leave on this journey. And on and on and on we go." William scythed his arm through the air. "Save your guilt for when we have her back, and then do what any man would and throw yourself at her feet and beg for mercy."

"She will not make me beg."

William snorted. "Do you know nothing of women?"

"Nay." God knew, he spoke the truth. His knowledge of women came from the Bible and Faye.

"Nay, I suppose you do not." William shrugged and gave a soft laugh. "I like you, Gregory, but I love my sister. I will not see her hurt anymore." He stared over at the castle. "There are many ways to strike a woman."

The unjustness of the last gagged him. Gregory wanted to lash out and belt the man for even suggesting he could, in any way, be compared with Calder or Hugo. He tightened his grip on his pommel and stayed his hand. Faye's tears that night in Bess's cottage had seeped through his tunic into the skin beneath. His failure to act had hurt her as surely as Calder's fists.

William nodded and kneed his horse forward.

Henry appeared at his side. He looked like a man with a grave message to impart.

Gregory groaned out loud. After Henry, there would be Roger. The men in her family chafed at having let her be hurt and now sought to redress the situation. Would anyone else in the camp like to have a go while they waited? The cook? The camp followers?

"She is a mighty one." Henry jerked his chin toward the keep. He gave Henry credit for a more politic approach than his father and older brother.

"I will not be returning to the Abbey."

Henry opened and shut his mouth as color climbed his cheeks. "Aye, well, she is my sister and we were wondering what would happen." They must have had a family war council or some such foolishness.

"I never liked Calder," Henry said. "I was much younger when he arrived to marry Faye. A man will often reveal to a child more than he does to another adult." It was the truth. He and Calder had met as squires and Calder always showed one face to his lord and another to his fellows. For his wife, Calder had worn an entirely different face. Hugo had a face to match his dead brother's.

Gregory's anger simmered and sputtered beneath the surface. Aimed more at himself than anyone else. Like a craven churl, he had never pushed Faye hard enough to make her leave. Seven years he had lived with the knowledge of what her husband did to her, and he had done nothing. His paltry excuse had been that he had no right to interfere between a man and his wife. His cowardice turned to bitter ash in his mouth. Calder had been his liege lord, and he had believed he owed the sod his loyalty. Ultimately, however, Faye had paid the price for that loyalty. He should have ignored her pleas for him to keep his silence about what happened at Calder. He should have snatched her and the boys up and taken them away. The list of his failures marched with grim purpose through his mind.

It hadn't always been as bad, not in the beginning. It had crept up on them over the years. The habit of ignoring the truth had crept along with it. In this, he and Faye had been in tacit agreement. He could not claim ignorance. He had known, had lain awake at night and burned for the bruises on her.

It had taken Faye that last beating, the worst, for him to override Faye's wishes and for him to insist he take her to Anglesea and break the code of secrets and silence. When they had arrived at Anglesea, she had not cited Calder's brutality as the reason to her family, but spoke of his association with the dead King John and how he plotted to overthrow her father. Gregory had kept his silence even then. Never again. There would be no more secrets between them. There were no good secrets.

Garrett joined them. "I believe it is my turn at the stocks."

Henry's lip curled in distaste as he eyed the nag Garrett rode. Garrett remained unmoved by any plea for him to give up Parsley and get a better destrier. Henry had offered to train a destrier for him, but Garrett was stubborn. Fierce determination not to be anything other than the man he was drew Gregory's admiration

"I have been told to ask your intentions." Garrett raised a brow at him.

"The others are ahead of you."

"Ah." Garrett nodded toward the keep. "So, how does this waging war against a keep happen?"

"Siege." Henry scratched his cheek as he considered the castle. "War engines, hot oil, archers, that sort of thing."

"Sounds painful." Garrett grinned.

"We will attempt to reach an agreement." Gregory's gut clenched. "And then, I kill him."

Garrett's grin widened into feral snarl. "Beatrice thought you might say that."

"She did?"

"Oh, aye." Garrett nodded. "She had her sword strapped over her belly and was ready to join us. It was only when I assured her you would be here, she agreed not to come."

Henry made a disapproving noise. "You should take your wife in hand."

"Tell me, Henry." The anger on Garrett's face came and went in a flash. "She was your sister for years before she was my wife. How did you manage to take her in hand?"

Henry grunted and colored to his hairline.

"Indeed." Garrett snorted. "That is what I thought. For you to even say such a thing shows me how little you know of women."

Gregory's face heated. His knowledge of women fell short of even Henry's he would wager. All this talk of his intentions made him uncomfortably aware of his ignorance. As a man of God, he'd never inquired more or furthered his education. Since he had rescued Faye from those brigands, his mind tormented him with all sorts of possibilities. Their encounter the other day had opened a door that would not stay shut.

Garrett eyed him quizzically. "Well, Gregory, that look on your face tells a story."

Heat flamed higher on his skin, and Gregory cursed. "I was merely thinking how little I know of women myself."

"Indeed." Garrett turned in his saddle. "Come on, then. I have the feeling this conversation will require some oiling with mead." He nodded at Henry. "And an absence of male relatives."

"Now is not the time." Gregory returned his gaze to the keep.

Garrett eyed it with him. "I do not think it is going anywhere. Come along." He thumped Gregory on the arm. "Come and keep me company while the mighty Sir Arthur makes his plans. I hate the waiting."

Chapter Twenty-One

The summons from Hugo started the churning in Faye's gut. He had some new humiliation stored up for her. She was sure of it. Faye followed Sir John into the hall with her head high.

People filled the hall to bursting. The noise of male voices near deafened her.

Sir John kept his gaze averted from her beaten face. With her right eye swollen to twice its size and her lip split and bloodied, she must present quite the picture. Come morning, the ache on her right cheek would blossom into a bruise. Simon remained upstairs, safe from Hugo for now. She'd brave this new humiliation and more to keep it thus.

Heads turned as she made her way through the throng to the front of the hall. Their gazes prickled across her skin. Let them look at her face and see what Hugo had done. The shame was Hugo's not hers. As they had stood aside when Calder had brutalized her, they now must face their cowardice again.

"My lady." Hugo sat at the high table. His leer roved her insolently as she drew closer. A smug smile crossed his face. "Welcome home."

Her stomach churned until she wanted to vomit. How she

would love to have that knife with her again and know how to wield it. She would carve the smile from his face and laugh as she did.

She and Sir John stopped at the foot of the dais leading up to the high table.

Hugo didn't invite her to sit. He meant to remind her of her place before the hall by having her stand in front of him like the lowliest serf. Faye squared her shoulders and let her gaze drift across the occupants of the hall. She addressed the hall at large. "I bid you good evening."

Heads ducked and glances shifted to the side. What a craven bunch, not even able to hold her stare.

Hugo stuffed meat into his mouth with his large fist. The fist he had raised against her and Simon. If she had the strength to make him pay for what he'd done, she would stuff Hugo's fist into his mouth until the sod choked on it. Grease dribbled over Hugo's chin and he wiped it with his sleeve.

Faye met the challenge in his stare.

"I have brought you to meet a friend." Hugo grabbed up his tankard and guzzled. Mead spilled over his chin and stained his tunic.

The hall hushed as two men shoved a girl into the hall.

Hugo's triumphant sneer spoke louder than any words.

Ruth stumbled and came down hard on her knees and huddled on the floor, her clothing torn, her face bruised and swollen almost beyond recognition. She hunched into herself and trembled as if she had no control. This was Ruth, sweet-faced, laughing Ruth with her big heart and endless patience. Bile rose in the back of Faye's throat. She pressed her hand to her mouth.

"No fond greeting?" Hugo chuckled.

Ruth's eyes gleamed dull and spiritless from her damaged face.

"What have you done?" The question wrenched from Faye.

"I thought I should make an example of her." A bench scraped as Hugo got to his feet.

Faye stepped toward the girl. "Ruth?"

Sir John touched her arm and shook his head in warning. Faye did not care. She stumbled the few feet separating them and knelt beside Ruth.

Ruth flinched and went still as Faye touched her.

"Oh, Ruth." Faye cradled the girl's face in her palms, afraid to cause more pain. So many words snarled in her brain that she could only shake her head. She had done this to Ruth. Ruth had helped save Simon and this was the result.

She noted each mark, each bruise and scratch on Ruth's once-pretty face and stored them away in her mind. Faye had shouldered Calder's guilt and shame too long. She would not do so again for Hugo. He had done this and for each hurt Ruth suffered, he would pay.

"Do you see, my lady?" Hugo's hand pinched her arm as he hauled her to her feet. "See what happens to those who betray me. Give the girl back to the men."

Ruth whimpered as her captors dragged her to her feet.

She couldn't help Ruth. Her helplessness jammed in her throat until she wanted to scream it out. Faye pulled at Hugo's hold. "Nay."

"You learn slowly, my sweet." Hugo tightened his grip.

"Sir Hugo?" Sir John shifted a step closer. A frown creased his brows. "The hall."

Hugo glanced to the knight and beyond.

Grim faces stared at them.

The pressure on her arm increased. She wouldn't give him the satisfaction of making her cry out.

Sir John jerked his head to without the keep. "Our larger concerns? Outside?"

"Get her away from me." Hugo flung her at the older man.

Sir John caught her, his grasp firm but gentle as he assisted her to regain her footing.

She slowed her churning thoughts and stilled the fear in her belly. Faye took a deep breath. Stout heart and clear mind, as her father said. These would win the day.

With a troubled frown, Sir John watched them take Ruth away. He had stepped in before Hugo could strike her. Discomfort flickered in the back of his eyes as Sir John motioned her to precede him from the hall. "My lady."

Sir John would never openly defy Hugo without some encouragement.

"She is a good girl, Ruth." Faye climbed the stairs with Sir John at her back. "I knew her family. There was some talk of her marrying a young carpenter from Upper Mere. A nice young man." Faye lingered as much as she dared. "Is there nothing you can do for her?"

"Nay." Sir John's voice held a definite note of regret.

"What he has done to her is horrible."

They cleared the final bend in the stairs and entered the upper passageway. The lord's solar loomed ahead. Once there, Sir John would lock her in again. Time ran out. "Will he do the same to me?"

"My lady?" Sir John's steps faltered.

Faye turned to him. "Hugo. Will he give me to his men to brutalize as they did Ruth?"

He paled, but his gaze shifted away and his frown deepened. "Nay."

"But you are not sure." If he would but look at her, the seed of doubt could be nurtured.

He stared at the wall beyond her shoulder.

"You cannot be sure of what he will do in his anger and his ambition."

Sir John took a step away. "You are a lady."

"And Ruth was a lovely young girl. An innocent who said her prayers every night and never let the men of the keep turn her head."

"She betrayed her lord." Sir John stiffened.

"Simon is her lord, and she did only what she thought best for him. Ruth believed a child should be with his mother." Faye allowed her anger to seep into her voice. "And this is her punishment. This agony she suffers."

He looked at his feet.

"Look at me, Sir John." He must see the truth.

Sir John dragged his gaze up to her face. A muscle twitched in his jaw.

"Look at my face and see what he has done to me." She pointed toward the solar. "And if that is not enough for you, look at my son's cheek. My son and your earl. Simon is the person to whom you owe your loyalty."

"Enough, lady." Sir John thrust his hand at the solar. "You do not know of what you speak."

"I know better than anyone of what I speak, Sir John." Faye held his gaze for a long moment. "You lived here when I did and you were not blind then, just as you are not blind now." She turned and walked to the solar.

Simon sprang from the bed as she entered. "Mama?"

"I am well, sweeting." She touched his bruised cheek.

Sir John's stare fixed on the purple mark on Simon's face. Let him look. Let him look and examine his conscience when he was done.

"Have you eaten, my lady?" Sir John stepped back into the doorway.

"Nay."

"I will bring you something." He shut the door behind him. The bolt slid home.

Trembling set in as soon as he had left. Poor Ruth. She couldn't shake the image from her mind. Hugo might be even worse than Calder.

"There is an army," Simon whispered. His face flushed as he motioned toward the casement. "Outside the walls, Mama, a huge army. Do you think it is grandfather?"

Faye ran to the casement. "Dear God."

Simon had not exaggerated. The army spread across the land

before the castle. Brightly colored pennants snapped in the breeze, a dragon proper on Argent. Her father's colors. He was here. Her father had come. She hugged Simon to her and knew not whether to laugh or cry. So she did both.

There beside her father the lion rampant, her uncles were here, too. They might not even be looking, but Faye waved at the tiny figures on the green. She waved until her arm grew tired. It gave her the sense of connection with them. She prodded Simon until he waved. "We are here," she wanted to shout. "We are here. Come and get us."

A tall, armored figure stepped out of one of the tents. He wore no colors. Gregory. She was sure it was him. She could not mistake his carriage or the set of his shoulders.

Faye strained out of the casement and waved more. Had she imagined the tall figure's head swung in their direction? Nay, he raised his hand. "He sees us." Joy bubbled up her throat in a sob. "It is Gregory, and he sees us." Faye grabbed Simon's shoulders and bent her head to his. "We will find a way out there, Simon. By God, we will."

* * *

Gregory sat silent on his horse beside Sir Arthur.

The men atop the gatehouse shifted out of sight. Presumably, one of them had gone to fetch Hugo. Sir Arthur insisted he would not speak with any other.

Some sense of awareness had made him glance up earlier, and he had seen the barest flash in the upper casement. Faye. She was alive. The gnawing dread muted to a manageable level. As long as she lived, then hope lived.

On the battlements, a figure appeared. Hugo. Gregory's blood surged. Would he could stretch across the distance and fasten his hands about the cur's throat and squeeze until his face turned black and his eyes bulged in their sockets. Wrench the life out of Hugo with his own hands.

"Well met, Sir Arthur." Hugo braced his hands on the crenellations either side of him. "And Father Piety, what a surprise that you are here, too."

"Whoreson," Sir Arthur muttered. If he were a cursing man, Gregory would be inclined to second that remark. "Let us get to it, Hugo," Sir Arthur shouted. "You know why we are here, send out my daughter and my grandson."

Hugo paused and grinned. "You mean my brother's wife and my ward. I am afraid not, Sir Arthur."

A well-aimed knife would pierce the dog in his gullet. However, it would rob Gregory of the satisfaction of watching the light die as he killed Hugo.

"Hugo, try not to be any more of an idiot than you have thus far shown yourself to be." Sir Arthur folded his arms over his pommel. "You know me, and you know I will not leave without them. I have with me a writ from King Henry giving me guardianship of Simon and Faye."

Hugo jerked and straightened. "I am the boy's rightful guardian. My brother desired it thus. And besides, the king mistrusts you. He would never support your claim."

"And yet, here it is." Sir Arthur waved a scroll in the air. "Brought to me by the hands of my wife's brothers." He motioned with the scroll toward the small knot of knights standing near the archers. Two of them wore the king's crest blazoned on their surcoats. The meaning, unmistakable, they rode with the king's blessing. Sir Arthur turned back to Hugo. "It seems the king, being no more than a boy, has strong feelings when it comes to a child being ripped away from his mother."

"I care not what you hold in your hand." Hugo threw his hands wide. "I still hold something of much more value to you behind these walls."

"Release them, Hugo, by order of the king," Sir Arthur called.

"Never." Hugo raised his sword. "If you can get in, you can have them."

"This is then your final word?" Sir Arthur's pose remained

relaxed, but Gregory sensed anger gathering within him. "Your willfulness will lead you into an act of defiance against the king?"

"The king has no place between a man and his family."

Sir Arthur threw back his head and guffawed. "The king has his place in every part of our lives." He turned to his oldest son. "Mark you, Roger. There stands a dead man."

Even from the distance, Hugo's rage seeped from him.

Hugo's anger would turn on Faye. "Beware." Gregory barely moved his lips as he spoke. "He will visit that rage on Faye and the boy."

Sir Arthur gave a tiny nod in acknowledgement. "I want to see my daughter," he called.

"Do you now?" Hugo leaned his shoulder against the stone. "And why would I allow that?"

"Look around you, boy." Arthur gestured to the sea of waiting men. "And ask how much choice you have."

Hugo laughed. "Look around you, old man. All those men will do naught until you can breach these walls. I would wish you luck, but in the circumstances, you will understand if I do not."

"Indeed." Sir Arthur slapped down his visor. "A little advise, Hugo. Run while you can." Sir Arthur motioned the archers forward. "Anything moves on those battlements, put an arrow in it."

Heads disappeared behind the crenellations, Hugo's with them.

"God's Bones." Sir Arthur jerked on the reins to turn his destrier. "As long as he has Simon and Faye the whoreson has us bent over a barrel."

Gregory wanted to howl his frustration. His impotence churned like ruined meat in his gut.

"We will get them." Sir Arthur dug his heels into his horse. "Never you fear, Sir Monk. I have faced larger keeps with lesser numbers, and I always prevail. Let his men chew that over as they wait for me to act."

"Aye." Garrett shot a quick glance at Sir Arthur. "Ask one who has lived to see the truth of that boast."

"You carp and whine like a woman." Sir Arthur flung at Garrett.

Garrett grinned and winked at Gregory.

Gregory stared at the stone standing between him and Faye. He had no smiles or winks to return. He clung to the image of that tiny hand waving at him. "I am coming." The sound of his voice startled him.

William clapped him on the shoulder. "She knows."

* * *

Hugo laughed at Sir John. The craven dog had the ballocks to question him. He would crush the man beneath his heel. "What did you say?"

Sir John faltered and drew a deep breath. "Sir Hugo, they outnumber us. If they breach the walls, they will overrun us."

Hugo curled his lip back. Cowardly whoreson, tucking his tail between his legs and trembling before mighty Sir Arthur of Anglesea at the gates. In his day, Sir Arthur might have been a great knight, but that day was long gone. Outside his gates stood a pitiful old man shouting his defiance. It made Hugo want to laugh. The old man bellowed and puffed up his chest like he had forgotten the march of time. No man was impervious to age and Hugo burned to remind him. The brothers didn't bother him one whit. Arrogant, drunk on their father's glory, and nothing more. He could take them all at once. He had waited long in Calder's shadow for what was his, and now he had it within his grasp, and he would never let it go.

"And what of the writ?" Sir John's questions threatened his good mood.

"What writ?" Hugo stared the man down.

"From the king." Another knight stepped forward. "To ignore it is treason."

The fools dared to challenge his authority. Hugo shot his fist out. His gauntlet raked the man's face and drew blood. Satisfaction surged as the man staggered back amongst the hens around him. "Hear you." Hugo met each man's gaze as they clustered before him. Cowards, the lot of them. When this was done, he would see them pay for their dissension. "There is no writ from the king. The old man lies."

"Why would he lie?" Sir John stood his ground. Good. He would go first. Strung up by his entrails from the battlements.

"Indeed." Hugo forced a smile. "Why does any man lie? To save his miserable hide. He fears us." He beat on his chest with his fist. One or two heads came up, shoulders stiffened by pride. Still, too many appeared uncertain. "The great Sir Arthur of Anglesea knows this is a fight he cannot win and he lies out of fear."

A ragged cheer broke out. Let that stoke a fire in their bellies. He needed them for now, useless sods that they were.

Sir John stared at him, his face blank.

What did he care? The man was as good as dead.

Chapter Twenty-Two

Full dark settled outside Faye's casement. The fires of the waiting army twinkled on the edge of the forest, her hope and her salvation.

Sir John entered the room with a serf. Grave lines carved his angular face like a tormented saint. The serf stoked the fire, whilst Sir John placed a salver of food on the table beneath the casement and stopped to stare beyond.

The serf scuttled from the room, shutting the door behind him.

"Your father is here."

"Aye." Faye hadn't expected him to speak.

"He brings a large force with him."

"Indeed."

Sir John's expression remained rigid, providing no clues as to his thoughts. His tense silence pressed down on her nerves until she wanted to scream at him to go or stay or say something. "He says he has a writ from the king making you and Simon your father's wards."

Father had saved them. She should never have doubted he would act. "Then we are to be released."

"Nay." Sir John turned from the window.

"But of course we must be released." Faye gaped at him in astonishment. The nightmare was over, her father and uncles had used their influence and the king had spoken.

"Hugo will not release you."

Faye laughed. It must be a jest. "He has no authority to hold us."

Sir John did not laugh with her.

A creeping chill spread over Faye's skin and she rubbed her arms. Of course Hugo would not release them. He wanted the power that came with being earl. As long as Simon was young, and Hugo could control him, that power would be Hugo's. She and Simon were little more than his chattel to do with as he wished.

"Hugo is arrogant." Sir John passed a hand over his eyes. "Your father has sworn retribution, but Hugo sits in the hall and drinks with his vassals."

The chill hardened into cold, icy fear. A drunk Hugo frightened her more than a sober one. Calder had lost reason when he drank. Not that reason had ever formed a huge part of Calder's thinking.

"He drinks heavily." Sir John strode to the door. "He celebrates his imminent victory against Sir Arthur. All the castle serving folk are required to attend him." He opened the door and shut it behind him.

Faye nudged Simon toward the food.

He ate with his typical boyish enthusiasm.

Faye smiled at her beloved son. Nothing stood between a growing boy and his dinner. The twinkling lights outside beckoned her, calling to her to come. A niggling sensation wormed into her brain. Something was amiss. Other than Sir John being strangely forthcoming. Faye froze. The door, it was the bloody door.

He had spoken of Hugo getting drunk in the hall, of all the servants being busy and in attendance. Then he had left. *The bolt.*

Her head reeled and she caught the wall for support. Surely, she was mistaken.

Sir John had left and shut the door. He hadn't slid the bolt into place to lock them in. She was so accustomed to the sound, that she didn't immediately register its absence. Her legs trembled as she crept over to the door. Hope constricted painfully in her chest making breathing difficult. Her hands shook as she put them to the latch and lifted.

The door swung open. Faye shut it again, quickly. Her heart thundered in her ears. Sir John had not bolted the door and the servants were in the hall. She stood for a moment, frozen by fear and indecision. The way was open. All she had to do was step out of that door.

Simon peered out the casement as he ate.

Faye paced into the center of the room. Beyond the door was the upper corridor. The chapel. The knowledge fisted her in the middle. Behind the altar lay the opening to a small crypt beneath. And from there—

Oh, dear Lord, her head grew light and the room spun. The crypt concealed a door that led straight to the postern gate. It would be guarded, for certain, with the army camped without.

She pushed the air out of her chest, stumbled to the edge of the bed and sat. If they were discovered, Hugo would be terrible in his anger and retribution.

Hugo was already a monster. If he didn't catch her escaping and kill her, he would kill her in this chamber, for sure, because she would never consent to marrying him. And if Hugo killed her, there would be nobody to protect Simon from him. "Simon." Her voice sounded as if it belonged to someone else, chill and faint. "We have to go."

Gregory paced the confines of the tent. Behind him Roger and Sir Arthur pored over a plan of Calder Castle and strategized a way past the towering walls.

William worked his steady way through a wine skin. The man had an unnatural ability to consume wine and remain coherent.

Garrett slept on Sir Arthur's cot.

Gregory's skin felt pressed over his bone, too tight. Faye was at Hugo's mercy and they waited. Waited for what? For Sir Arthur to find a way over those walls with minimum loss of life. Gregory understood that, but rest evaded him. As long as Faye stayed behind those walls, he wouldn't find peace.

"Gregory." Sir Arthur hailed him. "Come and tell us what you know of the keep."

Relief to be doing something, anything, propelled him forward.

* * *

Faye and Simon reached the bottom of the stairs and stopped. The only way to the chapel meant crossing the entrance to the hall. For Simon, Faye tucked her fear as deep as she could. As she approached the great double doors leading to the hall her hand trembled over the wall. The doors stood open and the roar of noise from within battered against her straining ears.

A serving woman rushed out of the hall, her face harried. Betsy's hands were filled with tankards as she hurried back to the kitchens.

Faye tugged Simon to hide him beneath her skirts and shrank closer to the wall.

Startled, Betsy stopped short. They were caught. Faye sagged against the wall before she fell. She tensed for Betsy's scream.

Betsy gave Faye a tiny nod and continued on her way to the kitchen. Faye blew the air out of her lungs in a rush. They needed to move quickly. The next person leaving the hall might not be as sympathetic.

She hugged the wall as she approached the entrance. Faye inched her head around the doorjamb. Smoke and people blurred into a moving haze. Faye jerked her head back. The drum of her heart muted the male voices. She grabbed Simon's hand in a tight grip.

Now.

They dashed across the clear space and stopped on the other side. Faye jammed her back against the wall, braced for the shout that would give them away. A woman shrieked followed by the crash of furniture and loud laughter.

She pulled Simon forward. The light dimmed this side of the hall. Few tapers had been lit and long shadows stretched between them. Faye hugged the shadows like a dear friend. The noise of the hall receded behind them, and she quickened her pace.

No men posted throughout the keep. They must be either on the battlements or in the hall. The chapel door stood just ahead.

Faye ran the final distance and grasped the latch. Holding her breath, she inched the door open. Absolute dark greeted her on the other side. The faint scent of incense hung in the air. They slipped inside and Faye closed the door behind her. On impulse, she bolted it. Not that Hugo made frequent visits to the chapel, but it might buy her precious time.

As expected, the chapel was empty. There had not been a resident priest at Calder Castle since Father Mathew had passed three years ago. Upper Mere relied on the services of the nearby monastery for spiritual guidance. Faye kept to the deeper shadows to the side of the chapel as they crept toward the altar.

No candles burned to mark the prayers of knights before battle. Behind the altar, the dark intensified and she stumbled forward, one hand clasping Simon and the other groping at the empty space.

Faye swept her hand before her. Surely, she must have reached the back wall by now? Her fingertips encountered stone and she edged to the right. Fabric. A tapestry of the Blessed Virgin concealed the passage. This must be it. She brushed the cloth aside. A slight breeze chilled the perspiration on her face. The opening to the crypt. She nudged the space ahead of her with her toes. Nothing. Forward, slowly until her toe dipped over the edge of the step.

She moved blind as the tapestry dropped back into place. Painfully, carefully, she inched down the stairs. First finding the lip and then a firm place for her foot before she moved. The descent drew on forever. It seemed as if she lost most of the night creeping from one stair to the other.

Simon stumbled and she gripped his hand until he regained his balance.

The stairs spiraled down into the crypt. She didn't think it possible, but the dark deepened as they descended. The dank, fetid air clung to her skin as they approached the crypt. She should have brought a candle.

"Mama." Simon's whisper bounced off the walls and echoed back at her. She squeezed his hand to silence him. "There are ghosts down here, Mama."

The Earls of Calder lay here. Faye suppressed her shudder. They were dead. The living Earl of Calder needed her to be brave. "Nay, Simon." Faye tightened her resolve. Something sticky brushed her face and a scream lodged in her throat. She held her breath and forced it down. There were spiders down here, too. Oh, sweet Jesu, and in all likelihood rats. She dared not increase their pace for fear of what they would stumble into in the dark. "Gregory told me a story when we were looking for you."

"Aye." His little voice quivered.

"Shall I tell you?"

Anything to keep the fear at bay.

* * *

Desperation. Gregory named the sensation twisting his innards and it grew stronger with each passing hour. With Faye and Simon in the castle, they dared not risk a protracted siege.

Sir Arthur had a team of men poised to scale the walls, and archers to protect their ascent. Their forces split into three and surrounded the keep from all sides. Hugo would pay for his laziness. Deep wells of shadow at the wall base gave them the advantage they sought. Hugo relied on the mere to the south and wall height to protect him. He should have considered how Sir Arthur had brought down past keeps.

To the west and east, the other forces set up large encampments, not hiding their presence and drawing the castle eyes in that direction. He and the scalers wagered their lives on distraction and the dark. It wouldn't hold for long. It didn't need to. Only long enough for Gregory and his men to get over the wall and open the gates.

Sir Arthur's engineers had taken a team of men into the forest to construct the trebuchets, should the first attempt fail. Everything that could be done was being done.

He'd forced himself to sleep for a few hours. A lifetime of being a knight had trained him to rest when he could. Around him the men crouched dead silent.

The moon waned above them in a clear night sky. Their ascent would begin long before dawn. The dark would provide cover, but increase the risk of falling. The scaling ladders lay concealed at the base of the highest point of the walls.

Savage satisfaction roared through Gregory. Hugo's stupidity would be Gregory's reward.

William nudged him. "It is time."

At last. Gregory put his shoulder to the scaling ladders. Over thirty feet in height, they would take more than one man to lift. A flaming arrow arced through the still night from Sir Arthur's camp, the signal to halt.

"What in God's name...?" William clasped his shoulder.

The crouched men murmured to each other.

Gregory nearly threw back his head and roared his defiance. He needed over that wall.

"Do not." William must have read his thoughts. "If my father calls us back, he has good reason." Gregory had an even better reason to get over that wall.

William's hand tightened on his shoulder.

Already the other men slipped back to the camp.

* * *

Faye couldn't believe it. The postern gate hung ajar. Outside the crypt, the moonlight seemed bright as noon. No guard at the gate, either. Sir John? Perhaps. No time to stop and count her good fortune.

She went first, tugging Simon behind her. At the first sign of danger, he knew to slip back into the crypt and wait for Sir Arthur's rescue. The walls of Calder loomed at her back. The land ahead dropped away to where the army camped; her father's army, her brothers and Gregory.

Her knees locked and her next step yawned before her. The quiet *snick* of the postern-gate lock forced her into action. Her savior had locked the gate behind them.

"Mama." Simon prodded her thigh.

Aye, they were not safe yet. She ducked low to the ground as they moved across the killing ground, still in range from the castle archers and not yet under the encampment's protection.

A shadowy form appeared before her. "Speak fast before I slit your throat."

Faye's scream died against his palm. Steel pressed against her neck, and she dared not breathe.

"Jesu." The steel dropped away. "Faye?"

Oh, dear God, Roger.

"You had best come with me," Roger whispered. Snatching up Simon, he half carried her as her knees turned to pudding. Over the front lines they went and straight to the command tent. Light stung her eyes as the tent flap opened and Roger dragged her inside.

"Sweet Jesu." A figure blocked the light before sweeping her into a rib-crushing embrace. Then the tears came and would not stop. She'd done it. Somehow, she'd escaped from Calder.

Her father's arms held her. Her face pressed into his hauberk. She did not even mind the hard metal against her sore cheek. She drew great breaths of leather, horse, and metal into her chest. The scent of safety, her father and home. Simon clung to Roger's shoulders, his face pale and tear streaked, but wearing a huge grin.

"You came." She dug her hands into her father's hauberk, part of her brain still sure it could not be possible.

"Of course I came." Emotion roughened her father's voice. "Why do my daughters never believe I will?"

Faye laughed and sobbed all at once. "You took too long."

"Aye." Sir Arthur kissed the top of her head. "But then I know war is not always fought at a run."

"Do you really have a writ from King Henry?"

Sir Arthur grinned. "Aye, William went to London and pled your case. You know William. He can talk the birds from the trees. We came as soon as we had the writ and could raise an army."

"I am extremely happy to see you."

"Sweeting." Her father grew misty-eyed. "I did not abandon you and your boy. You must know I would never do that."

"I know." Faye scrubbed the tears from her cheek. "I love you."

Sir Arthur coughed and cleared his throat. "Here now. Of course you do. You are my Fairest Faye."

"Only not so fair at the moment."

Sir Arthur studied her face, lingering over each injury. "He will pay, sweeting. Never fear."

"Let me see." Roger pushed in front of her. He took a sharp breath. "I am going to enjoy this."

"As will we all." Sir Arthur cupped her chin.

"How did you escape?" Roger asked.

"I had some help." Faye disentangled herself from her father. "Sir John left the door open for me and, I suspect, the postern gate. I do not think he supports Hugo's decision."

Roger's face split in a feral grin. "It appears Hugo's troubles are only beginning."

"What will do you now?"

Roger folded his arms over his chest. "You and Simon will leave for Anglesea at first light. We will stay and teach Hugo what happens to those who challenge Anglesea."

"A siege?"

"Aye." Roger grinned at the prospect. "And with the full blessing of the crown."

"How is Arthur?" She turned to her father.

"He is well." Sir Arthur touched her cheek. "He misses his mother, but between Mary, Beatrice, and Nurse they have him well in hand."

On the morrow she would see her youngest son. It was finally over. The blood drained from her face with relief and she swayed.

Sir Arthur hugged her to him. "It is done."

Footsteps scuffed outside the tent.

"Ah." Roger grinned at her. "It took him longer than I thought."

Chapter Twenty-Three

Faye caught her breath as the tent opened and Gregory stood there. She tried to take all of him in, in one glance. His gaze locked on her and stuck. "Thank you, Lord."

"Faye." Almost knocking Gregory out of the way, William barreled in behind and swept her into a hard hug. "We were moments from coming over the walls after you." William examined her face, lingering on her bruised lip and eye. "I see we did not come fast enough. Whoreson!" William's face tightened in fury. "He will pay for this as well."

"Gregory." Simon wriggled out of Roger's hold. "You should have seen us. We snuck through the chapel and into the crypt. There were ghosts down there, but we did not care. We were brave."

"Aye." Gregory's voice thickened, and he cleared his throat. "You were very brave."

"Come." Roger took the boy by the hand. "And we will find you something to fill that maw you call a belly." He leaned over Simon and sniffed. "And wash the stink from you."

"I do not stink." Simon stiffened.

"Aye, you do." Roger rumpled his hair. "And you can either

231

bathe here, or I will let Nurse catch a whiff of you on the morrow."

Her father and brothers left the tent with Simon. Alone with Gregory. Her legs melted to the spot. Part of her wanted to fling herself into his arms, but another part whispered caution. His stern face and tense carriage kept her at a distance. "I am sorry about Aldous."

Gregory flinched and nodded. "He was a good man."

The width of the battle tent yawned between them. The width of all they had never spoken yawned even wider.

"How did you do it? Escape." Stone-faced. How she had grown to hate his reserve.

"Sir John left the door open. I believe he opened the postern gate as well."

"Sir John?" Gregory nodded. "He was loyal to Calder, but his heart is in the right place."

"Gregory?" Words welled in her throat, but she could not find the right ones to speak. So much to say and yet no way to speak of it all.

"He beat you." Gregory spoke coldly and she shivered.

She touched her fingers to the bruise on her cheek. "It is not as bad as it looks."

"Jesu, Faye." He dropped his head, shoulders slumped as if he were beaten. "I know not how to do this?"

"Do what?"

"To beg your forgiveness." Faye gasped at the depth of anguish on his face as he looked up. He vibrated with it and his hands trembled.

"You are not responsible for what Hugo did." As he had for her, Faye longed to soothe the torment from him. To rest in his arms and comfort him, like he had her so many times. "Nor where you to blame for Calder before him."

"Nay." He balled his hands into fists. "I am not worthy. I cannot even count the ways in which I have failed you."

"Gregory…" She did not want his guilt. It was his love she craved.

"Let me say this. I must. We have gone too long with secrets and silence." His voice cracked on a deep breath. "I was there, Faye, for what Calder did to you for all the years of your marriage. I saw and I did not act."

"He was my husband." And she had been too shamed by what he had become—what she had become—to break her silence.

"Husband?" Gregory gave a bitter bark of laugher. "He was never your husband, Faye. I was that, in all but name and…" The other, the thing they never spoke of. Desire, lust, love. He scrubbed his fingers across his scalp. "I was the one you turned to for comfort. It was I who cherished and loved you, not Calder. And yet, I stood idly by while he hurt you. I should have acted years before I did."

She wanted to deny it, even opened her mouth to say as much, but his words cracked open a secret place within her. All those times she had left Calder and sought Gregory, had she not been waiting for him to save her? Aye, she had. And he had patched her up, shielded her from prying eyes, but always acquiesced to her desire to stay silent. Her anger wasn't rational, or even fair, but it was there beside the young girl who had wanted him so desperately to love her back and rescue her. "You believed you did the right thing."

The time for lies and evasions long past, they stood bare before each other.

"I wanted you to save me." The words hurt her throat as she said them. So long contained, they came out sharp and barbed. "I could not save myself, and I wanted you to do it."

"Aye." His jaw tightened. "In my heart I knew as much, but I hid behind my intended vows and my belief I was right. I told myself I honored marriage, but I was a coward. I knew if I gave in to what my heart desired most, I would have to face the lie of my future as a priest. This I could accept, but you paid the price."

"You are still hiding." The anger rose from a deep place she no longer had the strength to deny. "Now you are hiding behind your guilt and I am still standing before you."

"You are right." He threw his hands out before him in supplication. "Since Hugo took you, I have thought endlessly of what I would do if I finally had you safe. And now, I stand here, trembling like a child, too frightened to do what I most want."

His admission staggered her. Tall and strong and capable, every inch a warrior and at this moment beset and held frozen by his fear. And her. Her terror ran as deep, right through to the heart of her. Here was all she had dreamt of and desired. No more pretense and nothing but themselves holding them back.

Love. What a tiny word encompassing everything between them. All the pain and longing, all the missed chances and wasted time. *Love me*, her soul whispered. *Take me and love me and heal this between us.* Her legs remained rooted to the spot.

He took a small step toward her, and her heart leaped into her throat. "Forgive me," he said, his pain open and plain for her to read on his face. "Forgive me that I did not take you and shelter you the first time I saw Calder's mark on your flesh." Another step. "Forgive me for each hurt I allowed you to suffer and did not act."

She nodded, her neck stiff. The tightness in her chest unraveled the tiniest bit. Had some part of her always needed to hear this? How else to explain how she stood still and listened with her soul split wide open.

"Forgive me I had not the courage to tell you all you meant to me." He drew closer.

A sob burst from her. How she had longed to hear him say, just once, the words that would give her hope. The yearning had near torn her apart at times and still, she had clung.

"Forgive me that I left you when I should have remained by your side and been the man you deserved."

The pain seared through her. Faye crossed her arms to contain it. The pain of watching from that blasted casement as he rode away to the Abbey. He had not even turned to see her standing there, with her love on offer. If he had turned once, but he had kept riding. Away from her. Out of her life.

He stood right before her, the heat from him tangible on her skin.

"You never even faltered." The picture was seared in her mind. Gregory, back straight, as he rode away from her.

"I was too craven to turn. I knew if I did, I would never leave."

"Why?" Dear Lord, it hurt. She could not bear it. Faye folded into herself to protect her aching middle.

His hands warmed her arms. "I could not accept my love for you."

Calder had never come close to inflicting this degree of agony on her. She needed to strike out and protect the pain. "I have no forgiveness for you."

"Nay." He tugged her closer.

Faye wrenched at his hold. He had no right to hold her, speak to her this way, make her hurt this badly, when he would only turn around and leave her once again. "I cannot."

"I love you." He wrapped his arms about her. "Forgive me. Not because I deserve it, but because there has been too much pain between us."

"Nay." Even now, with all her old hurts rising to the fore, she wanted to rest her head against him and revel in the love he professed. *It is too late*, her hurt whispered.

"Forgive me that I failed to protect you from Hugo, like I failed to protect you from Calder."

He asked too much. She did not have it in her to give him what he asked.

He brushed his lips over her temple as he held her tight against his chest. "I love you."

Faye railed against it. Even as her female form cleaved to his, soft where he was hard, frail and weak where he was strong. She hated it and she gloried in it. She knew, if he hurt her again, it would end her. "Let me go."

"Nay." His arms made it difficult to draw breath. "You are the wife of my heart, and I can never let you go again."

She dug her hands into his waist. She wanted to shove him away and hold him closer.

"I will never leave you again. I will never allow anyone to hurt you, myself included. I give you my oath, Faye."

"The church?" They were all the words she had to ask the question clinging to her mind.

"God would not have blessed me with you, had he wanted me to join the church."

Faye's legs gave way. She had to be imagining this. She was still in Hugo's solar and she must have fallen asleep.

Gregory's chest pressed against her. His strength was all that held her standing. "You are mine and I am yours. Even if you never take me, Faye, I am yours."

Her dream, her dearest wish, her deepest longing. She was, finally, his.

And Faye wept.

* * *

Dear God, she smote him. Smote and smitten. He had brought her to this and each tear she shed burned through his tunic into his heart, every sob cut like a dagger. He vowed to take it away. Never again would this courageous, loving woman weep as if her heart might never mend.

The rightness of her in his arms rocked through him. Words could not come close to what rested in his center. Her cheek beneath his lips, wet with tears, a revelation. The smoothness of her skin, the taste of salt from her tears stirred him as nothing else.

He pressed his mouth to hers, needing to show her all he knew to be true.

Her lips opened beneath his. Benediction.

A primal surge coursed through him. His. For now, for always.

His shaft swelled, hard and thick, his ballocks tight and ready. Physical love had always been something only for procreation. How limited his view had been, mired in his ignorance and stubbornness. It was an elemental connection one soul craved with another.

He dipped into her mouth, to taste her essence and draw it into himself. His flesh hardened to the point of discomfort. Spreading his hands over her back, he learned the feel of her. So soft and warm, it hit him like a blow to his knees. He needed her. Hungered for her.

Her breasts pressed full and ripe against his chest. Gregory cupped them in his hands. Firm and round with her nipples jutting out, demanding his touch.

The man in him ripped free of control. Lust he could master, but this held him in its thrall. He marveled at the differences between them. The gentle curve of her hip into the fullness of her ass. How tiny her waist beneath his hands and how lush the rise of her bosom against his chest. She touched him, the power her hands wielded at odds with their size. She could bring him to his knees with the merest brush against his muscle.

She dug her nails into his skin, and he gloried in the proof she matched his desire. She kissed him with little pants and moans that reverberated through him, fueling the fire and driving it into a blaze.

Beneath his tunic, she touched his bare skin. Dear God, he would come apart if she did not stop. He would perish if she did. He wrenched his mouth from hers.

"Slowly," Garrett had said. "Love her slowly and carefully, see to her pleasure before your own." How did a man accomplish such an impossible feat when his flesh demanded nothing more than to lose itself in her sweetness?

He pushed her hair from her beautiful face, his hands too large and clumsy. Drinking in the sight of her flushed, silken skin, the fullness of her mouth, wet and swollen from his kisses. Her desire unmanned him. Her need matched his.

Slowly. It would kill him for certain. His hands trembled and ripped the ties on her bliaut as he loosened them. Clumsy hands.

She did not seem to mind. With fistfuls of fabric, she pulled his tunic over his head. As if he were a thing of marvel, she stared at his bare chest. Spread her hands over him, her face alight with delight.

He had to see her. Fabric tore as he pulled her bliaut over her head and then did the same with her chainse.

Nothing in all creation could be as perfect and as beautiful as Faye standing naked before him. His shaft throbbed insistently for him to bury himself in her.

Her breasts stood firm and proud from the gentle rounding of her belly. Between her legs, a pale patch of hair beckoned him atop the long, graceful sweep of her thighs. His hands stood out dark and rough against the pale silk of her skin, Her nipples, pale pink, between his dark, coarse fingers. They swelled and hardened to his touch and he stayed a moment and explored.

Pressing into his touch, she moaned. Inside his braies, she closed her hand around him. Sensation shot through him and he nearly spilled in her hand, again. Not this time. Slowly. God, give him the strength to give her the pleasure she gave him.

Over the curve of her belly and into the fascinating patch of hair he slid his hand.

She cried out, exposing the long column of her neck. Beneath his lips, her throat vibrated as he savored her skin.

She parted her thighs. His hand delved inside, as if it had its own mind. Wet, hot and silky, his fingers slid over her. He had to get inside. Every part of him strained to sink into her core.

He nearly cried out in protest as she stepped away from him. Like a slave, he followed her and her soft smile of challenge to the cot at the side of the tent. She laid down on her back and opened her thighs in silent invitation.

Bedamned. Glistening and pink, the naked core of her drove him to the precipice of control. His ballocks tightened at the base of his shaft, throbbing and ready to spill. Laying over her as one bewitched, he feared crushing her.

Her slim thighs bracketed his hips, bringing the tip of his shaft into contact with her wet heat. Instinct drove and he thrust. Sweet God, she wrapped around him in a moist, hot fist.

He couldn't hold it. He drove into her, deeper until he couldn't tell them apart. She gripped his shaft, hot, silken, and wet. Thinking ceased, it was only his flesh joined to hers as he thrust again. She whimpered beneath him, her hands on his ass pushing him deeper.

His completion curled up from his toes, fastened like a fist around his belly and into his stones. With a roar, he pushed as deep as he could and emptied into her. *His.* It surged through him until he had nothing more and collapsed boneless atop her.

* * *

Faye delighted in his weight. Intimacy with Gregory had been so different from her experience with Calder. No fear or pain or discomfort. She should be giddy with delight. Yet, something was missing.

Other women spoke of this. Good Lord, her mother had even told her to expect pleasure from coupling. She had always supposed there to be something wrong with her that she dreaded intimacy with a man. Through the kissing and the touching, she had experienced everything those women spoke of. The heat, the dizzying delight, the pulse throbbing at her core—all of it.

His flesh remained joined to where she still throbbed, wanting. The excitement had been intoxicating and heady. As if an exotic dish had been placed before her, for her to smell and see and delight in and then ripped away before she could taste. Blast. It had begun so well. She shifted beneath him, restless and incomplete.

Pushing onto his elbows, he gazed down at her. His face gentle and flushed with completion.

Her heart thrilled to see what she had wanted for so long. Like a nagging tooth, her woman's flesh pulsed.

He assessed her, and frowned. "I went too fast."

"What?" A little tendril of annoyance surprised her as it curled deep inside her.

Gregory pulled a face. "Garrett warned me that might happen."

"Garrett?" Faye gaped at him. Her cheeks flamed at the very notion. "You spoke to Garrett about us? About this?"

"Aye." He nodded. "He said it would get easier to control."

"You spoke of this to Garrett?" Even as she asked the question, she prayed he would answer differently this time.

"I wanted to make it perfect for you." He cupped her face between his large hands. "I have no knowledge of women."

Dear God in Heaven! She would never be able to look Garrett in the face again. Faye wanted to kick him. If he were not holding her pinned to this cot, she might have done just that.

Faye took the opportunity as he eased to her side and scrambled off the bed. She didn't get far before his hands on her hips hauled her back. Her back hit the cot and drove the air out of her.

"He said to let your reactions be my guide." Gregory frowned as if he were studying a difficult problem from all sides. Mortification washed through her and rushed heat to her exposed parts. She brought her hands up to cover her nakedness.

"Nay." He placed her hands by her sides.

"Gregory." The man had lost his mind. "Let me up."

He stroked the side of her neck and grinned down at her. "I think not."

Under his fingers, her skin tingled. His fingers drifted lower to her hardening nipples. Good Lord, only wantons responded in this manner. Yet the place between her thighs heated.

"You like this." His long fingers caressed her swollen nipples.

A bolt of heat shot between her thighs. She did like that. She liked it even more as his fingers continued to play with her.

"Tell me." His breath brushed warm against her neck as he whispered against her ear. "Do you like this?"

"Aye." It left her mouth as a breathy moan.

"And this?" He lowered his dark head and took her nipple into his mouth. That sent an even stronger wash of desire through her. She arched her back into the silky heat of his mouth.

"Aye?"

"Aye." She writhed against him. She needed more. Every part of her sensed there was more of this and yearned for it.

He dipped his hand between her thighs.

Her legs dropped open like the lowest woman.

He touched her center and other thoughts fled as his fingers brushed a place that made her jerk. With a low, contented growl he brought his fingers back to that place.

In counterpoint to his stroking fingers, her hips discovered a new rhythm. The thing she had been missing hovered closer and closer. Low moans of pleasure built in her throat and escaped her lips. Feeling spread through her belly, growing stronger and stronger, it drove her on relentlessly. It built and grew more insistent. Dear Lord, she would die from this. "Aye." She demanded, lest he stop now.

It hit her in a sudden wave of sensation and heat, curled into her muscles and shattered. Finally, she understood. The heat in her cooled, but she still could not move a muscle.

Gregory gazed down at her, a small smile on his mouth. "Aye?"

Indeed. A great big smile worked its way on her face. Aye, indeed.

"We will get better at this." He kissed her with heart-breaking tenderness.

"Is that what Garrett says?" As soon as she could work up any sort of ire, she would have strong words about him talking to Garrett. It might take some time.

Against her thigh, his shaft hardened. She tingled in response. If she carried on in this unchaste manner, she would be heading straight to hell. Then again, being chaste had never won her this soaring sense of wondrous. She wrapped her hand around his length. He groaned and dipped his head to kiss her. His tongue swept into her mouth.

If they were hell bound, at least they would make the trip together.

Chapter Twenty-Four

Gregory could not believe they were arguing already. Not an hour ago they had been wrapped around each other enjoying the benefits of Garrett's wisdom. Now, she stood with her hands jammed on her hips and her chin thrust out at him. "I am not leaving for Anglesea before this is settled."

"Faye, you cannot remain in the midst of a siege. We cannot risk you, again." Sir Arthur lost patience and his voice rose to a near bellow.

Normally, Faye was the image of her mother, but with her shoulders back and her chin thrust forward, she strongly favored Sir Arthur, as her father attempted to order her home.

"Think of Simon." William tried a different approach. He poured Faye a cup of wine and held it to her. "A siege encampment is no place for a boy and he has already been through too much."

"Do not use my child against me." Faye snatched the cup and downed the contents in one gulp.

William blinked at the goblet she held for a refill and then obeyed her silent command. He turned to Roger and raised one dark brow in challenge.

"And what of little Arthur?" Roger stuck his chin out. "He misses his mother. Surely, you would not remain here when you could see him?"

Gregory flinched at the low blow. She'd warned them not to use her children against her.

Faye gulped more wine. She turned to him, silently beseeching him for support.

He would have done so gladly, but he would not risk her again. It seemed he was going to have to beg her forgiveness for this as well. He wanted her out of the way and safe behind Anglesea's walls.

She read the refusal in his face and her shoulders slumped.

"I will see Faye safe to Anglesea." Garrett looked to him and not Sir Arthur for agreement. "I need to check on Beatrice and there is nothing I can do to help here."

Gregory hated to let her out of his sight. Bad things occurred when he left Faye under anyone else's protection, but he needed to see this finished with Hugo. There would be no future for him and Faye until this was done. He nodded.

"Good." Sir Arthur rubbed his hands together. "Get together an escort and leave as soon as you are able."

"My lord." Sir Arthur's squire entered the tent. "They are signaling for parley from the keep."

"Let them wait." Sir Arthur took the wine and poured himself a goblet.

Triumph surged through Gregory. They had Hugo beaten and the sod knew it. A siege might take months but would end in surrender. With Faye and Simon's escape, Hugo had lost his last pawn in this battle. None of the Anglesea party felt inclined to let the matter rest and go home. No mercy.

Faye's face hardened. "Tell him I want Ruth."

"We will get your girl." Sir Arthur turned to her. "This time, however, you need to trust me."

Faye hesitated before she nodded. Trust did not come easily to his Lady Faye, and what she had seen in Hugo's hall still gnawed at her.

Tension in the tent mounted as Sir Arthur finished his wine and poured another. William seemed to be the only one impervious to it as he sipped his wine. Either the man had deep thoughts or a great, gaping hole between his ears to remain so calm.

"My lord." Breathing ragged, the squire hurried back into the tent. "They are pressing for parley from the keep."

"Are they now?" From cheek to cheek, Sir Arthur moved the wine in his mouth. "William, where did this wine come from?"

William craned his head to stare at the tent roof. "I believe this one is from the monastery at Fairhaven."

"I like it." Sir Arthur took another sip.

Gregory bit back a chuckle. The wily Sir Arthur made a formidable foe.

The squire peered from him to William and back again, shifting his feet. Gregory pitied the boy.

"Tell them I require a gesture of good faith," Sir Arthur said.

The boy gaped. "My lord?"

"The castle." Sir Arthur waved a hand. "Tell them I require a gesture of good faith before I will parley."

"My lord?" The boy squawked and reddened to his hairline.

Sir Arthur leaned his elbows on the table and glared at his squire from beneath his unruly brows. "You. Go and tell the keep I require a gesture before I will parley."

"Me?"

"Aye, you. You have a voice. I have heard you use it often enough."

The unfortunate boy opened his mouth and shut it again. He glanced at William and back at Sir Arthur. "I am a squire, my lord."

"Do you think I am unaware of that fact?" Sir Arthur stood.

The squire jumped back. "Nay, my lord. It is just that I am a squire and we do not, as a rule, parley." The last words came out in a rush as if the boy could hardly believe his own daring.

"Now is your chance." Sir Arthur strode over to his cot and sat on the edge. "Go."

The boy left the tent at a run. He was back again a scant moment later. "What sort of gesture?"

"Tell that whoreson he has someone Lady Faye would like to see released. He has until I wake to comply or there will be no quarter when I take his keep."

The boy turned.

"And squire?" Sir Arthur stretched his length on the cot. "Make sure he believes I am in earnest."

"Aye, my lord." He left at a trot.

"Father?" Faye frowned at Sir Arthur. "You have me as confused as that poor boy."

"Are you still here, Faye?" Sir Arthur crossed his ankles. "Because I believe we agreed upon you returning to Anglesea."

"I—"

"Come along, Faye." William rose. "Let him get some rest. We can get you and Simon ready to travel."

Despite the situation, Gregory wanted to smile. Sir Arthur knew exactly what he was doing. Inside those walls, Hugo could seethe and simmer, but his fate rested in the hands of the man feigning sleep on his cot. He put his arm around Faye and drew her from her father's tent.

Her shoulders stiffened with resistance, but she allowed him to lead her out. "I am not leaving until I have Ruth with me."

Gregory nodded. He expected no less from his lady.

Outside the tent, an armed party readied itself for travel. They were experienced men and Gregory trusted Garrett to see Faye to Anglesea safely.

A shout arose from the men nearest the wall.

"Stay here." Not trusting her, he remained where he was, waiting for Faye's nod. He wouldn't put it past her to scale those walls on her own.

Faye's lips thinned. "I swear I will stay here."

William strode ahead of him. He pointed to the small gate within the larger gates that opened. A figure staggered out as if being thrust.

Shock held him frozen. He had believed Faye, but seeing Ruth in the flesh sent the anger rushing through him afresh. Hugo was not a man. He was a savage beast. The entire litter of Calder offspring should have been drowned at birth.

William walked toward Ruth.

"Cover him." Gregory motioned the archers. William had more ballocks than good sense. A member of Sir Arthur's family would be welcome target practice from the walls. Then again, the men in this family never expected others to do what they would not do themselves.

Around him the archers nocked their arrows. The creak of drawn bows a soft ripping in the air. William hoisted the girl into his arms. She lay limp and broken across his chest as William brought her back to the camp.

Gregory sensed Faye beside him. He grabbed her arm as she tried to slip past him. There were still archers on those walls, and it would be like Hugo to put an arrow through Faye because the opportunity presented.

Faye stepped up to William as he drew closer. "Ruth?"

Ruth stared at Faye with dead eyes that had seen too much. Fury rekindled in Gregory. How could any man inflict this sort of pain? For this, too, Hugo must pay.

Faye stroked a stray lock of Ruth's hair from her face. "You are safe now, Ruth."

Gregory made a quick prayer for Ruth's broken soul.

"Father Piety!" Hugo's bellow carried through the quiet evening.

Gregory tensed. Calder's favorite joke of an evening had long since worn thin. One more mark in the tally against Hugo.

"I see you, Monk." As he stood in clear view of the battlements, this was no great achievement. Gregory turned to face the walls.

"I have an offer for you." Hugo's head appeared between the crenellations. How easy it would be to instruct the archer to put an arrow right between his eyes. Sir Arthur had the best archers in the land, trained as well as any Welsh longbow man.

The nearest archer raised a brow in question. At this distance the arrow would punch straight through the back of Hugo's head. Gregory shook his head and faced the walls. "What is your offer?"

Faye gasped.

"An end to this." Hugo gestured the army camped at the base of the keep. "With minimal loss of life." Sieges were long, protracted, and messy and the body count would grow before this was done. Gregory braced for what came. Hugo saw this as his last opportunity to enact some vengeance.

Faye dug her fingers into his arm. He would wager she made much the same guess.

"A challenge," Hugo yelled.

Aye, Gregory did not need to be a prophet to see that one. Let Hugo declare his intuitions, the deceitful cur. "A challenge?"

"Man-to-man." Hugo thumped his chest and thrust his fist at him. "Between you and me."

"To the death?"

"Nay." *Damn!* "A challenge to surrender."

"Why would we do that?" From behind them, Sir Arthur's boomed. "Your surrender is merely a matter of time."

"Aye." Hugo came back quickly. He must have been thinking on this. "But many within the keep will sicken and die before I do. You know this as well as I, old man. Would you see your grandson's keep whittled to the sick and dying?"

"I am going to make him eat that 'old man' from the end of my blade," Sir Arthur said. Sir Arthur would have to wait his turn. Gregory had some words of his own to feed Hugo. "If I lose,

Sir John will open the keep." Another face appeared beside Hugo. "You know you can trust him."

"Done!" Gregory yelled before anyone else could speak. He wanted this, with every fiber of his being. The chance to meet Hugo in open combat.

"Are you addled?" Faye glowered at him, pinching his arm so hard he winced,

"I will not lose." Hugo was a good swordsman, but he was better. Much better.

"He knows that." Faye jerked her head in Hugo's direction. "The only reason he challenges you must mean he has some knavery planned."

Gregory drew in a deep breath before he responded too curtly. "I know that, Faye." Concern for him was writ clear across her face. Her love soothed his nipped pride. "There is no doubt Hugo has something planned, but I am wise to him."

"Then why would you take this risk?" She loaded the question with all that had passed between them. Why would he risk leaving her again? Why would he risk his life when they had only now found each other? Always, the past stole between them like a thief to rob their future. It ended. Now.

Gregory cupped her cheek. Her skin was finest silk. "I will not lose." He put as much reassurance as he could muster in the simple statement. "I have too much to risk through losing, much more than Hugo."

"It would bring this matter to a swift end." Sir Arthur came up beside Faye.

She turned on her father. "Gregory could die."

"He will not." Sir Arthur smiled at her. "He will fight, and we will watch for trickery." He gestured to William, Roger, and Garrett standing behind him. "Trust me. Trust your man."

* * *

Faye trusted Gregory with everything she had, but asking her to condone a challenge between Gregory and that beast was too much. She understood Hugo, better than any of them. For him to issue such an open challenge could only mean he was sure of the outcome. As one, the men in her family faced her, calm certainty on their features. They meant her to draw confidence from them, but she could not. They did not understand.

"Please." She must try to reach Gregory. He knew Hugo almost as well as she. "Do not do this."

His face settled into implacable lines. "I must." Always so blasted stubborn. Faye wanted to shake him, to beat on his chest until it cleared his deaf ears.

"My lady." He turned her to face him. *Accept this,* his steady regard entreated her. "I cannot call myself a man, your man, if I do not take this opportunity to avenge the wrongs he did you."

Men and their pride and vengeance. It angered her enough to scream. How could vengeance comfort her if Hugo killed him? "You do not have to risk yourself to be my man. You are that already."

"I must do this. Will you give me your blessing?"

Faye railed within. Even should she deny him, it would not stop him. She could see it in the determined lines of his face. Gregory would do this, will she or nil she, with or without her blessing. She had no choice. To send him into the challenge thinking her wroth with him. Nay. To have him distracted by her anger when he fought for his life. How many times had her mother faced this moment? If Lady Mary could do this, then so could she. "You have my blessing, always."

Relief flooded his features and his mouth softened into a smile. He kissed her forehead. "Trust me."

Faye clung to him. She wanted never to forget the feel of his lips on her skin, the strength of his arms beneath her fingers.

"I must prepare."

She tightened her grip. "Will you not wait until daylight, when you can see better."

"Nay." He stepped back.

The small space of air between them made her chest ache. She needed to draw him close and keep him with her. Her face near cracking with the effort, she nodded and smiled. "Go with my love."

"In an hour." Sir Arthur shouted to the keep. "Gregory will meet you here in one hour."

"I will be there." Hugo's voice floated down to them.

Of course he would. It filled Faye with an unshakeable dread. She kept her feet where they were as Gregory strode beside Roger to prepare.

An arm settled about her shoulders and William stood beside her. "You are a woman of remarkable courage."

Nay, she was a terrified and stupid woman. She should call Gregory back, refuse her blessing, insist he not do this. Perhaps plunge the sword into Gregory herself before Hugo did. Anything would be better than watching him do this awful thing. She merely shook her head in denial.

"Aye." William clasped her to his side. "You are. We are strange creatures, we men."

Faye glared at him. Did he want to debate with her now?

William chuckled and shook his head. "We are so many parts, but pride forms the greatest piece of the whole. It is a wise and brave woman who understands this."

"But I do not understand."

Gregory disappeared into the tent behind Roger. There he would don hauberk and helmet, pick up a shield and sharpen his sword. She hated fighting and all that came with it.

"Every blow you have suffered and every hurt is carved on his soul like a seeping wound." William touched his finger to the bruise beneath her eye. "Every time he looks at this, he sees only his failure to prevent it. Now, you gift him with absolution."

William spoke true, she knew it in her heart, but still it rankled. "You do not know this."

"I do know this." William glanced back to where Ruth

huddled, a solitary heap, beside the fire. "When I look at her, I feel it." He thumped his chest. "In here. How much worse would it be if she was the woman I loved?"

"I will see to Ruth." What else could she do?

Chapter Twenty-Five

Gregory tested the haft of his sword. His hand curled around the grip like a second skin. He belonged here. The sword his old friend.

Hugo entered the field.

By mutual agreement, they dispensed with shields. Blade against blade, short and brutal, to the point of surrender. Around them, a ring of men watched, silent and grim. Hugo had brought a party of ten and they stood to one side of the circle. On the walls of the castle, archers waited, bows at the ready. Braziers cast flickering orange light across the field. Daylight would have been better, but Gregory was done waiting. This ended tonight.

Hugo stood a few inches shorter, but built compact and powerful. The cur was fast and light on his feet. Blade gleaming with reflected light from the brazier, Hugo took up a fighting stance, weight balanced between his feet, sword raised, testing the air before him like a serpent's tongue.

Hugo favored his right foot, his balance off. Gregory assumed fighting stance and fixed his stare on Hugo's shoulders. The blade was a mere extension. The blow would start there before the blade moved.

Shifting his blade through the air, Hugo circled.

Gregory couldn't afford to let the flickering blade distract him. He shut out the sounds of the men, the torchlight, the smell of wood smoke.

Hugo lunged, feinting to his shield side.

Gregory blocked the blow, held the bind long enough to gauge its strength and twisted his wrist.

Hugo danced back out of range.

The next blow came at his head. Gregory parried and thrust, testing Hugo's reflexes. Hugo's sword blurred and blocked.

They danced free.

They were matched in speed. Gregory had the advantage of reach. He cut to the left.

Hugo twisted and hit him on the weak, pushing his sword away.

Not as quick to that side. Gregory tucked the information away.

Hugo leaped free and came at him in second ward, sword raised for the head blow.

Gregory blocked, twisted to weak and released.

Hugo swept to his right.

He would need to be faster than that. Gregory parried to the left, ducked low and swept in from below. Hugo stumbled out of the way, slightly weaker on his left leg. Gregory pressed the small advantage in a rapid succession, left, right, overhand left and bind.

Sweat coated Hugo's top lip, and his glare gleamed feral. He hesitated in the bind as if his strength waned. Hugo had grown soft. Gregory shoved him out of the bind onto that weaker leg and closed again. Swift to the shoulder, blocked only in time, but not fast enough to prevent first strike. Gregory's sword glanced off the mail of Hugo's upper arm.

Hugo hissed, his lips tightened, and a flicker of real fear crossed his face. No blood, but that would hurt. Gregory came in fast before the other man could recover, forcing Hugo to fight off the left foot, leaving him to block cross body and testing that bruised arm.

Face tight with rage, Hugo growled. Craven pig did not like his opponents to fight back.

Gregory danced out of the way, toying with him, inciting that anger. Hugo lunged, angry, sloppy, thrusting forward and compromising his balance. Gregory ducked and let the sword carry over his head, exposing Hugo's chest. Gregory's sword sheared into metal, deep enough to cut the flesh over the ribs.

Hugo bellowed and swept blindly and backhanded. Gregory leaped clear before the blow arced through the air. Gregory thrust at the open left flank, straight for the belly.

Searing agony burst across Gregory's shoulder blade and down his sword arm. He staggered forward, his thrust dying. Gregory barely stopped his sword tip from embedding into the ground.

He'd been stabbed from behind. His mind struggled to absorb the new information.

A commotion broke out around them.

Keep your eye on the danger, man.

Hugo grinned and attacked. Jesu, he had no strength to his sword arm. Gregory got the block up in time to save his neck, but struggled to hold the bind through the pain in his back. Hugo's blade inched toward his neck.

Nay, this would not be how it ended. He kicked out blindly and hit Hugo's leg. The man stumbled and Gregory ducked out of the bind.

His fingers went numb around the sword hilt. Sticky wetness seeped over his back and down his side. An inch lower and the knife would have hit his heart.

Cold, hard rage flooded him. His blood ran down his back. He had moments to end this. He grabbed the hilt with both hands. He had lost the advantage of speed and balance, and his strength waned with each heartbeat.

Hugo pressed hard, his blows coming thick and fast as he sought the opening.

Gregory's head grew light. Not now. He shook his vision to

clear it. *Concentrate. Find the weakness.* The kick to the leg had cost Hugo.

Gregory danced wide, his feet clumsy and heavy beneath him. He dropped the point of his sword. Victory gleamed in Hugo's stare as he raised to second ward, Hugo's favorite strike position.

Elation surged through Gregory. Double handed he hit Hugo's exposed flank, his sword cleaving straight through mail and into muscle.

Hugo's eyes bulged. His sword dropped from his fingers and thumped to the ground by his side. Whoreson! Gregory thrust and twisted, driving the blade deeper and opening the wound wide. Done. Power surged through his muscles in a clean, satisfied sweep of rightness. He twisted again, reveling in the agonized rictus on Hugo's face.

"Kill him." Hugo's fingers tightened around the edge of the embedded sword. His stare swung wildly among his men. "Archers. On the wall. Kill them all." Hugo swung his head to his men. His glance whipped from one to the other, entreating, demanding.

Sir John turned his back first. The others followed.

Hugo dropped to his knees.

Head light, knees weak, Gregory staggered back. Strong arms steadied him.

"Treacherous bastard." Roger's voice. "Never saw the knife."

"Gregory." He pushed back the closing blackness. Faye's face swam into sight above him. He must be on the ground. Tears tracked down her ivory cheeks. "Gregory."

He wanted to tell her not to cry, but his tongue swelled in his mouth and wouldn't move.

Her soft hands cradled his face. Warm and wet, her tears dropped on his cheeks.

Tired. So very tired. Gregory closed his eyes.

* * *

"We need to get him help." Roger drew her away from Gregory.

They raised Gregory's limp form between them, taking care not to jostle him. So much blood, too much blood. The hungry ground swallowing Gregory's life drop by precious drop.

"Help me." Fingers plucked at her hem. Hugo. His face ashen, dark gaze pleading with her. "Pain. End it now."

Faye stared down at him. "Does it hurt?"

His breath rasped between his bloodless lips. "Please."

Savage, blinding satisfaction coursed through her, and Faye staggered beneath it. She plucked her skirt from Hugo's grasp. "Good. When you get to hell, give Calder my regards."

* * *

Faye cared not whether it was still night, or if day had broken. She sat in the still monastic infirmary and counted the rise and fall of Gregory's chest. As long as he breathed, she would not give up hope. Roger and William had rushed Gregory here after Bess declared him beyond her skills, the monastery near Calder the closest point to get help.

Dear God, he would not die. God would not be so cruel. Except God must be wroth with her. She had done the unthinkable and taken one of God's men for her own. Worse, she had been angry at God over Gregory's choice.

From outside, the melodic rise and fall of the monks singing the mass drifted over her. Her father had taken Simon back to Anglesea with him. Simon had wanted to come, but Sir Arthur had firmly led the boy away.

Strips of linen swathed Gregory's upper chest, pale against the dark of his skin. He lay still, his pallor horrible.

The whisper of slippered feet across stone announced the arrival of one the healing monks. "My child." He had a deep, raspy voice that grated along the edges of her nerves. "You must eat."

Faye wanted to fling away the offending hand. She forced

herself to remain still. Eat? When Gregory lay here and fought for each breath? Even the thought of food turned her stomach. She had done this to Gregory. In startling clarity, she recalled each word of her conversation with William. Gregory had fought for her. He had taken Hugo's life to avenge her. Her chest tightened into a dull ache, reminding her she needed to draw breath.

"We pray for him," the monk said. "We pray for the soul of our brother." *He is not your brother. He is my love.* Her jaw locked around the words and she bowed her head. *And I am Eve, leading Adam into temptation.*

The monk drifted away to tend to somebody else. A dry, hacking cough broke the silence.

The monk's voices rose in song. *Réquiem ætérnam dona ei Dómine; et lux perpétua lúceat ei Requiéscat in pace. Amen.* The requiem for the dead. Over and over again, echoing in her head. She wanted to scream at them to stop. Don't pray for his soul as if it is already departed, pray for his life. Pray for a miracle. *Too much blood*, they said. Lowering their voices as if she would break if they spoke louder.

"God." Her throat dried and she coughed. She could not anger God now. "Dear Father in Heaven." Her mind emptied as she tried to pray. Someone had to pray for Gregory's life. "You cannot let him die."

It was not right. Regrets crowded out the words of her prayer. She should never have allowed him to help her when Simon was taken. Never have forced him to take her with him. Never have let him fight for her. If he had remained at the Abbey he would be alive now and with his brothers in prayer.

"Dear Heavenly Father, spare him." The five words echoed again in her mind, receding with each echo until she could only repeat "spare him, spare him, spare him" in one looping litany in her mind. "I am sorry I took him from you."

At the Abbey he had been safe. All his life Gregory had wanted to be a monk. *Temptation* he had called her. Temptation, the evil that had inserted itself between God and Gregory. "Spare him and I will make this right." There must be some mercy in God's heart for one of His own. "I will give him back to you." She halted that line of thinking. How arrogant she had grown. "He was never mine. I took what was yours, but I will not anymore. Only please, let him live."

"Faye." Roger's hand clasped her shoulder. "They need to tend the wound, and you must come away."

"I cannot." She shrugged him off. If she left, Gregory would forget to fight. She needed to be here to watch for death.

"Faye." His hand returned to her shoulder, harder this time. "They are monks and they need to bathe him. They must remove his coverings to do so, and you are not his wife."

Roger's hand curled around her upper arm and tugged her to her feet. The edges of her vision darkened and she swayed on her feet. Bathe him. Prepare the body for the last rites. "He is not dead."

"Aye, Faye, he lives."

"They why do they bathe him?"

"For cleanliness, sweetheart. They need to do this."

"They will not take him away?" She scoured her brother's face for the truth.

"Nay." Roger nodded. "Not while he lives. Come now, you have not eaten in two days."

Two days? She had been here for two days. "He cannot be alone."

"William will remain while they tend him." Roger nodded to where William stood on the other side of the bed. William's beautiful face lacked his charming smile.

Her brother must not fail her in this. "Do not leave him."

"I will not leave him." William nodded. "I will stay right here until you return."

"Come." Roger's arm circled her shoulders as he led her from the infirmary.

Sunlight confused her after the dimness of the building. Her world lay shattered at her feet and the sun shone as brightly as ever.

"Here." Roger led her to a pond in the center of the courtyard. He helped her sit on the low stone wall surrounding it.

Fish flashed in the sunlight as they darted away from her shadow. From the meadow beyond a blackbird trilled a happy song. It seemed strange, as if it did not belong. The water cooled her fingers as she trailed them in the pond.

Roger set some fruit and cheese beside. Faye laughed at it. Everyone insisted on her eating. How ridiculous. She couldn't seem to care what happened to her, but Gregory must live.

"I will not allow you back to the infirmary until you have eaten." Roger took a seat beside her. Boxing his ears would take energy she didn't have, so Faye ate a plum and some cheese. Her boys needed their mother. Roger gave the food a pointed glance and she took more cheese.

"He is a strong man." Roger held out a peach to her. Sweet juice flooded her mouth as she chewed and swallowed to please Roger. "I have seen wounds on a battlefield you would swear fatal and men have survived."

Faye nodded because Roger meant to be kind, but she would wager he had seen many more wounds kill. She raised her face to the sun's kiss. Nurse would fuss over freckles. Faye drew the sunlight into her very being, as if she could carry it deep enough within to banish the dark place.

Running feet snapped her back to the small courtyard. A monk appeared at the door to the infirmary, a smile split his beaming face. "It is a miracle." He threw his hands up in the air. "God has answered our prayers."

Faye's heart lodged in her throat. She grabbed for Roger's hand and held it. "Gregory?"

She reached the man ahead of her brother.

"He is awake." Tears glistened in the monk's brown eyes. "We were bathing his wound and he groaned and then he woke. It is a miracle."

"I prayed." Faye ran down the dark infirmary corridors behind the monk, her feet pattering against the stone floor. "I prayed that God would spare him and he has."

"You made a powerful prayer, sister." The monk clasped her hand. "God has heard your prayer and granted you a miracle."

Nay, not a miracle. Faye approached the bed with her heart pounding in her ears. Gregory moaned. Was his color better already?

The raspy-voiced monk smiled. "He will live, my lady."

Faye collapsed against Roger. Gregory would live. It was more important than anything. Pain pierced her middle and she folded her arms about herself before she shattered. The deal was done. God had sent her a sign, an answer to prayer. A scream lodged in her throat and died there. She must not fight this. All her willfulness had led to this point. This was her test. She could not fail. For Gregory, she must find the strength to leave.

Chapter Twenty-Six

F aye viewed the walls of her childhood home as if she saw it anew. Anglesea had not changed, but she had.

Riding beside her, Roger and William still did not understand why she had waited only long enough to ensure Gregory was out of danger before she left. They pestered her with questions. She explained and explained and still they argued. Why did she not stay and speak with Gregory? Why did they not wait until he could ride and then bring him home together? They could not understand and it hurt too much to speak of it constantly. God had taken Gregory back. Her bargain was made and she would honor her part. Without honor, she was nothing.

Dear God, she ached. No respite from the tearing pain inside. She'd left her heart at the monastery. Her dreams and hopes, all gone. The tang of the sea brought the sense of homecoming to her.

Lady Mary stood with Nurse in the bailey. In her mother's arms—Faye's heart leaped—little Arthur.

"Mam!" He shrieked and bounced.

She barely waited for her horse to halt before she leaped from the saddle. William turned to assist her, but she hit the ground at a run.

Arthur must have grown an inch since she was away. Faye all but snatched her baby out of Lady Mary's arms.

He wriggled and squealed. His chubby arms grabbed her neck in a strangle grip. Faye breathed in the sweet, sticky scent of little boy and relished the strong little body wriggling in her arms. Dear Lord, she had missed her baby. For Arthur and Simon she would find a way to smile again. Hearts did break. The pain in her chest stabbed as if from a hundred tiny shards of glass.

"Where you been, Mam?" Arthur took her face between his hands and turned her to face him.

"I went to fetch your brother home."

"Simon." Little Arthur beamed at her.

"Aye, Simon." Holding him tight to her, she greeted her mother and Nurse in turn.

"Merciful Heavens!" Nurse clapped her hands to her chubby cheeks. "You look a sight."

"I think she looks splendid." Her mother touched Faye's short hair. "I am so proud of my fearless daughter."

Beatrice waddled out of the keep, larger than Faye had ever seen a gravid woman look. Hovering at her back came Garrett and then her father with Simon and Henry. Her family. Tears pricked as Faye took them all in. The people she loved most in the world, gathered around her in love. All except Gregory. There would be life without Gregory. And there would be joy, again. There had to be. Not today, though, and probably not for a goodly number of days to follow. She jammed a happy smile on her face. "I am glad to be home."

Lady Mary narrowed her blue gaze on her face. "Later," she said as she led the way into the keep. "We will speak later."

* * *

Faye donned her best bliaut of finest rose samite as she joined Anglesea in the hall. A long bath in lavender water, followed by a goodly dose of Nurse's fussing had pushed back the dread knot in her stomach.

She stopped outside the hall and smoothed the frown from her face with her fingers. It did no good to wear your anguish on your face. In the hall, the evening meal surged forward in a joyous celebration of homecoming. People packed the hall until it heaved with activity.

"Well met, my lady." Faces turned to her, smiling and happy to see her.

She wove through the trestle tables, answering their questions, responding to their good wishes. All the time, her heart was missing. Miles away with a man who was no longer hers. Faye sat with a smile pasted to her face and pretended. Eating only when Nurse watched her, she pushed food across her trencher.

Simon dashed from person to person, reliving each moment of his adventure. The tale grew wilder and more daring each time he retold it. Little Arthur dozed in her arms. She should take him upstairs to his cot, but it had been too long since she'd held his sleeping weight nestled against her. It didn't hurt as much when she held one of the boys.

She left the telling of their tale to William. Her brother had a flare for these things and she could not, yet, speak of it.

Ivy slipped onto the bench beside her. The girl grew more beautiful each day. She had filled out in the time she had lived at Anglesea and the haunted look no longer lurked in the depths of her moss-green eyes. "Nurse and I have placed Ruth with an old crofter's widow," Ivy said. "It will be a long time before she is able to be amongst people."

"Will she recover?"

Ivy shrugged. "That is up to her." Ivy would know, having suffered something similar. Faye had new respect for the girl sitting beside her. She knew Ivy's story, most of them did, but the image of Ruth brought it rushing back to her.

"Is Tom here this evening?" She couldn't dwell on the sadness, or she might never stop.

Ivy's pale cheeks tinged with soft color. "Nay, he has a cow calving and he likes to be there when they do."

"He is a good man," Faye said.

Ivy giggled and Faye gaped at her. She had never heard the like coming from the other woman.

Ivy caught her staring and choked off the sound. "How do you fare?"

Faye opened her mouth with her prepared answer. There would be no more staring out of casements and sighing. One of these days, if she tried hard enough, she believed there would come a time when it wasn't such an effort. She made the mistake of looking at Ivy before she answered. The woman's stare was uncanny in its ability to see what lurked beneath. "It is done."

"Is it?" Ivy turned to survey the rest of the hall. "Because you have decided it is so?"

That surprised a bitter laugh out of Faye. Decided? Nay. There had been no deciding in this matter for her. She had made her bargain with God and Gregory lived. That would have to be enough. "Gregory will return to the Abbey." Merely saying the words twisted inside her like a dull blade.

"He said so?" Ivy gave her a loaded glance. "William said you left before you spoke to him."

Faye glared at the back of her brother's head. William had loose lips. "Gregory nearly died."

"Indeed."

What was it about Ivy that made a body want to confess? She would have made an excellent priest had she been a man. "I promised God if he survived, I would not stand between Gregory and his calling again."

Up went one of Ivy's dark brows.

Faye squirmed and Arthur murmured a sleepy protest. She stroked his back to settle him. Ivy needn't make it sound foolish. Ivy had no idea how much her decision cost her. "As I finished my prayer, the monk announced Gregory was awake. It was a mira-cle." Let Ivy chew on that before she looked doubtful.

Ivy made a soft noise of disbelief in the back of her throat. "Miracle or not, I would have said his calling is a matter for God and Gregory to decide."

"You were not there." Anger surged through Faye. Who was this girl to pass judgment on this?

"Forgive me." Ivy's face softened into a smile. "I meant no disrespect."

Faye's ire died as fast as it had flared. "Nay, the fault is mine. I have not yet made peace with this and I must if I am to continue to have any sort of happiness in my life."

"Aye." Ivy fiddled with the edge of the table. "I am a simple woman, Lady Faye. I was born to a family who could barely afford to feed the mouths they had. When I was fourteen, my father gave me to Rudd to do with what he would."

Faye nodded. Rudd was the animal who had used Ivy as a whore. Tom had killed him and Faye was glad of it.

"Happiness, in my experience, is in short supply and when seen, should be reached for and held as close as you can."

The woman spoke in riddles that made no sense to anyone. Ivy was a fine one to be handing out advice. "Like you do with Tom?"

Ivy started and then threw back her head and laughed. "Well said, my lady."

Ivy's laughter tugged her in. Good Lord, she had grown sharp-tongued. It was not like her.

"What are you two laughing about?" Beatrice lowered her bulk to the seat on Faye's other side.

"Our own foolishness." Ivy helped Beatrice to settle. There must be more than one babe in that enormous belly of Beatrice's.

"Oh, aye." Beatrice pressed her fists into the small of her back. "I could do with a good laugh about now."

Ivy's smile disappeared. "You are not well?"

"It is my back." Beatrice shifted her weight. "It has been paining me all day. It goes and then it comes back, but it seems to grow stronger as the day passes. I was not able to eat a thing."

Faye tensed and looked to Ivy.

Ivy met her stare. "All day?"

"Not every minute." Beatrice screwed up her face. "Merely on and off throughout the day."

Excitement tingled through Faye. See, there was life within her. She had been just the same with her boys. "You should have said something earlier."

"Why?" Beatrice stuck her bottom lip out and glowered. "I am as big as a cow, and I am not surprised my poor back is complaining."

"Sweet Bea." Faye could not keep the grin from her face. "Unless I am very much mistaken, you are having your baby."

* * *

Exhaustion dragged at her legs as Faye entered her chamber. It was a happy sort of tired.

Beatrice had delivered her child with very little difficulty. Not that the curses spilling from her sister's lips gave indication of the ease of delivery. Good Lord, but Garrett had taught her sister some interesting words. Faye might try some out for herself one of these days. A little boy. Or rather, a large and lusty boy. Beatrice and Garrett were still battling over a name, while Beatrice worked her way through an enormous breakfast.

Beyond the casement, dawn stretched her arms in a blush of pink and orange and gilded the sea. Dark still framed the cliff marking the western edge of Anglesea demesne. Right there, the thin needle of the spire of the Abbey would appear as the day strengthened. Would Gregory return there or would he choose to remain at the monastery where he healed?

Sadness welled up and threatened the joy of the night's events. Faye pushed it aside.

No more sad Lady Faye.

Chapter Twenty-Seven

Heartache, Faye discovered, bore a remarkable similarity to tooth ache. It nagged away at the back of your mind until you nearly screamed to let it out. She kept busy. With a new baby in the keep, there seemed to be always something to do and not enough hands to do it.

Faye tied the apron over her gown and wrapped a kerchief around her hair. Not her best look, but who cared in any case.

"Ergh!" She annoyed herself with those little vipers of self-pity that crept into her mind.

Garrett and Beatrice had finally settled on the name Richard for their child. It was a fine name, strong and noble.

William had acquiesced to Sir Arthur's assertion that it was time to marry. The search commenced for a suitable bride. The wily brain of her father already worked on turning William's marriage to the family's advantage. His entreaties to Roger had fallen on deaf ears. Roger flatly refused to marry, while Henry had announced his intention to join the Holy Wars. With nothing helpful to offer regarding arranged marriages, Faye stayed out of the bride discussions. Secretly, she agreed with Roger that a person should be allowed to find their own mate. Some did, they just didn't get to keep that mate.

Dear Lord, there she went again. Nurse would accuse her of having her lip dragging along the ground. A fortnight, fourteen days and fourteen long and near-sleepless nights. She ate because Mother and Nurse would be on her like a pair of hornets if she did not. She went through the motions of speaking and smiling. Her boys were a blessing, a reason to rise in the morning and make her way through the day.

Verily, it was not all bad. People treated her differently since her return, particularly the men of the keep. They no longer skirted her as if she carried a dread disease. These days they sought her out. Now that the truth was out, nobody expected her to mourn Calder and she didn't have it in her anyway. Widows enjoyed a freedom not accorded maidens and matrons. What a pity she feared she would be old and wizened before she got around to enjoying her liberty.

Faye pushed her shoulders back and entered the hall. No time for moping when she needed to oversee the removal and beating of the tapestries. Mother said they were fine for another month, but the telltale glimmer of webs meant spiders and she could not abide spiders. Spiders reminded her of the inn and the night Gregory...

A group of men enjoyed a respite from arms training at a trestle. Faye returned their greetings with a polite smile and closed on them. Anglesea had a surfeit of strong, fine-looking men. Household knights, visiting vassals, even knights from her uncles were often in their hall. "I have need of some assistance."

They shot to their feet as if their braies were on fire. A young knight with a naughty twinkle in his eye squared up to her. "Anything, my lady Faye."

She barely suppressed the flinch as he called her "my lady Faye." What else was he going to call her? She could hardly insist no one ever call her "my lady Faye" ever again. Pitiful. Her huddle of champions would not be happy when she had them up a ladder and taking down those tapestries. "I need to have those tapestries aired."

To a man their faces dropped as they turned to study the tapestries.

"You have but to ask." The twinkler gave her a roguish smile. "If it is within my power, it is yours." Aye, and that wink promised a lot more.

"Woman!"

Faye froze, her stare stuck on the tapestry image of her father astride his destrier. Her mind had snapped. It was the only explanation, because that sounded exactly like—

She turned. "Gregory?"

He looked wonderful. A trifle pale and thinner, but she drank in the details. Dressed in hose and a surcoat he stood inside the screen's entrance and glowered at her.

"Good morrow the hall." The rotund figure of the Father Abbott from St. Margaret's trotted into view.

A deep bass chorus of male responses came from her group of champions.

"Gregory?" Words emptied out of her mind like water from a leaky bucket.

Gregory's grave, beautiful face was stiff with...anger? "I thought I would find you here."

"He insisted on coming." The Abbot tutted his disapproval. "And he should not be traveling yet."

"Gregory?" Dear God, was she going to keep saying his name until she made herself scream? "What are you doing here?"

Gregory glowered at her.

"You may well ask." The Abbot tucked his hands into his sleeves. "We tried to stop him."

Gregory stalked toward her, his brows lowered in a thunderous scowl. "You left."

"Aye, well I—"

"You what?" He stopped right in front of her.

Her traitorous mind stuck on how marvelous he looked. All other men paled in comparison. His shoulders so broad, he stood strong and tall with his jaw set in stone glaring at her. She wanted to touch him, to reassure herself he was really here. "I left you to return to your calling."

"I heard." The depth of his anger pierced her happy bubble. Gregory wasn't merely angry, he was furious. "Father Patrick gave me your message."

Father Patrick must have been the monk from the infirmary. "I believed it the right thing to do."

Gregory snorted. *Snorted?* Her supreme sacrifice of wrenching out her heart and stamping on it, walking about as if she were only half-alive and Gregory snorted.

"Enough!" Gregory motioned the Abbot over with a curt jab of his hand. "Do it now."

She was asleep and this a dream. It was the only explanation that made sense. Faye pinched her thigh. Nay. Gregory was still there, with the Abbot beside him and her thigh now sported a bruise.

"Do you not think you should ask first?" The Abbot frowned at Gregory.

"Nay." Gregory jabbed a finger at the men behind her. "They can stand as witness."

"Witness to what?"

"Our marriage."

She had definitely lost her mind. They would come to lock her away in one of the turret rooms and bring her food cut up in bite-sized pieces.

The Abbot shook his head in disapproval. "Sir Arthur should be here."

"You are right." Gregory glanced at the "witnesses." "You." He selected the rogue. "Go and fetch him and get the rest of the family while you are about it. Let us see this thing done right."

"Stop." Faye grabbed for the man's arm. Her head whirled so badly she needed everything to halt so she could catch up.

"Now." Gregory growled.

The man swallowed and slid out of her grasp. He left the hall at a run.

"What are you doing?" Her voice seemed to come from a distance. "I cannot marry you."

"I told you she would say that." Gregory glared at the Abbot.

The Abbot nodded and took her limp hand in his. "And why is that, my child?"

"He belongs to God." The blood drained from her head and she clung to the Abbot before she fainted. The idea had lost none of its sting.

"Because you made a bargain with God?"

The compassion in the Abbot's face nearly undid her. "Aye."

Gregory growled and shook his head. It was easier to keep her gaze on the Abbot.

"My child." He squeezed her hand. "I do not believe our Lord makes those sorts of bargains."

"But Gregory recovered. It was a miracle."

"Indeed it was." The Abbot smiled. "But possibly more thanks to the miracle of God creating such a fine, strong man and giving him the best reason in the world to live."

"I gave him back to God." Faye floundered under the Abbot's steady, sure gaze.

"So we understand, and I must warn you he has much to say on the subject." The Abbot jerked his head toward Gregory.

"What in the name of God is happening here?" Sir Arthur's bellow bounced off the walls. He saw the Abbot and flushed. "Begging your pardon, Father Abbot."

"Bless you, Sir Arthur." The Abbot went pink.

Sir Arthur's gaze swung to Gregory and a huge smile lit his craggy face. "You took your time."

"I had a hole in my back." Gregory grinned back.

Sir Arthur made a rude noise. "That wouldn't have stopped me."

"Hush now, Arthur." Lady Mary held her hands to Gregory. She stretched up and kissed him on the cheek. "We are prodigious glad to see you."

Clearly, Faye was the only one still in possession of her wits and it behooved her to take command of this situation. "I have no idea what is happening." It came out as more of a wail. So much for taking command.

"Marriage." Gregory put the Abbot gently aside. "Yours and mine. Right here and right now."

"I—"

"Before Hugo rises from the dead and snatches another member of your family. Before another rogue band of outlaws holds you to ransom. Before the seas boil up and swallow Anglesea whole, you and I will be married."

"You did not ask me."

The Abbot raised his gaze to the roof, the picture of righteous innocence. "I said you should ask."

"If I ask," Gregory spoke to the Abbot, but watched her, "she might start mumbling inanities about miracles and bargains with God."

Faye never mumbled and she, for certain, never mumbled anything inane. She opened her mouth to set him straight.

"I have your permission." Gregory glared at Sir Arthur and it was not a question.

"Oh, aye, aye." Sir Arthur waved his hand. "Marry the girl."

Girl? Marry the girl? As if this matter was already decided.

Gregory nodded to the Abbot. "You may proceed."

"There is the matter of the new decree, my son." The Abbot raised his brows and pursed his lip.

"Indeed." Gregory frowned. "I am going to marry this woman, any objections?"

A chorus of nays greeted this. A lone, "aye" floated over from the diminutive figure of Ivy.

The Abbot's mouth dropped open as he swung to gape at her. "What is your objection, my child?"

Beside Ivy, Tom turned to glare down at her. "Aye, what is your objection?"

"He has forgotten the most important part." Ivy pointed at Gregory.

"What part is that?" Tom folded his arms over his chest.

"He has not said he loves her and without her, his life is incomplete. A girl needs to hear these things." Ivy slid Tom a sidelong glance.

With a wry smile, Tom rubbed the back of his neck. "Does she now?"

"She most certainly does." Ivy smiled softly at Faye.

"Indeed she does." The heat in Gregory's gaze melted her insides. Dark eyes full, his love for her was clear to read. She wanted to leap and gambol about the hall, the happiness in her burst so strong.

The Abbot thrust his chin at Gregory. "Get on with it, then."

"I love you." Gregory wrapped his fingers around her nape and tugged her forward until his forehead rested against hers. "I will not live without you. Marry me."

Not quite a question, but she didn't mind. "Aye."

"Now are we going to get to the wedding," Roger said.

"I love a good wedding." William grinned.

Roger punched his shoulder. "Good, because yours is next."

* * *

Married again. Faye giggled at the "bridal chamber" Beatrice had created with scattered flowers across the silken bed coverings and woven through the hangings. A meal rested on the chest beneath the casement: sweetmeats, cakes, honey, and wine. Her sister had the heart of a true romantic.

Faye poured a goblet of wine. A bathing tub rested before the hearth, full of steaming water and wafting the scent of lavender throughout the chamber. Smiling, she loosened the ties on her plain, dun-colored bliaut. She had married still wearing her apron and her kerchief. She dropped the bliaut to the floor. Her oldest, most threadbare chainse went the way of the bliaut.

For her first wedding, she had worn costly velvet, adorned with a sapphire girdle. That wedding had been jammed full of all the pomp and ceremony of two great houses uniting. She pushed the memory aside. In this chamber tonight, only the future held sway. She preferred this kind of wedding, and the future that now stretched before her.

Carrying her wine to the tub, she positioned a stool to place the goblet beside her as she bathed. Her father and brothers kept Gregory in the hall. Plying him with drink and making a great game of keeping him from their chamber. He would be some time getting rid of them. She slid into the hot water and lay her head back.

"Thank you." She whispered her prayer to the silent room. The gratitude swelled in her chest and brought tears with it. Her joy was eight years in the making and now that it was here, it humbled her.

"I am almost certain a crying bride is not a good omen."

Faye jumped and swung her head. Gregory stood beside the tub. The man walked like a cat. She gathered her scattered wits. Sudden nerves fluttered in her belly, which was ridiculous. "You escaped my family?"

"I have a pressing need." He crouched beside her and took a sip of her wine.

"And what was that?" The way he looked at her heated her skin even more than the water.

"We have wasted too much time already, my Lady Faye." He stroked her damp cheek. "Are you going to be in there much longer?"

Faye rose to her feet. "Nay."

Gregory's gaze swept a long, slow study of her nakedness. Faye warmed under his regard.

"You are beautiful," he said. "I should sweep you into my arms and carry you to our bed but—"

"You have a hole in your back." Faye stepped from the tub.

He stood. "Ivy has cautioned me."

"Ivy has grown positively garrulous." Faye indulged her need to touch and placed her palms to his chest. Warm, strong man flexed beneath her touch. "You appear to be wearing too much clothing."

"You could be right." He reached for the bottom of his tunic and tugged. A wince crossed his face.

"Let me." Faye pushed his hands away, took the bottom of his tunic and raised it inch by careful inch. A trim waist widened into his chest and further to the straight line of his shoulders. Faye eased the tunic from him. Dear Lord, what a beautiful man. She traced the swell of muscle across his chest with her fingers and dipped lower. His belly contracted at her touch and intriguing ridges and dips formed on the flat plane. Hers, all hers. Faye spread her hands across his smooth skin. A lifetime of being able to explore him spread before her like a never-ending feast. She untied his belt and let it drop to the floor.

"Should I be doing something?" He groaned as she slid his chausses from his slim hips.

"You are doing exactly what I want you to."

His shaft stood stiff and engorged from the dark patch of hair between his thighs. She curled her fingers around him. An answering rush of wet heat flooded the apex of her thighs.

His breath snagged as she stroked. His dark head dropped forward to his chest to watch her touch him. "Slowly." He groaned through his clenched jaw. "We need to go slowly."

Faye laughed. "Slowly?" She did not think so, not with the way her nipples ached for his touch and her woman's place throbbed with need. She led him to the fanciful bower created about their bed. "Come."

Faye lay back, arching her back like a wanton beneath his dark, heated gaze. He followed her down, his skin pressed to hers along her entire length. Rising to his elbow, he smoothed her hair from her face.

"Your wound?" Carefully she wrapped her arms about his waist, pressing his shaft closer to the join of her thighs. This was where she needed him the most.

"My wound is not what aches now." He dipped his head to plant hot kisses along the column on her neck.

Faye tugged his hair to raise his head. Impatient for his kiss, she fastened her mouth on his. The taste of him swept through her. She could never grow tired of this, not if they both lived to be old and decrepit. Taste and touch embedded into the very deepest part of her. Another time, they could go slowly and learn each other limb for limb. Now, she needed him inside of her. Faye opened her legs and wrapped them about his hips. "Love me."

Gregory settled his weight over her. His gaze held hers as slid into her. The rightness of it made her cry out. This was how they both belonged, from this day forward.

"I love you," he said. "And I cannot fathom what made me believe I should be a monk."

It came from deep within her, an uprising of the sheer beauty of the moment and a sound of total abandonment that fit like the final thread in their tapestry.

And Faye laughed.

aye sighed at Simon's petulant expression.

"I will not." The eight-year-old, Earl of Calder glared at the serf before him. "I am the earl. You should not bother me with this."

Nay, indeed. Her son would not speak to anybody in that manner. Simon needed taking in hand. Since they had returned to Calder, Simon, the new Earl and Gregory his guardian, her son had moments of sheer willfulness.

The serf cowered before Simon, too accustomed to cowering before a cruel master. "Aye, my lord."

"Enough." Gregory rose and nodded to the serf. "Thank you, I will deal with this."

"Simon is in trouble." Arthur sang out happily. Faye feared her youngest had the right of it. Well-deserved trouble at that. Gregory wore his sternest expression as he dismissed the servants from the hall.

"I do not want to bless the harvest." Simon's expression chilled Faye slightly. There were moments when he resembled his sire too much for her peace of mind. Nay, Simon and Calder might look the same but they were cut from different cloth.

"It is important to them." Gregory motioned Simon to stand.

"You are lord here now and that brings many advantages, but also responsibilities."

Simon glanced around them and sighed. Gregory's point was well made.

Faye had rid the keep of any sign of Calder and Hugo. Handsome carvings adorned the walls and complimented the red stone. She had commissioned a large window of stained glass that filled the space with jewel-bright light. Barely a week ago, the stone masons had finished installing it. It depicted a bearded, gray-haired man standing in the forest, a stag at his back, a wolf at his feet and a badger beside him. The figure's deep blue eyes seemed to gleam kindly at whoever looked at the image. The earthy scent of sage freshened the rushes.

Simon dropped his head. "But they make me stand for hours and it is hot."

"They labor all year to bring the fruits to your table." Gregory put his hand on Simon's shoulder. "They ask only that you acknowledge their effort."

Simon grumbled beneath his breath and nodded.

"The worth of a man," Gregory said, "is not in how he treats his equals, but in how he treats those who have no choice but to serve him."

Simon nodded. Faye's heart went out to him. It was not always easy to be eight and have the mantle of earl resting on your young shoulders. People bowed and scraped wherever he went. It was up to her and Gregory to guide Simon into his role.

"I will bless the harvest," Simon said.

"And?"

"And beg Black Peter's pardon."

"Good." Gregory thumped him on the shoulder. "You make a fine earl."

Simon peered up at Gregory. "Can we go swimming first?"

"Aye, swimming." Arthur bounced to his feet.

"Only if my Lady Faye will join us." Gregory smiled at her. It never failed to thrill her. Married over a year and he could reduce her to pudding with just one smile.

"Please, Mama." Simon turned his sorrowful gaze on her. The artful little dissembler.

"A lady does not cavort in woodland pools." Faye sniffed repressively.

Arthur giggled.

Faye leaped to her feet. "Let us be off!"

"And afterward," Gregory said from behind her. "Simon can join the men at the harvest."

"You mean work with them?"

"Indeed." Faye tugged Arthur with her. "It is the least you can do after you spoke that way to Peter."

"Gregory." Simon rolled his eyes. "A lord does not work alongside a serf.

Gregory took her hand and led them out into the bailey. "He does today."

* * *

Books in the Sir Arthur's Legacy series, start with **Sweet Bea** and then **My Lady Faye**. They can be read standalone, but you always get a little extra if you read the series in order. Sir Arthur's Legacy continues, in Book 3, **Conquering William**.

* * *

An Inconvenient Marriage.

William of Anglesea is the free-spirited brother, the charmer, and the diplomat of Sir Arthur's brood. He has little doubt he can use his silver tongue and winsome smile to sweet-talk his way through his new marriage of convenience. But the alliance he's entered into quickly reveals itself to be a rather inconvenient arrangement.

Tarnwych Castle is in shambles, its people near to starving, and not least of his challenges is Alice—his intriguing new bride.

Raised in duty and service, Alice of Tarnwych hides her fire beneath a prim and rigid exterior. Thrice widowed and thoroughly disillusioned with men, her only wish is to have a child of her own to love. But the more time she spends with her captivating new husband, her heart—and body—begin to desire more.

When Alice's behavior takes a dark, disturbing turn, and frequent accidents make it clear someone is intent on ending William's life, he vows to save Tarnwych and find the truth. He hopes to convince Alice to choose a tantalizing future with him over the rigid, long-held beliefs of her past. Together, they must navigate the chaos swirling around them, a danger that threatens their happiness.

* * *

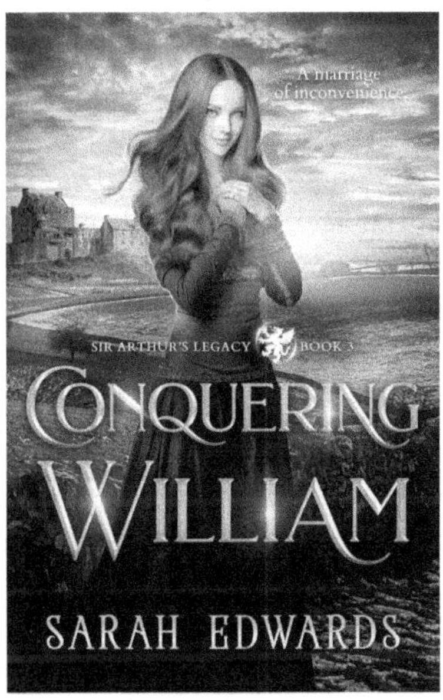

Read Conquering William

* * *

Chapter 1

If she lived to be a hundred, Alice never wanted to attend another wedding, particularly not as the bride. The odor of roasting meats almost undid her, and she took a long draught from her water goblet. A bride did not vomit all over her wedding feast.

Her father, face ruddy with wine, sidled up and pinched her side. "God's teeth! Smile, you stupid wench. I have found you a good 'un this time. Far better than a whey-face like you could hope for." Goblet held high, he strode away, sprinkling wine across the heads of those he passed. His forced laughter grated on her ear.

To her right, her groom drank from his goblet. In a deep, smooth voice, he murmured to his mother on his other side. As he shifted, his muscular thigh pinned her skirt to the bench.

Loathe to draw his attention, Alice tugged the dull brown wool.

He inclined his head with a smile, moved his leg, and freed her skirt. "I beg your pardon."

God save her from her beautiful husband. "No matter."

"May I serve you more water?" Eyes deeper blue than the lake beneath the castle twinkled at her. Candlelight gleamed off his dark hair and clung to his finely etched face.

"Thank you, but nay."

With another smile, he turned back to his mother.

She would prefer if he did not smile so much. Or did not smell so appealing. His subtle woodsy-sweet spice teased her every time he leaned nearer. He did quivering things to her innards. How could she hope to hold a man such as this? Atop the scarred table, their trencher sat between them, still full of mutton, gravy oozing into a brown puddle on the table. It couldn't be worse. Her father had outdone himself this time. Four husbands he'd chosen for her and this one, by far, the most daunting.

Aye, but William of Anglesea would make fine children. Tall, strong boys, broad and powerfully built like their sire, and girls to take after his mother and sisters. A child of her own. A downy head nestled against her breast, a tiny body cradled in her arms. She touched her palm to her flat, empty belly, and put her hand back on the table before anyone could notice. Even whey-faces had dreams.

About the Author

**Sarah Edwards is also published under the name
Sarah Hegger**

Born British and raised in South Africa, Sarah Hegger suffers from an incurable case of wanderlust. Her match? A hot Canadian engineer, whose marriage proposal she accepted six short weeks after they first met. Together they've made homes in seven different cities across three different continents (and back again once or twice). If only it made her multilingual, but the best she can manage is idiosyncratic English, fluent Afrikaans, conversant Russian, pigeon Portuguese, even worse Zulu and enough French to get herself into trouble.
Mimicking her globe trotting adventures, Sarah's career path began as a gainfully employed actress, drifted into public relations, settled a moment in advertising, and eventually took root in the fertile soil of her first love, writing. She also moonlights as a wife and mother. She currently lives in Ottawa, Canada, filling her empty nest with fur babies. Part footloose buccaneer, part quixotic observer of life, Sarah's restless heart is most content when reading or writing books.

Hegger's utterly delightful first Ghost Falls contemporary is what other romance novels want to grow up to be." – Publisher's Weekly, Best Books of 2017

"The very talented Hegger kicks off an enjoyable new series set in the small Utah town of Ghost Falls. This charming and fun-filled book has everything from passion and humor to betrayal and revenge." –
Jill M Smith, RT Books Reviews 2017 – Contemporary Love and Laughter Nominee

Becoming Bella

"Hegger excels at depicting familial relationships and friendships of all kinds, including purely platonic friendships between women and men. Tears, laughter, and a dollop of suspense make a memorable story that readers will want to revisit time and again."
Publisher's Weekly, Starred Review

"...you have a terrific new romance that Hegger fans are going to love. Don't miss out!"
Jill M. Smith – RT Book Reviews

Blatantly Blythe

"Ms. Hegger has delivered another captivating read for this series in this book that was packed with emotion..." Bec, Bookmagic Review, Harlequin Junkie, HJ Recommends.

Nobody's Fool

"Hegger offers a breath of fresh air in the romance genre." – Terri Dukes, RT Book Reviews

Nobody's Princess

"Hegger continues to live up to her rapidly growing reputation for breathing fresh air into the romance genre." – Terri Dukes, RT Book Reviews

"I have read the entire Willow Park Series. I have loved each of the books ... Nobody's Princess is my favorite of all time." Harlequin Junkie, Top Pick

Also by Sarah Edwards

Sports Romance

Ottawa Titans Series

Roughing

Contemporary Romance

Passing Through Series

Drove All Night

Ticket To Ride

Walk On By

Ghost Falls Series

Positively Pippa

Becoming Bella

Blatantly Blythe

Loving Laura

Willow Park Romances

Nobody's Angel

Nobody's Fool

Nobody's Princess

Medieval Romance

Sir Arthur's Legacy Series

Sweet Bea

My Lady Faye

Conquering William

Defying Roger

Henry's Honor

Love & War Series

The Marriage Parley

The Betrothal Melee

Western Historical Romance

The Soiled Dove Series

Sugar Ellie

Standalone

The Bride Gift

Bad Wolfe On The Rise

Wild Honey

www.ingramcontent.com/pod-product-compliance
Lightning Source LLC
Chambersburg PA
CBHW071219210726
48293CB00002B/496